Cassidy wasn't sure what to expect the following morning as the pale pink sun finally decided to push some weak tendrils through the overhanging canopy of the woods, but it certainly wasn't this.

"Don't drop your shoulder," Thomas barked as Cassidy threw a slim, sharp knife at him. Unfortunately, she had recently discovered that not only were her knife-throwing skills less than stellar, but throwing things at an apparition was completely pointless. Thomas seemed indifferent to her mental turmoil. "Now try it again. And this time concentrate."

"I *am* concentrating." She gritted her teeth and pressed the blade into her leather-gloved hand so that the point was facing her. Then she drew back her arm before throwing it forward. Once she released it, the metal blade spun as it flew through the air before landing harmlessly on the sodden leaves that covered the dark, damp dirt, nowhere near the apparition of Thomas.

OTHER TITLES YOU MAY ENJOY

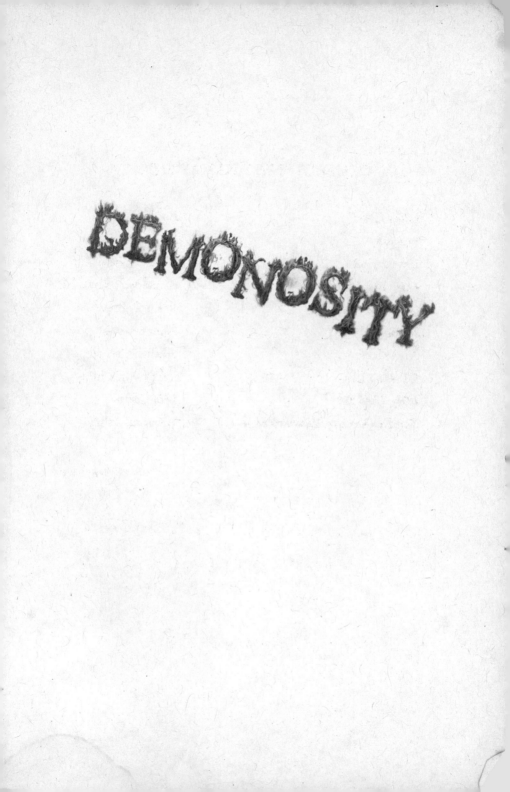

DEMONOSITY

AMANDA
ASHBY

speak
An Imprint of Penguin Group (USA) Inc.

SPEAK
Published by the Penguin Group
Penguin Group (USA) Inc.
375 Hudson Street
New York, New York 10014, U.S.A.

USA / Canada / UK / Ireland / Australia / New Zealand / India / South Africa / China
Penguin Books Ltd, Registered Offices: 80 Strand, London WC2R 0RL, England

For more information about the Penguin Group visit www.penguin.com

First published in the United States of America by Speak,
an imprint of Penguin Group (USA) Inc., 2013

LIBRARY OF CONGRESS CATALOGING-IN-PUBLICATION DATA
Ashby, Amanda.
Demonosity / Amanda Ashby.
p. cm.
Summary: Thomas Delacroix, the spirit of a fourteenth-century knight, needs a
contemporary girl to help him protect the Black Rose, a powerful ancient force,
but popular, quirky high school junior Cassidy Carter-Lewis is not happy about being chosen
to train before dawn and battle demons at parties, the mall, and even school.
ISBN 978-0-14-242397-4 (pbk.)
[1. Demonology—Fiction. 2. Spirit possession—Fiction. 3. High schools—Fiction. 4. Schools—Fiction.
5. Knights and knighthood—Fiction. 6. Family life—California—Fiction. 7. California—Fiction.
8. Humorous stories.] I. Title.
PZ7.A7993Dem 2013
[Fic]—dc23
2012042252

Speak ISBN 978-0-14-242397-4

Printed in the United States of America

1 3 5 7 9 10 8 6 4 2

The publisher does not have any control over and does not assume
any responsibility for author or third-party websites or their content.

As always, I would like to thank Jenny Bent and Susan Hawk for continuing to have my back and help me become a better writer. A big thank you needs to go to Karen Chaplin for believing in this book right from the start and to the amazing Kristin Gilson for helping me to bring my demon knights to life! Also to everyone else at Puffin for all of their support. To Sara Hantz and Christina Phillips for continuing to put up with my crazy. To my husband Barry Holt for being a fount of knowledge when it comes to history. And finally to my lovely sword guy, Caleb Chandler. Thank you for letting me pick your brain and for helping me with all of my many, many questions and for being so happy to discuss the best way to kill medieval demon knights! Any mistakes are well and truly mine.

O N E

France 1310

Thomas de la Croix was not someone who scared easily, but as the smell of decaying flesh, rancid blood, and black magic caught in his nostrils, he felt dark tendrils of fear clutch at his chest. His grip tightened on his sword—the only gift his true father had ever given him—as he forced himself to concentrate on the horde of demons that came crashing through the cloister entrance. Their poleaxes and shields clanked violently as they pushed against one another in their haste to reach the doorway that Thomas and his companions were currently guarding.

Over in the corner, the monks cowered in a huddle, their heads barely visible above their coarsely woven cowls, but Thomas ignored them. Instead, he concentrated with an intensity that belied his seventeen years. He ignored everything but the demons as they tore across the tiled abbey floor, their amber eyes ablaze with swirling colors of liquid fire, their once-human faces now distorted beyond recognition as the siren call of the thing that Thomas had sworn to protect lured them ever forward.

He held his ground, aware of the cold steel of his helmet against his brow. For three years, ever since the bitter night in Landévennec, Thomas and the other knights had been on the run as they protected the Black Rose from the many demons who now desired it. Three long, torturous years they had managed to protect the alchemist treasure that offered not only immortality but also unlimited power and strength to whoever should harness it. Unfortunately, as Thomas well knew, if the demons succeeded in their mission, then the world would be over. Not something that he was prepared to let happen. He had lost everything he cared about in the last three years, but he would make sure that those losses hadn't been for naught.

The first of the demons reached him, but before it could even open its mouth, Thomas thrust his faithful sword deep into its chest. The runes engraved on the steel buzzed with energy and helped the blade to slice through the thick skin until it penetrated the beast's heart. Thomas ignored the demon's look of surprise as the fire swirled out of its dying eyes, and he used the giant, limp body as a shield to stop the next demon from reaching him.

He staggered and almost fell as the enraged demon slashed at the flesh of its fallen comrade in order to get past. Thomas's muscles howled in protest and he clenched his jaw before finding the extra strength to push the dead creature backward, causing the demon behind it to go crashing to the ground. As soon as it fell Thomas was down on his knees thrusting his sharp dagger deep into this demon's neck, slitting its throat until dark blood spilled out onto the abbey floor.

If Thomas didn't already know that he was condemned to the bottom of the Great Wheel, then surely this latest sacrilege would secure his place. But again he reminded himself that it mattered not. As long as the Black Rose was safe, he would take whatever the Great Wheel chose for him in this life and the next.

To one side, Symon was struggling to stop another of the demons from snapping his neck. In a flash Thomas was beside him, using his shoulder to shove the giant creature away from his fellow knight. The pair of them then stepped forward in tandem, and both drove their swords past the demon's shield and deep into its chest. It immediately crumpled onto the abbey floor, joining its fallen comrades.

Thomas wasn't sure how long they fought, but finally the onslaught was finished. Over where the massacred demons lay, the all-too-familiar sickening stench of the blood magic that the demons used to bolster their strength rose upward, like steam on a winter's morn. Thomas ignored it as he turned back to his men. Etienne had fallen, and the gaping red slash where his guts had once been told Thomas that he was no more for this life. But the three other knights with whom he had come were still standing and looking to him for direction.

Thomas didn't hesitate as he stalked over to the altar and

picked up one of the beeswax candles, of much finer quality than most nobles would see at their dinner table. Without preamble he threw it onto the pile of corpses and watched as the demon flesh burst into flames.

Watching the long fingers of fire lick across the ancient beams that were strutted across the ceiling until they, too, burst into flames, the monks moaned in protest. Thomas dismissed their looks of condemnation. A church that could afford beeswax candles instead of tallow ones could afford to be reconsecrated and rebuilt once the filth of this night had been burned away.

"We need to leave now," he said, marching toward the door. He nodded for his men to join him just as the roof went up in another burst of flames. In the distance he could hear one of the monks crying out "*enfant du diable,*" but Thomas shrugged off the insult just as he had been doing his entire life. Besides, while he was sure that the devil had given him many sins, he knew that his eyes—one pale blue and one dark brown—weren't a gift from the ruler of hell, but rather from his long dead mother who, according to his old nurse, was similarly afflicted.

"Thomas, you go too far," Symon said from next to him, his face ashen as the wailing monks followed them out into the safety of the cool night. "Is this how you repay their hospitality? By burning their church to the ground? Where is the honor?"

"Honor?" Thomas spat as he marched across the cobbled courtyard, oblivious to the burning abbey that he left behind.

Instead, he focused on the small outbuilding that concealed the entrance to the monk's hidden vault. "You were told when you joined the Brotherhood that there would be no tourneys, no spoils of war, no glory. There is no honor in what we do, Symon. There is only duty, and the sooner you learn this, the better. Besides, you know as well as I do that the only way to truly kill a demon is to burn it."

"Yes, but there was another way to have stopped this battle. If you'd listened to me, then the demons wouldn't have come here and the church would've been saved," Symon persisted, causing Thomas to yank the helmet from his head and run his hand along the long, angry scar that covered the length of his cheek.

"Only a coward would consider *that* an option," he said in a cold voice as he twisted the crude steel handle of the door and then used his shoulder to push it open. The monks had shown them the secret vault two days earlier when they had taken sanctuary, and Thomas had decided it was the safest place for them to keep the Black Rose.

"Who are you to call me coward? I have ten more winters than you, *garçon*," Symon snarled, as he tried to emphasize Thomas's youth.

"*Oui*. And yet I've still killed many more demons than you have, *old man*," Thomas retorted with a withering glare. "Now, enough of this. We need to get Armand and the Black Rose and leave this place before word reaches more of the Demon Lords and they decide to—"

However, the rest of the words died on his lips as he

dropped his shoulders and stepped through the low door-frame, only to discover there was no sign of Armand or the dull wooden box that housed the most dangerous artifact in the entire kingdom. Thomas scanned the deserted room, his horror mounting as he noticed the crudely drawn circle etched into the dirt floor; the flickering candles, burned down almost to their wicks; the smell of Eastern herbs and spices that hung in the air. Then he saw the bowl of blood in the center and his horror turned to ice-cold rage.

"What have you done?" His voice was little more than a whisper as he pulled off his gauntlets and tightened his fingers. "Where is Armand? *Where is the Black Rose?*"

"We did what needed to be done," Symon said in a defiant voice as he pushed his meager chin high into the air. "While we were fighting, Armand invoked the ritual and sent the Black Rose to find its vessel. The ancient books all said the best way to protect it is when it's housed in human flesh. This was how it was always done until the Brotherhood came along and decided that they could do it better."

"He *what?*" Thomas's voice echoed around the stone vaults and hung in the air like an unsheathed sword.

"You heard me. He did the ritual. We can't keep running forever, Thomas. It's been three years, and there are only six of us left—no, five, now that Etienne has fallen. And the Demon Lords keep turning more human flesh into demon minions. They are like a plague that will not end. Someone had to take the lead."

"And that someone is *me*." Thomas could almost feel his

mismatched eyes blaze as he kicked over the bowl of blood and sent it flying across the room, dripping its unholy essence down one whitewashed wall before finally coming to rest on the dusty ground. "I am the grandmaster now, and not only have you disobeyed me, but you've made a mockery of every knight who has given up his life to protect the Black Rose. If my foster father was still alive, he would kill you where you stand."

"We made the right decision," Symon insisted as his hand nervously clutched at the hilt of his sword, no doubt wondering if Thomas shared the late Hugh de la Croix's views on betrayal. But instead of reaching for his own weapon, Thomas threw his gauntlets down on the floor in an angry gesture.

"Tell me, Symon, do you know *why* the Brotherhood stopped allowing the essence of the Black Rose to reside in a human vessel?"

"Because they grew arrogant and didn't want to relinquish power to anyone? Because they liked feeling important? *Just like you do*. How do we know that the Black Rose hasn't corrupted you, too?"

The muscles around Thomas's jaw twitched, but still he didn't reach for his sword. "Actually, it was because we couldn't control *where* the Black Rose would go to find the vessel. Sometimes east. Sometimes west. Once it went back in time. Problem enough when it was only mortal men who were chasing after it, but once the Demon Lords, with their blood magic and their ability to travel through the ether, joined the hunt, it was impossible. We can't match them for ability, and we can't risk leaving the Black Rose unprotected. Not even for a blink of an eye."

"We *haven't* left the Black Rose unprotected," Symon insisted. "We have sent forward a guardian. We went through all the ancient texts, and we found a way. Where the Black Rose goes, Armand will follow. He has the grimoire, so that he can keep the vessel safe, just as our ancestors before us did. The old ways are not the wrong ways, Thomas. You must see that now. The Black Rose will be safe, and all of our running will be at an end."

For a moment Thomas felt the room start to spin. Then he regained his composure and strode across the dusty floor to where the leather traveling satchel was lying on a stool. He snatched it up and shook it, only to discover it was empty.

The grimoire was the one thing that stood between the Brotherhood and the demons. It was a large leather-bound book, and not only was it infused with power, it was possessed of all the magical rituals they needed to fight and ward off demons.

And now it was gone.

Thomas dropped the leather satchel to the ground and spun back around. "You fool! What have you done?"

"I told you, we can't keep running. This was the only way. We need to trust Armand. He will keep the Black Rose safe."

"Armand will be dead by the time the vesper bell rings on

the morrow," Thomas retorted in a cool voice, and suddenly Symon's arrogance started to falter as his face paled.

"Wh-what? Armand is going to die? Are you certain?"

"As certain as night follows day. The magic from this circle, though powerful, is not enough to keep his body together. Even with the blood of whatever pathetic vermin you drained and all of the laws of nature that you violated, it's still not enough. The whole reason the Brotherhood stopped doing the ritual was because we couldn't travel through the ether to protect the Black Rose. So what say ye now? Now that you know the Black Rose is lost in time and unguarded?"

"What have I done?" Symon let out a horrified groan as he awkwardly dropped to his knees and lay prostrate on the dirt floor, his plated armor protesting as he did so. "Forgive me. I have failed you."

"Yes, you have, but since I am not your confessor, it's not my forgiveness that you should seek," Thomas snapped, his voice rough as he signaled to the other knights to gather up their meager belongings. "Now get to your feet. We need to find the grimoire and a new guardian to keep the Black Rose safe from"—he paused for a moment, stumbling over the words—"from the demons. Otherwise, we will all be doomed."

TWO

Now

There were many things that sixteen-year-old Cassidy Carter-Lewis was good at. Unfortunately, decision making wasn't one of them. And when she said not good, she actually meant disastrous. But in her defense, she was a Libra, so it totally wasn't her fault. *After all, when your star sign was a set of scales, you knew that you were off to bad start.* Not that it was any consolation to her right now as she looked over the multitude of crystals, candles, and silver trinkets on the vending cart on the lower level of the mall. Indecision clawed at her, and it wasn't helped by the bored-looking cart owner, who kept glancing at his watch to let her know that he would be closing soon. *No pressure then.* Cassidy gulped and grabbed two of the healing crystals that had been sitting in a basket and waved them in front of Nash's face.

"Okay, so tell me the truth, do you like the green one or this silvery black one best?"

"Green." Nash didn't bother looking up from the leather-bound book that he was reading as he leaned against the side of the cart with the kind of casual ease that Cassidy could never hope to muster.

"Are you sure you're not just saying that so we can go home?" Cassidy put the crystals down on the counter and pushed the book away from Nash's face. As she did, a group of girls who had been halfheartedly inspecting some Halloween-inspired masks suddenly looked over with interest.

Not that Cassidy was really surprised, since girls *always* looked at Nash with interest (and so did a lot of guys, for that matter), because the simple truth was that with his pale blue eyes, sooty lashes, and alabaster skin, which looked as if it had been carved from marble, Nash Peterson was a divine specimen of heavenly perfection, not to mention a certified genius, and someone had to be dead not to admire him. Unfortunately, they might as well be dead for the good their attention to Nash would do them, since at the age of twelve Nash had declared that he was asexual and despite all the interest he attracted wherever he went, four years later, he hadn't shown any signs of changing his mind.

In fact, as far as Cassidy was aware, she was the only girl who hadn't fallen for him. But that was probably because she had known him since fourth grade, when he had helped her finish her science project, resulting in her very first A-plus.

"Of course I'm saying that so we can go home," he immediately agreed, oblivious to the attention he was receiving. "Cass, we've been at the mall for two hours looking at crystals. *Two hours.* I do believe that this is what

Dante meant when he described the ninth circle of hell, because look at this place. It's devoid of warmth, life, and light. In fact, I can feel the coldness creeping into my veins already, trying to isolate me into an eternity of icy solitude and suffering, where time has no meaning and there's no relief from the torment."

Okay, and the other reason they were such good friends was because Cassidy was the only person who didn't think it was weird that Nash quoted Dante like most people quoted *Glee*, and that he was more comfortable reading about how the Renaissance astronomers made the lenses for their telescopes than going to a school football game.

"Is there any chance that you might be exaggerating?" Cassidy inquired as the girls, finally realizing that Nash wasn't going to acknowledge them, sulkily moved on to another vending cart.

"Fine, so perhaps it's not the ninth circle," Nash grudgingly agreed before he glanced around the mall at the ugly mosaic walls and the tinkling fake fountain just to the left of them. "But it's definitely the fifth or fourth. Can you please just choose one you like?"

"It's not about what I like," Cassidy reminded him as she randomly picked up a large amethyst cluster and inspected it. "I need to try to figure out what my dad would like."

"Your dad would like you to buy something. I'm shutting in five minutes," the vendor called out as he started to pack away some mood rings, causing Cassidy to tighten her grip on the amethyst; her dad would be anything but happy if he knew what she was doing.

In fact, he had specifically told her that he didn't want any get-well cards, stuffed animals, or flowers. And while technically she wasn't buying any of those things, she knew he would still hate the idea that she was fussing over him just because he was going to have knee surgery tomorrow. But despite his assurances that he was going to be in the hospital only overnight and that after about six weeks of physical therapy he would be back to his best, Cassidy couldn't help but worry. Which was why she was determined to find the perfect good-luck present. Something that—

"Hello. I'm not getting any younger here," the vendor snapped. Cassidy quickly put the amethyst back, her eyes moving past the gaudy Halloween trinkets and quickly skimming over the collection of temporary tattoos, and . . . *Actually, that wasn't such a bad idea.* She paused to take a second glance at the tattoos.

Her dad had been threatening for years to get a tattoo. Obviously, right now wasn't the best time for him to get a real one, but a temporary one would be *perfect.* She picked up the first packet. The tattoo was of two black roses branching out like a love heart, their twisted, leafy stems in perfect symmetry with each other.

"Are you serious?" Nash leaned toward her and raised an eyebrow. "A tattoo? Won't your mom go ballistic?"

"My mom isn't the one having surgery," Cassidy reminded him. "Plus, my dad will love it. What do you think?"

"Weelllll," Nash admitted as he examined the tattoo for a moment before handing it back. "It is quite appropriate. Did you know that, while the Victorians considered the black rose to be a mark of death because it didn't actually exist in nature, the Irish thought of it as a symbol of hope in their efforts to break away from the red rose of England?"

"Nash, you're a genius!" she said. Her dad was originally from Belfast, and though his brogue had been watered down from years of living in California, he still considered himself an Irish son.

"I *am* pretty amazing," Nash agreed.

"And so completely modest," Cassidy teased as she waved the tattoo in the air. "I do like it, but I think I'd better test it first in case it looks stupid once it's on."

"Please, you're killing me," the vendor moaned.

"Don't worry. I'll pay for it, and then if it's good, I'll get a second one." Cassidy thrust a ten-dollar bill at him before he could say anything else.

"Are you seriously going to put it on now?" Nash looked at her, and even the cart vendor was eyeing her with interest.

"Of course. Why not?" She gave Nash the packet and instructed him to open it while she fumbled around in her oversize purse, which was filled with far too many things. Nash had long ago commented that just because she was bad at making decisions didn't mean she had to carry her entire wardrobe and makeup collection in her purse. Not that he had complained last week when he needed a tape measure to determine if the model ship he wanted to buy would fit in the backseat of his mom's car. It was also handy for when she wanted to apply a temporary tattoo—it didn't take her long to fish out a bottle of water and a makeup pad.

She quickly squirted some water onto the pad and then took the tattoo from Nash. She pressed it onto the inside of her arm and then smoothed it over with the damp pad. A minute later she peeled the back off.

Her whole arm tingled as she inspected the tattoo.

The body of the two roses was inky black, and the leafed stems seemed almost to be moving and twisting on her arm. More important, as she looked at it, instead of the indecision that normally plagued her she felt an overwhelming sense of rightness. She loved it, and so would her dad. She held up her arm to admire it one last time when Nash nudged her.

"Why is that guy staring at you?"

"Where?" Cassidy looked up to see a disheveled guy over by the escalators staring at her intently. He was dressed like an extra from some B-grade King Arthur remake. She let out a groan. "Actually, I think the real question to ask is: Why is someone wearing armor at a mall in Southern California?"

"It's not armor," Nash corrected as he narrowed his eyes with interest. "It looks like chain mail to me. Oh, and he's coming over here."

She let out a sigh. While Nash, with his stunning good looks and his complete indifference, managed to attract attention from just about everyone, Cassidy, with her thick, dark, auburn-colored hair and mossy green eyes, seemed to attract only the weirdos. In fact, being approached by a guy wearing armor, or—she hastily corrected—chain mail, probably wouldn't even make it into her top five weirdo encounters.

She braced herself as he finally reached them. Up close, she realized that he was probably only in his early twenties, but the long, matted blond hair that hung limply around his pale face made him look older. He was sweating profusely, no doubt from the heavy chain mail that was smeared with dirt and oily black smudges, and there were two red, feverish spots on his sallow cheeks.

The guy pointed to the tattoo on Cassidy's arm and began to speak in a rapid-fire language that she didn't recognize. *Yup, definitely weird.* Cassidy stared at him blankly, which only caused him to speak faster. She shot Nash a helpless look.

"Do you know what he's saying?"

"No, actually, I don't." Nash, who went to stay with his grandmother in Italy each summer and spoke three languages, looked surprised. "I mean, most of it sounds like mutant Latin, but then a few of the words are undeniably French. I think he is saying 'Armand' over and over again, but apart from that, I've got nothing." He turned to the guy. *"Armand. Parlez-vous français?"*

This seemed to piss the guy off more, and he stabbed at Cassidy's arm, speaking even louder.

"Nash, you know, this is getting creepy, and—" Cassidy

started to say, but before she could finish, the guy stopped yelling as a flash of pain seemed to ripple across his pale face. He doubled over, clutching at the tarnished chain mail, as if trying to claw it away from his chest, his breath coming out in ragged gasps. As he straightened and elbowed his way past her, her large purse slipped off her shoulder and landed in a messy heap on the floor.

Cassidy probably would've landed on the floor, too, if Nash hadn't stuck his hand out and steadied her. But instead of stopping to see if she was okay, the guy melted away into the thinning crowd of late-afternoon shoppers.

"Okay, so what just happened there?" Cassidy rubbed her shoulder.

"No idea." Nash shook his head as he gallantly dropped to his knees and gathered up the various lip glosses and notebooks and so on that had spilled out when the guy had knocked into her purse. Then he stood up and handed the purse, once more filled with Cassidy's belongings, back to her. "But it was definitely unusual."

"I know, right?" She slung the bag back over her shoulder and scanned the crowd, but despite the fact that he looked like a homeless guy in full body armor—they saw no sign of him. "So what should we do now? Do we report him to security? Call the police?"

"And tell them what? That some dude spoke to you in a strange language and was dressed like a weirdo?" the vendor chimed in from where he continued to pack up his cart. "Because, hello, news flash: this is the mall. It's like a magnet for guys like him. And you know, considering that he actually had on both his shoes and showed no visible signs of body lice, that almost makes him look normal for around here."

"Normal? He knocked my purse off my shoulder," Cassidy protested.

"Not exactly illegal. Did he take anything?" the vendor asked, looking remarkably indifferent to the whole situation.

"Well, no," Cassidy was forced to reply since, if anything, her purse felt heavier than it had before, not that she was going to give Nash any more to tease her about. "But what if he goes and freaks out someone else? Are you seriously saying that we shouldn't do anything?"

"No," the vendor corrected in the same bored voice, "I'm *seriously* saying that I don't give two hoots *what* you do as long as you don't drag me into it. Now, are you going to buy another tattoo or not? Because it's my bowling night, and I want to get out of here."

Cassidy was about to open her mouth again before she realized that he was probably right. The mall was full of weirdly dressed guys.

"Fine," she muttered as she handed over a twenty-dollar bill and waited for her change. All that mattered was that she had found her dad the perfect present.

THREE

It was almost dark by the time Nash dropped her home in his mom's late-model Ford, which he seemed to love driving just a little bit too much for someone who was supposedly all about the romantic and philosophical ideals of the Renaissance period. Cassidy waited until his taillights had disappeared down the street before she walked up the path to the neat single-story house in which she had grown up. She grabbed the doorknob, her own tattoo tingling as she did so.

"So how did your trip to the mall go? Did you buy a new dress?" Her dad limped up the hallway, looking like he always did. His dark hair, with its odd gray streak, was pushed back from his face to reveal tanned skin with just a small scattering of wrinkles around his calm navy eyes. But despite his serenity, she knew he found it frustrating that his tennis habit had been reduced from playing three times a week to just watching matches on television, because every time he moved, it was painful.

"Not exactly." Cassidy shook her head, not least since most of her clothes came from the vintage shop down at the strip mall. At first, she had started going there to piss off her mom, who was fastidious to a fault, but after a while she'd grown to love the idea of having something that no one else had. Plus, without as much choice, it made decision making a lot easier. Then she realized that her dad was looking at her, so she fumbled around in her overloaded purse until she found the packet of tattoos. "I was actually there to get something for you."

"I thought that—" he started to say, but she quickly cut him off.

"Don't worry, it's not stuffed and doesn't involve balloons, fluffy bunnies, or sappy poems that mention the word *heart*," she promised as she handed the packet over. She caught her breath as he studied it in the same thoughtful manner he used for everything. "According to Nash, in Ireland the black rose is a symbol of—"

"Hope," her dad finished off, and then grinned. "And I love it."

"Well, that's lucky." Cassidy returned his smile and held up her arm so he could see the matching one. "Because I got one, too."

"And it looks good," he said when he had finished

inspecting it. "But Cass, if I wear this tattoo, you have to promise that you'll stop worrying about tomorrow. It's a simple operation, and I'll be signing up for tap-dancing lessons before you know it."

"All surgery carries risks," Cassidy corrected him in a stern voice, quoting something that she'd read on the Internet.

"You know what I mean." He put his hands on her shoulders, his navy eyes wide and earnest. "So, what do you say? Will you stop worrying if I wear it?"

"Fine," she relented. Especially since Nash, whose dad was a doctor, had been telling her the same thing for the last week.

"Good. Now, if I remember correctly, you owe me a game of Halo. Unless, of course, you're trying to wriggle out of it for fear of being beaten," he said in a teasing voice, which Cassidy found ridiculously comforting, since her dad had never managed to beat her once, not even when Nash had dared her to play with her eyes closed.

"Darn, you saw through my cunning plan," she countered as the pair of them headed toward the small den, the familiarity of it all washing away the last of her concern. However, it didn't last long—before they got even three paces, the sharp beep of the garage door opening rang out, and her dad came to a halt.

"Sounds like your mom's home from work. Which reminds me, I forgot to tell you that she's made dinner reservations for the three of us. For sushi."

Cassidy's happiness immediately evaporated and was replaced by annoyance. "Sushi? Dad, you hate sushi, and if she had paid any attention to us in the last *five* years, she might've known that."

"Don't be like that." Her dad shot her a cajoling smile. "She's trying."

"Yes, very trying," Cassidy retorted before reminding herself that stressing her dad out the night before he went into the hospital wasn't part of her game plan. Especially since her mom would probably manage to do that all on her own. "Fine, sushi it is. Yum."

"Thanks, honey." Her dad looked grateful. "I know it's hard for you to understand, but I really am happy that she's back."

Well, at least one of us is, Cassidy thought, just as the door leading from the garage to the house opened and the citrusy scent of her mom's perfume caught in her nose. Her mother's reddish-brown hair, so like Cassidy's own, was tamed into a neat chignon and she was dressed in a pencil skirt and plain blouse that Cassidy was pretty sure she ordered in bulk online to save her the bother of shopping.

"Hello, you two, I hope you're both— Good grief . . . what is this?" she demanded in distaste, her eyes immediately honing in on the tattoo packet before dismissing it with a shrug. "So anyway, Cassidy, I was speaking to Joanna Thompson today in the office."

Cassidy let out a weary sigh. *Here we go again.* Up until two months ago, Cassidy didn't have an opinion on Colin

Thompson, apart from the fact that he went to her school, wore dorky T-shirts, and spent too much time in the science labs. However, ever since her mom had moved back from Boston and set up a new office here in California, she had hired Colin's mom, Joanna, to do the administrative work, and now it seemed as if there was a never-ending series of conversations about what Colin was doing.

"Yes," her mom continued, either oblivious to Cassidy's annoyance or merely choosing to ignore it. "Colin was telling her all about the school production. Why didn't you tell me that Raiser Heights High is going to be doing *Romeo and Juliet*?"

"Er, same reason that I didn't tell you that the Jell-O was green today," Cassidy retorted, still stung by her mom's harsh reaction to, then dismissal of, the tattoos. "Because it's no big deal."

"Of course it's a big deal," her mom corrected as she started to sift through the mail in her ever-efficient manner. "Your college applications need to show that you're well rounded. Being in the school production would go a long way to helping you with that," she continued, settling into her current favorite topic: How to Bug the Crap Out of Cassidy by Discussing Her College Future. All. The. Time. "I think you should consider it."

"Thanks, but no thanks. Besides, school plays are lame."

"Don't be ridiculous—there's nothing wrong with being in the school play. Tell her, Ben," her mom directed as she finished sorting the mail into neat piles.

"Nope, I'm sitting this one out." Cassidy's dad held up his hands and shot her a sympathetic look. "I did drama only to pick up girls and have fun, not because I wanted to look well rounded. And speaking of girls, if I'm going to take the pair of you out tonight, I'd better go and make myself look presentable. What time's the reservation for?"

"In half an hour," her mom said, which was all the excuse Cassidy needed to retreat to her bedroom and try not to think how much nicer it would've been if it was just her and her dad sitting in front of the television eating pizza.

❖   ❖   ❖   ❖   ❖

Cassidy was sure there must've been a time when Becca Carter had been normal, but unfortunately, she had no knowledge of it. Even when Cassidy was a kid, her mom had worked long hours in the office, and it was Cassidy's dad who had done the school drop-offs, the PTA meetings, and the dance recitals (okay, there had been only the one before Cassidy realized that nothing was worth experiencing that horrendous stage fright).

At least back then they'd still had some semblance of being a family, but then her mom had left her job as CEO of a shoe company and had started working for the large manufacturing business that Cassidy's great-grandfather set up, spending more and more time in the head office in Boston, until soon she was virtually living a separate life. From time to time there had been talk of Cassidy's going

East to spend her vacations, but her mom had always been too busy with work, so they'd settled for a few Skype calls and Thanksgiving.

And that's how it had been for the last five years.

Until two months ago, when her mom had suddenly reappeared back on the West Coast, declaring that she was setting up a California branch and that, while she was at it, perhaps they should give the marriage another shot.

It had been a nightmare ever since.

Cassidy began to pace, trying to lose the unsettled feeling in the pit of her stomach. Normally, her bedroom, with its long wide windows, the wooden floors, and the muted apricot and pale green tones soothed her, but tonight it wasn't working. It probably wasn't helped by the fact she could hear her mom in the bedroom across the hall, giving her dad a play-by-play of some problem at work.

She clenched her fists. Her dad was going into the hospital tomorrow. Cassidy was pretty sure that he didn't want to hear what Bill in sales had done. She didn't want to hear it, either, and so she thrust her hand into the cavernous depths of her purse, searching for her MP3 player so she could block out her mom's voice. After several moments of fruitlessly fishing around, she realized that perhaps Nash had a point about how much stuff she kept in there.

Finally, she turned the purse upside down so that the contents spilled out across her comforter, where she finally discovered the small player, the cord of her earphones tangled up in her hairbrush. Unraveling it didn't take long, and she quickly stuck the earbuds into her ears and turned it on so that her mom's nagging voice was washed away by the sound of Florence and the Machine.

The tension eased in her shoulders as she scooped everything back into her purse. Lip gloss, magazines, the snow globe of the Eiffel Tower that she'd bought for Nash last week at a thrift shop and had forgotten to give him, a large leather-bound book—

What? Cassidy stared at the book and blinked.

Since when did she have a large leather-bound book in her purse?

She felt the lines across her brow gather together as she picked it up. It weighed a ton, which explained why her purse had felt so heavy, but it didn't go very far in explaining *what* it was doing in her bag. The tattoo on her arm prickled, and she unconsciously rubbed it before inspecting the book more closely.

The battered cover was cold and rough under her fingers, and the sensation sent an uneasy shiver racing up her arms. The title was long gone, and all Cassidy could see was the faint outline of where the words had once been embossed into the reddish-brown leather.

The coarse paper crackled under her touch as she opened it, but she hardly noticed as she stared at a black-ink diagram of circle upon circle, minute images or random words printed within each ring. She chewed her lip as she studied the images, but they were obviously meant to be understood only by a genius like Nash.

Cassidy let out a groan.

Of course. Nash. This was Nash's book.

He had been reading something at the mall, and he had obviously gotten tired of carrying it. It wouldn't be the first time he had slipped something into her bag. She rolled off the bed and put the book on her desk—no way was she lugging it to school in the morning. Instead, she reached for her cell phone to text him, but before she could finish her message, the hairs on her arms prickled and she was hit with a strong feeling that she was being watched.

An uncomfortable sensation made its way to her chest, causing her heart to pound in a rhythmic fashion as she cautiously moved over to the window and peered out.

The dark night was broken only by the dim glow of the neighborhood lights, but there was nothing unusual out there and so she drew back the white drapes in relief. She had obviously been listening to too many of Nash's creepy stories of how Renaissance doctors used to go and dig up bodies from the cemetery.

"What are you doing?"

Cassidy jumped at the sound of her mom's voice and she spun around in annoyance.

"Jeez, Mom, haven't you heard of knocking?"

"I did knock," her mom retorted as she glared at the earphones. Cassidy quickly yanked out the earbuds and let them dangle around her neck. "How many times have I asked you not to turn your music up so loud that you can't hear me? I'm sure it's damaging your ears."

Cassidy bristled. "My ears are fine."

"Well, I just wanted to check on you. We're leaving in ten minutes. Are you going to get changed?"

"No." Cassidy looked down at the pale cream dress she was wearing. She'd found it at her favorite vintage store last week, and while it had taken a while to decide whether to spend the twenty bucks on it, she was pleased she had. Not just because the Victorian neckline was cool and it looked good with her Dr. Martens, but because it obviously pissed off her mom. Now *that's* what she called value for money.

"Fine." Her mom merely shrugged as she walked into the room, her sharp gaze catching sight of the contents of Cassidy's purse, still covering half of her bed. She looked at the items with distaste for a moment before holding up a thin book. "I've just found this for you. It's an old copy of *Romeo and Juliet*."

"I told you that I didn't want to do it." Cassidy only just resisted the urge to stamp her boot on the wooden floorboards. "I don't want to think about my college application yet. I'm only sixteen."

"Yes, and the choices that you make today will affect your future," her mom retorted.

Cassidy raised her eyebrow at her. "Really, Mom? You want to talk about choices with me?" She folded her arms in front of her, and her mom had the good manners to blush, since, while Cassidy might struggle with making the most basic decisions, her mom suffered from no such affliction. Hence, her ability to dump her family for *five* years and live in Boston. And then, just as casually, to change her mind and move back as if no time at all had passed. Oh, yeah, her mom knew all about making choices.

"Okay, honey. I'm not here to fight with you. Besides, I'm sure your father would be pleased if you did it. It's his favorite Shakespeare play."

Just like sushi is his favorite food.

Cassidy didn't bother to answer. Especially since she'd watched Baz Luhrmann's version at least a dozen times when she'd gone through her Leo phase and her dad had never even blinked an eye at it. However, her mom seemed to take her silence as some kind of tacit agreement, and she carefully put the book down on the corner of the messy bed.

"All I'm asking is for you to consider it. And now, if you're ready, it's time to go. We don't want to be late." Then without another word she left the room, and Cassidy reluctantly followed her. It was going to be a long night.

F O U R

"You look like shit." Nash glanced up from the book he had been studying, once again oblivious to the group of girls who were whispering and pointing at him.

"Gee, why don't you tell me what you really think?" Cassidy dumped her purse on one of the many wooden tables dotted around the back lawn of Raiser Heights High and then joined him on the narrow bench seat. The school was a large redbrick box full of well-dressed, badly behaved, middle-class kids who looked pretty much like middle-class kids from every high school across the United States. Cassidy and Nash tried to avoid the school and the other students as much as they possibly could. Especially since it would be Halloween soon, and that just seemed to make everyone act more freakish than ever.

"You don't pay me all that money to lie to you," Nash protested before rubbing his chin. *"Oh, wait, you don't pay me at all."* Then he leaned forward and studied her face before pushing back a strand of her thick, dark red hair and shooting her a concerned look. "Tough night?"

"You could say that." Cassidy sighed as she tried to remember a time when she had been just a normal person who hung out with her friend and talked about algebra tests—okay, so in Nash's case, he preferred to talk about the Medicis and how they had proved that art and politics could exist side by side, but details schmetails. Her point was, since her mother had moved back in, she had not felt normal. "My mom dragged us all out for sushi."

"Sushi? You and your dad—heathens that you are—hate sushi," Nash reminded her in an unimpressed voice, since his own food tastes were slightly more highbrow than Cassidy's.

"Thank you. Unfortunately, the sushi actually ended up being the high point in a truly craptacular night."

"So I gather they didn't change their mind about your tagging along today?"

She gave a frustrated shake of her head. It had been an ongoing argument for the last week, and despite her best efforts, neither of her parents would relent. She had tried again this morning, purposely waiting until her mom was in the shower before she made her dad a cup of tea— something that he claimed every Irishman needed before he could even consider opening his eyes. But if she had hoped that she might persuade him when her mom wasn't around, she'd been wrong, and the party line was that it would be stupid for her to miss any school for a routine operation. Then he had pushed the tea aside and reminded her that he could only drink water before his operation.

"Oh, and if that's not bad enough, she also wants me to audition for the school play."

"She obviously doesn't remember the dance recital disaster." Nash widened his pale blue eyes in surprise.

"She thinks it will be good for my college applications," Cassidy explained as she angrily traced her finger around some of the carved graffiti.

"Not if they see you act it won't," Nash retorted.

"Exactly," Cassidy agreed in a dark voice. "Still, it was fun to see how pissed off she looked when dad put the tattoo on this morning."

"I'll bet." Nash grinned in appreciation before he jumped up and shot her a dazzling smile. "Don't move, I just need to see a man about a horse."

"Not going anywhere," Cassidy assured him as he sauntered over toward George Dennison, an eleventh-grade science geek with whom Nash liked to trade anecdotes from time to time. She watched Nash pause for a moment to dust off his black trousers, which were tucked into a pair of heavy boots, before adjusting his crumpled gray double-breasted shirt. She couldn't help but admire how above high school Nash was.

Then she froze as she once again had the eeriest sensation that someone was watching her.

She quickly swiveled around. To the left of her was a group of juniors, but they were busy studying something on the iPad that one of them was holding up. She rubbed her eyes, reminding herself that staying up all night worrying about her dad obviously wasn't good for curbing her paranoid tendencies.

Out of the corner of her eye, she saw a slight movement coming from the thick shrubbery that separated the parking lot from the front of the school yard. The hairs on the back of her arms prickled, and the tattoo on her arm felt warm against her skin. That was twice now. Did that mean it wasn't merely a figment of her imagination? The leaves rustled again. She craned her neck, hoping to see something, anything to let her know that—

"Oh, please, I thought you were over that moron." Nash reappeared, carrying an armful of books while wearing a look of disgust on his gorgeous face. "I mean, did he or did he not dump you faster than a bag of trash?"

"What?" Cassidy, who was still trying to figure out if there was someone hiding in the shrubbery, forced herself to turn back to where Nash was tapping the toe of his heavy black boot, looking anything but happy. "You do realize that I don't have any idea what you're talking about," Cassidy said with a frown.

"Reuben, of course." Nash nodded over to the group of juniors that Cassidy had been looking at moments earlier. Except this time she realized that it wasn't just a group of preppy girls; there was actually one guy lounging in between them all, looking like the cat who'd just caught the biggest canary ever. Reuben. Why wasn't she surprised?

His emo hair, which had once been surfer-dude blond, was

now dyed pitch-black and was poking up in all directions, with what could only be described as glue.

"I promise that I didn't even see him," Cassidy said, while silently cursing herself for not realizing that her ex-boyfriend was in the vicinity. Shouldn't she have some kind of radar for that? Like: *scumbag fifteen paces to the right*?

"Really? Because if I have to give you the talk again about what a morally bankrupt douche bag Reuben Salinger is, then I'll do it." Nash put down the books and folded his arms.

"You don't." Cassidy shook her head as the girls got to their feet and bounced toward the main entrance, with Reuben following at a more sedate saunter, too caught up in the moment even to notice that Cassidy was there. Which was fine by her. If she ever had to talk to her ex-boyfriend again, then it could only mean that every other male on the planet had been killed in some kind of freakish virus incident.

Not that she was really sure if she could even count him as an ex, since they had dated for only two weeks. Then she had been late to meet him at a party, which, for Reuben, was apparently code for "okay to shove your tongue down the nearest cheerleader's throat."

"Stop reliving it," Nash commanded with uncanny insight, considering his complete lack of sexual desire. Then he mellowed. "So if you weren't looking at Mr. Tosspot, then who *were* you looking at?"

Oh, just the imaginary, invisible thing that I thought was watching me, Cassidy considered saying, before deciding that Nash had enough worries about her without adding "delusional" to the list. Instead, she merely shrugged. "Just thinking. Anyway," she added as she suddenly caught sight of the book that he'd put down on the wooden table, "looks like you've been busy."

"I'll say. George's dad has a first edition of Boethius's *Consolation of Philosophy*. I mean, Cass, this is like crack to my people. Which is why, *mia bella*, I need to put this bambino in my locker."

"Fine." Cassidy was well used to Nash's unnatural excitement about all things book-related. Then she remembered about one book in particular. "Oh, and that reminds me. Nice one dumping that enormous thing in my purse yesterday. It weighed a ton."

"Your purse always weighs a ton. Not to mention the fact that it defies the laws of quantum physics," Nash countered before frowning. "But what enormous thing are you talking about?"

"A book. You know—big and leathery. Looks like it's about a million years old. You were reading it yesterday afternoon at the mall."

"No." Nash shook his head, causing his shiny brown locks to flop around his chiseled face before he dumped his leather satchel next to George's book and searched around for something, eventually pulling out a tattered brown leather book and waving it in her face. "*This* is what I was reading yesterday at the mall."

"What?" Cassidy widened her eyes as confusion danced across her brow. "It wasn't your book in my purse?"

"Of course not." Nash looked at her like she had just asked him to pull off his ear and pickle it. "Are you insane? This treasure cost fifty bucks on eBay, and I've seen what the inside of your purse looks like. Why would you even think that?"

"Er, because of the large leather-bound book that I found in there last night," Cassidy said as Nash put his book back into his leather satchel and held out his hand. Next thing she knew, she was being hauled to her feet as Nash nodded toward the school entrance.

"Okay, I'm intrigued," he said as he glided down the corridor. Cassidy never got sick of watching how people just seemed to melt out of his way. "How did it get there?"

"I've got no idea," Cassidy said as someone's backpack hit her arm. She paused for a moment and rubbed it before they finally reached his locker. "I mean, up until a second ago, I thought it was yours."

"So what's it like? And when you say old, how old, exactly?" Nash's clever eyes shone with excitement as he deposited the Boethius in his locker before carefully selecting a book to get him through "the monotony that is Mrs. Miller's Health class." He tucked his selection into his satchel and raised his eyebrows as the second bell rang out. "Well, I'm waiting. Details, please?"

"I don't have details. It just looked like a book. A big old leather book. Oh, and there were loads of diagrams in it. None of which made sense."

"That settles it," Nash said in a firm voice. "I'm coming

over to your house this afternoon to see this mysterious book. *Oh, crap. We've got to go.*"

"What?" Cassidy found herself being tugged in the opposite direction from their class. She ground in her heels and folded her arms, but before she could say anything else, she caught sight of Celeste Gilbert and three of her friends all marching directly toward them. Cassidy turned to him in surprise. "Um, since when do you know Celeste and her crew?"

"Since never," Nash retorted in a low voice, his head cocked as if trying to calculate the statistical probability of being able to run away before they reached them.

"So why are they heading in our direction?" Cassidy asked with interest.

Nash let out a sigh. "For some reason she's got it into her head that I would make the perfect Mercutio. She seems to think that my natural good looks will help bring in a bigger audience, and she keeps nagging me to come to auditions next week."

For a moment Cassidy just stared at him, and then she burst out laughing. "That might just be the funniest thing I've ever heard," she said, trying and failing to imagine Nash taking part in a group activity. It was just too ridiculous for words, since "playing well with others" wasn't exactly one of Nash's strengths.

"I'm pleased that you find it so amusing," Nash retorted. "But right now that's not really helping me."

"Sorry," Cassidy mumbled as Celeste finally reached

them and stood so that her pert cleavage was aimed directly at Nash. Cassidy had to fight to stop herself from laughing. The truth was that, while just about every other sophomore guy would die to have Celeste Gilbert give them the time of day, she had managed to pick the one guy who was immune to that sort of thing. Cassidy was sure that there was a life lesson in there somewhere.

"Nash, anyone would think you were trying to hide from me." Celeste pushed past Cassidy as if she wasn't even there so that she could lay a hand on Nash's arm. Nash flinched.

"Nash, is that true? Have you been hiding from Celeste?" Cassidy grinned, earning her a nudge in the ribs from her friend. However, Celeste still didn't even acknowledge Cassidy's presence. Instead, she took out a flyer (from where Cassidy didn't know) and pressed it into Nash's hand.

"Of course I haven't, Cassidy." He gave her a dark look. "I've just been busy. Very, very busy."

"Well, you're going to need to make some time because the auditions are on Monday after school, and I won't take no for answer. You would be so perfect for the role," Celeste said with the authority of one who was used to getting her own way. Then she gave him one last searing look with her wide blue eyes and nodded to her friends that it was time to go.

Cassidy watched them all leave before she turned to him and grinned. *"Oh, Nash, you just have to do it. You do, you do,"* she mimicked, earning herself a withering glare just as the final bell rang.

"Do I look like I'm laughing? If you tell anyone about

this, I will make you catch the bus for a week," he informed her.

"Okay, I've had my moment." Cassidy held up her hands in surrender before wrinkling her nose. "How does she even know you?"

"I've got no idea." He shuddered. "Ever since last week she's been trying to corner me. She's very persistent."

"Probably because she's not used to guys ignoring her. I bet she sees you as a challenge."

"Yes, well, not as challenging as I find her." He shuddered again. "And now we'd better get a move on before we get a tardy slip."

✢ ✢ ✢ ✢ ✢

At the end of the day Cassidy sat cross-legged on a patch of grass by the parking lot, staring at the blank screen of her cell phone. She knew she would see her dad soon when Nash took her to the hospital, but she also knew that if her mom didn't text to tell her how it had gone, then she was probably going to go insane. Seriously, how hard was it for the woman to pick up her cell phone?

Cassidy moodily grabbed another Cheez Doodle and popped it into her mouth while wishing that she'd bought Pringles instead. As she chewed, she looked around for Nash. She'd had an art class for last period while he'd had advanced geekoid-something-or-other class, and now she was waiting for him; he had his mom's car, which meant she didn't have to catch the bus.

She pushed her sleeve back and looked at the black rose tattoo. It was still tingling, and at least three people had thought it was a real tattoo. Not that she cared. She was just about to run her fingers over it when a faint gust of wind raced around her. Cassidy looked up just in time to see a single brown feather floating lazily in the air. As she watched, it softly came to rest in her lap.

Without thinking, she picked it up and unconsciously brushed it across the back of her hand. The down was soft as velvet and the color of the darkest chocolate, shot through with swirls of pale gray. It was mesmerizing, and she found herself getting lost in the rich tapestry of colors and—

"Man, there you are. I've been looking all over for you," a voice suddenly said, and before Cassidy knew what was happening, Reuben had flopped down on the grass next to her, his skinny, denim-clad legs stretched out in front of him. Cassidy blinked for a moment as she realized that she'd been so lost in her own private world she hadn't even noticed him approach. As she dropped the feather back into her lap she thought she heard the rustle of wings, but when she looked up into the nearby tree, there was nothing there. Then she realized that Reuben was staring at her expectantly, a familiar expression on his face. Her stomach lurched, and suddenly all thoughts of the feather were forgotten.

"What do you want?" she demanded, while privately cautioning herself to ignore the way his cheap aftershave still managed to make her go all Pavlov's dog whenever she smelled it. Thankfully, Reuben seemed indifferent to her confusion as he gave her his trademark smile, exposing what Nash liked to call his genetically unfortunate teeth.

"That's what I like about you, Cass, you're so modest that you don't know your own charm. I just thought it would be nice to hang out again. It's been too long. And . . . oh, hey, Cheez Doodles." He leaned over and popped one into his mouth before giving her a friendly nudge on the shoulder.

"Er, Reuben, you do remember that we don't date anymore, which I'm fairly sure means that you're not allowed to help yourself to my Cheez Doodles."

"Don't be like that, Cass." He tried to reach over for another one, but Cassidy smacked away his hand. "After all, we were so great together. In fact, I'm not sure why we even broke up."

"I do believe that it was because you found your tongue stuck down Natasha Bennett's throat and then a week later it was down Tracey Marsh's throat. And after that, I think it was either Katie or Katrina's throat—I always get the Hobson twins mixed up. Now, why don't you go sit with all of your preppy friends, since they seem to be enjoying Kiss an Emo Boy Month as much as you are."

"I can't," he suddenly said in a sulky voice. "They're all, 'Travis said this. . . . Travis said that. . . . Travis has a cute butt. . . . Travis has the best tan.'"

"What?" Cassidy blinked at him. Reuben was many things, but random wasn't normally one of them. She narrowed her eyes. "Are you on drugs?"

"I think he's talking about the new guy, Travis Lenoir,"

Nash said as he wandered toward them with the same effortless, casual ease with which he approached everything.

"Yeah, well, if you ask me, he sounds like a dick." Reuben pouted.

"Lucky no one asked you then." Nash gave Reuben a dismissive glare, not bothering to hide his disdain—though sometimes Cassidy wasn't sure if it was because of how Reuben had treated her, or because Reuben had once had the audacity to tell Nash that Leonardo da Vinci was a hack.

"Yeah, well, I don't know why you're so smug, Nash Peterson, since no one is looking at you anymore, either," Reuben retorted.

Nash shrugged. "Difference is that I don't give a damn. Now piss off, Reuben, and go find another rock to climb under, or—"

But before he could finish, Cassidy's cell phone signaled that a text message had come through. Her hands were shaking as she opened it, and then she turned to Nash and grinned, oblivious to the fact that Reuben was still there. She held up the screen so he could see the message:

```
The surgery all went well. I'll
tell you all about it when you get
here.
```

F I V E

"Cass, stop smiling. There is nothing pretty about my having to wear a pink hospital gown," her dad grumbled an hour later, but Cassidy couldn't help it. She had been scared of walking into the room in case he looked different, but he looked exactly the same—well, except for the gown—which really was bright pink. Plus, according to the doctor, the partial knee replacement had been a total success.

"So can you really come home tomorrow?" She perched on the side of the bed, careful not to bump his heavily bandaged knee.

"Yup." He nodded to the crutches that were leaning against a nearby chair. "I've got a physical therapy session here at the hospital in the morning, but then they'll do home visits for the rest, and if it all goes well, I should be back on my feet in a few weeks. Looks like your tattoo really worked."

Her mom, who was over in the corner filling out hospital forms, muttered something, but Cassidy ignored her as her fingers automatically went to her own tattoo, which was still tingling. She was just about to ask if his tattoo felt tingly, too, but before she could a nurse bustled into the room with an array of tablets for him to take.

After that they hung out with him until visiting hours were over. Thankfully, her mom had yet another crisis at the office, so Cassidy was able to spend the rest of the night IMing with Nash and giving him a play-by-play of just how great her dad was feeling.

❖   ❖   ❖   ❖   ❖

She was still smiling about it the next morning as her Health teacher droned on about the importance of a well-balanced diet. Next to her, Nash—in his own unique way—appeared to be listening intently while in reality he was discreetly reading the large leather-bound book that she'd found in her bag after their trip to the mall. She probably would have forgotten to bring it for him if he hadn't made her get up during their IM conversation and put it directly into her purse before she forgot.

He had hardly said a word to her since she had given it to him earlier. However, unlike Nash, the rest of the class was fidgeting and yawning as Mrs. Miller moved the discussion on to exercise. Cassidy idly played with the long feather that she'd found, running the length of it down her cheek before turning her attention to the invitation Nash had thrust at her earlier.

It was for Cade Taylor's Halloween party.

As always, it was addressed to him not her, and the number of times she'd just tagged along as his "plus one" didn't bear thinking about. Not that that would be happening for this party, since she had no intention of going. She folded up the invitation and leaned over Nash's shoulder to see if he'd found anything exciting in the book, when a murmur echoed around the room. Cassidy looked up to see a tall guy walk over to Mrs. Miller and hand her a note, at the same time giving her a jawbreaking smile.

Cassidy widened her eyes. Since the whole Reuben disaster, she hadn't been paying much attention to guys— which was actually quite easy, since, with the way she dressed and her refusal to wear more than a smear of lip gloss, not too many of them were beating a path to her door. But there was no denying that the guy standing at the front of the class was completely gorgeous, with a beauty that might rival even Nash's own.

However, while Nash was all alabaster skin, gothic punk clothing, and brooding good looks, this guy was like bottled sunshine, with warm dark eyes, a tangle of wild curls, and was that a hint of a dimple? Also, unlike Nash's tall, thin frame, there was nothing skinny about this guy. Judging by his wide shoulders, slim hips, and defined chest, he would probably be signed up for one of the many sports teams by the end of the day. Finally, Mrs. Miller, who seemed to be just as mesmerized as everyone else in the class, coughed.

"Class, this is Travis, and he'll be joining our class beginning today."

So that was Travis. Suddenly, Cassidy understood just why Reuben had been so pissed off yesterday, since there was no way his dyed hair and faux-emo talk could ever compete with Travis. Mrs. Miller pointed to an empty seat a row away from where Cassidy was sitting, and Cassidy watched, fascinated, as he slowly made his way over, looking slightly uncomfortable with all the attention he was commanding.

Boy, did Cassidy know that feeling. Well, not because she was a new guy with movie-star good looks that everyone wanted to drink in, but rather because, just after her grandfather had died a little over five years ago, there had been talk that his electronics company had been borrowing money from the workers' pension funds.

Of course it had all been a big lie, but no one seemed to care about that, and for a week or so Cassidy's family had been the news du jour. Thankfully, not long after that the costume for the school mascot—an oversize badger—had gone missing, and the whole thing about Cassidy's grandfather had faded away. But she had never forgotten how much it sucked to be the center of unwanted attention.

As Travis walked past he looked at her, his mesmerizing dark eyes full of confusion. Cassidy shot him a sympathetic smile while resisting the urge to reach out and squeeze his long, tapered fingers, which were so close to her they were almost brushing the desk.

Travis paused to study her face, a curious expression tugging at his lips as his dark eyes drilled into hers, as if trying to convey something important to her. She wasn't sure what it was, but it made her skin tingle, and by the time he had moved past her, her whole face was flaming so much that she was fairly sure there was steam coming out of her ears.

She turned her head and watched him casually slip into the seat he had been allocated, stretching his long, muscular legs out in front of him. He looked at her again, and Cassidy felt her cheeks burn so brightly that she spent the rest of the period with her eyes fixed firmly on Mrs. Miller, who was reminding them about an upcoming quiz.

When the bell finally rang, Cassidy gathered up her things just as Nash, who hadn't even seemed to blink since Travis had joined the class, suddenly leaned over. "Okay, so what the hell was *that* about?"

"Wh-what do you mean?" Cassidy feigned surprise as she busied herself with putting her pen into her purse.

"Oh, you know, all the smoldering eye contact that was going on between you and our new guy, Mr. Lenoir," Nash said, as Travis made his way to the door before turning and once more staring at Cassidy. This time there was no denying the yearning expression on his face. Then he turned and disappeared into the hallway, and Nash coughed. "Exhibit A."

Cassidy's face once again started to burn with a combination of excitement and confusion. "So you saw it, too?"

"You'd have to be blind not to," Nash informed her as he carefully put the leather book into his satchel and stood up. "So what's the deal? Have you already met him or something?"

Cassidy shook her head so quickly that her thick hair swung into her face. "No, I'd never even heard of him until Reuben talked about him yesterday. So what do we know about him?"

"Well, I know that he seems to like girls with reddish-brown hair who wear their grandmother's clothing and refuse to polish their Docs."

"It's not my grandmother's," Cassidy retorted as she glanced down at her seventies-style dress, which she'd pulled in at the waist with one of her dad's old leather belts, while totally ignoring the boot-polishing comment. "And that's not what I meant. Do you know what he's doing here and how long he's going to be around?"

"Why, so you can ask him to prom?" Nash asked, and Cassidy lightly punched him in the arm as they walked toward the quad to eat their lunch in peace and quiet.

"Yes, Nash. I want to ask him to prom, and then we can get married and have lots of children. That's what happens when teenagers stare at each other for five seconds."

"Well, not wanting to pick apart a long-held tradition of angst and pain, but my way would actually be a lot more sensible. Think of all the time and effort it would save."

Nash slung his arm over her shoulder in a companionable manner as they walked.

"What, so then everyone would have more time to spend reading books on ancient astronomy and science?"

"Exactly. All this love business just gets in the way of things, although, from a theoretical perspective, it does make for interesting study. Perhaps if you and Travis go on a date, I could tag along and observe."

"Not in this lifetime," Cassidy assured him as they reached their favorite table outside and slung their bags onto it before sitting down. Nash pulled out an expensive lunch box that was no doubt filled with his favorite tapas, while Cassidy got out a far less exciting sandwich. "Not that anything's going to happen. I mean, did you see how gorgeous he was? He's hardly going to be interested in me, and even if he was, I've got far too much going on even to consider it."

"Hey, I might not feel the normal urges, nor understand how they work, but even I know a hot, hormonally charged look when I see one," Nash corrected her. "Now, if we've finished talking about this, do you want to hear what I've discovered about your mysterious book?"

"You can understand it?" Cassidy immediately put down the mutilated ham with mustard sandwich that her mother had forced upon her that morning and flushed as she realized that she'd been so distracted by the unexpected attentions of Travis the New Guy that she'd completely forgotten about the mysterious book.

"Not exactly." He shook his head as he carefully lifted the

book out of his satchel and opened it up. "The closest I can guess is that it's written in some kind of Middle French."

"But you speak French," Cassidy reminded him.

"That is correct," he agreed. "But I don't speak this, which is why I'm thinking it's Middle French. A bit like how Chaucer's *Canterbury Tales* is written in Middle English."

"If you say so," Cassidy said, since while she'd vaguely heard of Middle English, she wasn't really quite sure what it was. Then she paused for a moment as something finally occurred to her. "Wait, that crazy guy at the mall the other day. Didn't you say he was speaking a weird language?"

"Exactly." Nash gave a pleased nod of his head, as if happy that she'd finally figured out what point he was trying to make. "So while I have no idea *why* he gave it to you, I think we've solved the mystery of *how* you got it. Remember he knocked your bag over. He must've slipped it in then, and because of all the junk you carry around, you just didn't notice."

Cassidy let his comment slide, mainly because it was true. Instead, she took a bite of her squished sandwich and chewed it for a moment before frowning. "So what do we do with it? I mean, you know more about old books than I do, but I'm pretty sure it must be worth loads of money. Should we be taking it to the police or something?"

"I'm not sure whether a theft like this would even be reported to the police; there's a good chance that the owner probably bought it on the black market in the first place. But you're right about the value. Not only do the cover and the paper seem genuine, it really is in the most remarkable condition. Whoever owned it must've kept it airlocked to preserve it like this. Anyway, if you don't mind a trip after school, I know an antiquarian bookseller who might be able to help us."

"Of course you do." Cassidy gave him an affectionate grin, since when it came to weird old stuff, Nash *always* seemed to know someone or other.

"What can I say?" He gave an unrepentant shrug as he turned the page and gestured for Cassidy to admire the black-and-white etching in front of him. At first, it looked like a big hot mess of spirally squiggles, with line upon line of tiny writing woven into it. But the more she looked at the diagram, the more the spirals seemed to shimmer and move in front of her. Cassidy's stomach knotted, and the tattoo on her arm prickled.

If she didn't know better, it almost looked like a pair of eyes. Cassidy immediately slammed her own eyes shut, but instead of cutting off the image, it seemed to bring it more intently into focus, until a pair of pale amber eyes burned in her mind, swirling like a torrential whirlpool, staring at her with such a searing intensity that Cassidy felt herself shake under the weight of it.

"Earth to Cass." Nash's voice caused the piercing eyes to vanish into a wisp of nothingness, and when she opened her own eyes again, the squiggle on the page was once again just a vague blur. She blinked once more and then shot Nash an apologetic smile.

"Sorry, I'm not sure what happened there," she said, trying to shake away the eerie sensation that the strange eyes had left behind. "Er, so what were you saying?"

"I was just telling you that your cell phone's beeping."

Cassidy immediately pulled her cell phone out of her pocket and studied the screen to discover that she'd missed a call from her mom. Crap. Not that she normally wanted to talk to her, but today was different. There was no answer when she called back, so she was forced to go into her voicemail. However, as she listened to her mother's efficient, clipped tones, she could feel her own face getting darker and darker; by the time she dropped her cell phone onto the table, Nash was looking at her in alarm.

"What's up? Are they home from the hospital yet?"

"Oh, they're home all right. But it turns out that Dad is feeling *so* well that my mom's decided to go into the office for a few hours," Cassidy said in a tight voice, still not quite able to process the message her mom had left. "He's on crutches and is meant to keep his knee elevated and rested. What's so important that she has to leave him alone in the house like that? Does she think the whole office building will fall down if she's not there? And she even had the cheek to leave a list of things I would need to cook spaghetti for dinner. I mean, if she's not going to bother coming home, why should I cook what she wants me to cook?"

"Yes, but you love spaghetti." Nash's face clouded over with confusion.

"That's not the point."

"Okay, so what *do* you want to cook?"

"I don't know." Cassidy gave an impatient shake of her head. Out of all the decisions that she hated making, deciding what to eat was at the top of the list. Then she let out a sigh. "Anyway, I don't want to fight. I'm not mad at you, I'm mad at my mom. But this means that I won't be able to come with you this afternoon to see your book guy. If you want to take the book with you, though, then that's fine."

"Are you crazy?" Nash looked at her in shock. "Howard's an antiquarian bookseller, not a Good Samaritan. There's no way I'm going to take the book with me. It would be like walking into the mob with a bagful of cash and diamonds and expecting them not to want it. A big no-no. It's much better if I just show him a few blurry photographs and then casually ask him some vague questions."

Cassidy raised a surprised eyebrow. She hadn't realized that the antique-book business was quite so cloak-and-dagger, but before she could say anything, the bell rang. She waited patiently while Nash quickly snapped a couple of photographs on his cell phone, and then they both hurried to fifth period. Besides, Nash would either find the owner of the book or he wouldn't; right now she had bigger things to worry about.

S I X

"Do you ever get the feeling someone's watching you?" Cassidy's dad asked later that night as they sat in the living room eating their dinner. Her dad was resting on the couch, his leg out flat in front of him and his empty pasta bowl on the small table beside him. Her mom still hadn't returned from whatever "work emergency" she was dealing with, so it had been just the two of them eating the spaghetti that Cassidy had grudgingly made. More because she couldn't be bothered to decide what else to cook than because she thought her mom's idea was a good one. However, at her father's question, she immediately looked up.

"Why?" She put aside her own pasta bowl as she remembered the eerie sensations she'd been feeling lately, and the burning eyes that had been emblazoned in her mind. Just thinking about it made the hairs on the back of her arms stand up, and she gave a little shiver. "H-have you noticed something?"

"Actually, I have. It's my daughter, and she seems to be watching my every move," her dad retorted in a dry voice. Cassidy let out a private groan. Talk about getting her wires crossed.

"I'm not watching your *every* move," she protested before raising her hands in defeat. "Okay, fine. But I'm worried about you."

"Cass, you can't keep looking at me like I'm made of cotton," he said, and she saw the hint of the temporary tattoo peeking out from under his shirtsleeve. It should've made her smile, but she couldn't quite muster one.

"Yes, well, if I don't do it, then who will?" Cassidy retorted as she pointedly glared at the empty chair where her mom normally sat and then over to where his crutches were lying on the floor.

"We've talked about this. I'm fine. The surgery is over, and in a few weeks I'll be crashing your school disco and embarrassing you in front of your friends with all of my slick moves."

"I'm pretty sure that discos haven't existed since 1985," Cassidy pointed out before letting out a sigh. "But fine, point made. I'll stop being so overprotective."

"And stop giving your mom such a hard time?"

Cassidy went to open her mouth in protest. Especially when she thought of the large stack of printouts on the kitchen bench that her mom had left for her. There were dozens of articles on college applications and why it was good to show diversity. However, then she remembered that stress was the last thing he needed, and she let out a reluctant sigh. "And I'll stop giving Mom such a hard time," she dutifully repeated.

"Thank you." He nodded as he reached for his crutches. "Now, we should really do these dishes."

"Don't you dare!" Cassidy jumped to her feet and gathered up the bowls before he could even think about standing up. "You can sit there and reminisce about your glory days as king of the disco," she commanded, before walking out to the kitchen and loading up the dishwasher.

It was almost eight o'clock, and despite what her dad said, she still thought that it was wrong of her mom to have not come home yet. Cassidy shook some detergent into the machine and tried to stay calm, but it was hard when she was so pissed off. After all, what was so important that her mom had to stay at work for so long? And if this was what it was going to be like from now on, then why didn't her mom just stay in Boston? All she was doing here was bossing everyone around and giving orders.

She turned the machine on with a thump and was just about to walk out of the kitchen when she caught sight of a large handwritten note stuck to the refrigerator: CASSIDY—TAKE TRASH OUT.

For a moment Cassidy glared at it. Especially since over the last five years her mom probably hadn't even known what day the trash was collected. Then she caught sight of the wedge of paper sitting on the bench. The printouts she was meant to be reading, complete with color-coded Post-it notes attached to them. Suddenly, she smiled. *Oh, she would take out the trash, all right.*

She grabbed a plastic bag and gleefully scooped the offending articles into it, then hurried outside and down along the side of the house. The large tree in the neighbor's yard threw *Edward Scissorhands*—style shadows across the concrete as she made her way along the path. Nash would say that she was being completely irrational and probably passive-aggressive to dump the articles her mom had left for her, but all Cassidy knew was that it also made her feel as if she had some small sliver of control. Plus, it would totally piss off her mom when she found out.

Cassidy grinned some more as she emptied the papers into the recycling bin. She had just flicked the lid shut and was about to open up the gate to drag the bin to the street when she heard a scratching noise from somewhere behind her. Her excitement at defying her mom disappeared as the hairs on her arms stood up, and fine tendrils of fear clutched at her heart. It was the same feeling that she'd had several times during the last two days. The feeling that someone was watching her.

Part of her wanted to believe it was because tomorrow was Halloween. But the other part of her—the part that her brain seemed to be listening to—wasn't so sure.

This time the scratching was louder, and Cassidy unconsciously edged away from it. In the process she managed to stumble back into the bin; she watched in dismay as it fell to the ground with a thud, spilling plastic bottles and papers out onto the path in front of her. She ignored the mess, her breath catching in her throat. But apart from a soft breeze that was blowing against the surrounding trees, there was no sign of anything and—

Whatever Cassidy was about to think next disappeared from her mind as a violent flap of wings sounded in her ears and she looked up to see an enormous bird on one of the lower branches of a nearby tree. Its wings were spread out in an eerie silhouette against the crescent moon as it turned its pale heart-shaped face toward her. Inspecting her with a pair of dark, swirling eyes that sat above its noselike beak.

Cassidy shuddered as a single feather leisurely floated down to the ground. It was almost identical to the feather that had fallen into her lap the previous day, and Cassidy found herself helplessly following its progress until it finally landed just by her scuffed-up Docs.

Two feathers? The hypnotic amber eyes that she kept thinking were watching her? She wasn't a genius like Nash, but she knew all these things had to mean something. It's just that she had no idea what, and despite the fact that every single nerve in her body was screaming at her to go inside, she looked back up into the tree.

The owl spread out its wings and pushed its talons against the gnarled branch, and for one awful second Cassidy thought it was going to launch itself at her. But instead it sprang off the branch and glided down to the other end of the path, effectively blocking her path.

For a moment it just stood there, feathers shimmering

and glowing in front of her very eyes; before Cassidy quite knew what was happening, the owl was gone and in its place was a body. A person.

A guy.

Cassidy was past screaming. She was past thinking. She was past taking any kind of action. All she could do was stand there and stare helplessly at the figure in front of her. He looked about her age, perhaps a year or so older, and his dark hair was cropped close to his head. His strong brow was knit in powerful concentration, and he was dressed in a coarse, collarless shirt, which reached well below his thighs and was ripped and stained.

As he walked toward her, she could clearly see a jagged, angry scar running down one side of his face. It was brutal, but then as he got closer, she discovered that even more compelling than the horrendous scar were his eyes. One was the palest of blues and the other a swirling brown color, and they were staring at her with such intensity that Cassidy felt incapable of looking away.

Then he spoke. "My name is Thomas de la Croix, and we don't have much time."

That was when she finally started to scream.

SEVEN

Cassidy clamped a hand over her mouth to try to muffle the sound of her scream, because whoever or *whatever* this thing was, there was no way she wanted to make her dad come out to check on her when he was supposed to be resting. Instead, she used her teeth to bite down hard on one finger, in the hope that the pain would cause the vision in front of her to disappear. It didn't work, and when she looked again, his disconcerting gaze was still fixed firmly on her.

He looked annoyed, and strangely enough, it was that which finally helped Cassidy to get herself under control. She dropped her hand back down to her side and took a deep breath. There had to be a logical explanation for what she'd just witnessed.

"What are you?" she said, her whole body still shaking from the shock.

"I told you"—his voice was laced in an accent that she couldn't quite place—"I am Thomas."

"I didn't ask *who* you are. I want to know *what* you are," Cassidy repeated, as she unconsciously took a step backward to try to avoid his uncompromising stare. To try to give herself some space in which to think. "I mean, you were an owl, and then you were . . . Well, then you weren't an owl. Are you some kind of shape-shifter, werewolf thing?"

"I am not a beast," he said in a low voice, and it was obvious from the way his jaw was clenched that patience wasn't one of his virtues. "I'm a knight of the Brotherhood of the Black Rose."

Black Rose?

The tattoo on her arm burned in response, and once again she heard a voice calling out to her. *Pick me. Pick me.* She took another step away from him until the rough plaster on the exterior of the house was rubbing against her sweater and into her spine. She thought of the crazy guy at the mall. Armand. His accent had been almost identical to Thomas's, and he had kept pointing at her temporary tattoo.

She let out a small gasp. "He gave me the book on purpose?" Her mind was spinning as she tried to connect the dots, but it was a puzzle that didn't want to be solved. Where was Nash's brilliant mind when she needed him?

"*Oui.* Armand would have been desperate. He came here to protect the Black Rose, and when he discovered his mistake, he would've been looking for another guardian who could handle the burden. There must have been something about you that called out either to him or to the grimoire."

"Wh-what's a grimoire?" Cassidy was almost too scared to ask.

"It's the most important book that the Brotherhood possesses, and it is the heart of our magic."

Cassidy was silent.

She had been forced to sit through more than her fair share of strange conversations with Nash, most of them full of names and places that she'd never heard of before. But right now this Thomas guy was making Nash's conversations sound like watercooler stories. It was ridiculous, and she'd heard quite enough of . . . *well, whatever it was.* She edged her way along the wall, hoping to slip past him, but Thomas quickly blocked her way, his mismatched eyes cold and clinical.

"You must listen carefully," he said, a guarded expression on his tense face. "Perhaps if I start at the beginning, it will make more sense."

Doubtful, Cassidy thought as her mind raced, trying to decide if she could get out through the gate that led through to the front yard. Unfortunately, her gate-jumping skills weren't what they should be, and she doubted she would have time to unlock it. She took a deep breath and tried to stay calm.

"The Black Rose is an essence. A very powerful essence that offers immortal life and unlimited power to whoever inhales it. It was created by alchemists before they realized that everything comes at a cost, and that the Black Rose also brings madness, pain, and destruction. That is why the Brotherhood has sworn to protect it from the men and demons who desire it."

Essences? Immortal life? Demons?

Cassidy, who was still struggling to deal with the owl-transforming-into-a-guy thing, blinked. He had to be kidding, but when she inspected his face, she got the feeling that he never kidded. About anything. Ever. She hugged her arms around her chest.

"As yet there has been no way to destroy the Black Rose, and those who covet it are growing ever stronger." And still the disarming eyes were staring intently at her.

"A-and what's any of this got to do with me?" Cassidy croaked, ignoring the way the fake tattoo on her arm was blazing. She wasn't sure how much longer she could keep things together.

"The Black Rose is currently residing in an unknown vessel. A corporeal body. *A virginal human body.* The vessel and the Black Rose need to be protected from those who desire it. That is where you come in. You must be the guardian. I need you to find the virginal vessel and the Black Rose and protect them until the moment of the next solstice, when you will send it back."

"Send it back *where?*" The words were out of her mouth before she could stop them.

"Back where it belongs. Back where we can keep it safe. Back to the year 1310."

"*What?* Are you insane?" Cassidy felt her jaw drop. So far, she had been doing a good job of not giving in to the hysteria that was threatening to rise up from her belly. Not when faced with the owl turning into a guy. Not when hearing of the demons and the immortal life. But now she was being told that she had to send something back through time. Her whole body began to shake as she stared at the loose woolen shirt he was wearing before she remembered the other guy from the mall, who had been wearing chain mail. How was this even possible?

"That is something I've often been accused of. But my mental state is not the issue here. I have explained what I need you to do, and the sooner we start your training, the better," he said, but Cassidy just stared at him blankly, causing him to bristle with frustration. "I *need* you to take this seriously. Whether you like it or not, you are the next guardian."

"I'm sorry." She had finally managed to find her voice. "If you really were from the fourteenth century, then why can I understand you? According to Nash, you all spoke differently back then. Even the writing in that book was different."

"The grimoire."

"Fine. Book . . . grimoire. What's the difference?"

He gave an impatient shake of his head. "*Non*. The grimoire is the reason you can understand me. All the power and knowledge of the Brotherhood lie within the covers."

"What? So by touching a book, I can go all BabelFish?"

He ignored her question. "It only works when the

grimoire chooses to accept your touch. But since we are standing here, it is obvious that it has now done so. That is why you can understand me when I speak and why you can see me. You will also find that you can now read the text."

Again, the tattoo on her arm began to blaze as the hysteria in her belly turned to dread. Not because of how ridiculous he sounded but because some of what he was saying made sense.

"And how can you understand me?" she croaked.

"It's not important," he assured her, his mismatched eyes blazing with a passionate intensity that made her shiver. "What *is* important is that you start training to find and protect the Black Rose immediately, because it won't be long before the demon knights discover that it has been lost. You have a lot to learn before the solstice if we are to succeed."

"Stop saying that." Cassidy shook her head. "Because it isn't going to happen. I'm not going to be a guardian of anything. Besides, there must be hundreds of people who would do a better job of it than I would."

Thomas didn't disagree; instead, he merely shrugged. "The grimoire has chosen you."

"Yes, but it chose me only because I had a stupid fake tattoo on my arm." Cassidy pushed back her sleeve to show him her arm. "Your book made a mistake. Anyway, if it's such a big deal, then why don't you do it, huh? After all—"

Thomas abruptly cut her off. "Touch me," he said, and Cassidy widened her eyes.

"Wh-what?" she asked in alarm, since, despite the surreal

nature of the whole conversation, up until now she hadn't felt in danger. But it suddenly occurred to her that she had no idea what he was capable of. She edged her way farther down the wall, once again feeling the uneven plaster digging painfully into her spine.

"You heard me. Touch me," he said, his voice not brooking any argument, and Cassidy found herself stepping toward him, purposely avoiding his hypnotic gaze. He held his arm out to her. She took a deep breath before finally reaching out to him. She could almost feel the heat radiating off his body, as his intense eyes stared down at her, and—

Her hand sliced through the air as if he wasn't even standing there.

She whipped her hand back as if she'd been bitten, confusion stinging at her eyes. Thomas didn't say anything. He just stood there, his brow taut with impatience. She reached forward again, this time for his chest, but once more her hand was greeted by nothing but air.

"I don't understand." She rubbed her fingers, her eyes never leaving his face. "Are you a ghost? Why can't I touch you?"

"I am no shade," he assured her. "Though many have tried to put me in my grave. Unfortunately, I cannot travel through time. I am where I have always been. You can see me because I have projected a vision of myself to you," he said, his voice still filled with impatience. "However, to do so requires a lot of effort. Magic."

"Okay." Cassidy shut her eyes for a moment as she

tried to make sense of everything. "And the owl?"

"The owl is real and exists here in your world. I am not part of it, and it is not part of me, but my power is such that I can bind with creatures if I choose. It is a lot less exhausting than appearing to you as I am now. So I connect with the owl to find the things that I seek."

"Like me?" she croaked as she realized why she'd had the eerie sensation that someone had been watching her.

"Like you," he agreed in a calm voice, as if it was totally okay to go all stalker dude when it was for a good cause.

"What about the guy at the mall? Armand? I felt him. He knocked my purse off my shoulder. He wasn't an apparition. He was real," Cassidy said, while trying to stop herself from drowning in the overload of information. Thomas bowed his head, and she had the distinct impression he was swearing, but when he looked up, his face was blank.

"Armand thought he could defy the laws of nature and travel through time. He wanted to follow the grimoire and protect the Black Rose as he had sworn to do, but he didn't understand his limitations, and thus, he paid the ultimate price."

"He died?" Cassidy gasped as she recalled his unnatural pallor and the feverish red spots on his cheeks.

Thomas gave a curt nod of his head. "He was a fool, and his foolishness has cost us dearly," Thomas spat. "The Black Rose and the grimoire are here, and we, the knights who have sworn to guard it, are there. *Now can you see my problem?*"

"Not really." Cassidy shook her head so that her long hair went flying into her face. She quickly pushed it out of her eyes. "If you can't time travel, then how can anyone get it?"

Thomas let out another faint string of expletives. "We use magic to help us fight the demon knights, but our magic is earth-based and pure. Unfortunately, those who covet the Black Rose don't share the same beliefs. They use blood magic. Slicing the veins of innocents corrupts almost as surely as the touch of the Black Rose. It also gives them power. And not only will blood magic let them travel through time, it will help them trace that which they seek. And if they succeed, they will be even more dangerous. More deadly. More . . . *unthinkable.* Now, please. Our time is limited. The demon knights will soon find the grimoire, and unless you stop them, they will also find the Black Rose. I *can't* let that happen."

Despite the fact that he wasn't really there, the intensity in his face was so overwhelming that she could almost feel the force of his emotions shimmering out through the apparition. As surreal and unbelievable as the situation was, she had no doubt he was telling the truth. Cassidy felt the familiar confusion that often happened to her as she tried to make up her mind. *If the Black Rose really was half as dangerous as he said, then—*

"Cass, are you out there?" her father called as the outside light flicked on. A moment later he appeared at the top of the path, leaning forward on his crutches.

"Dad, what are you doing?" Horror rose in her throat,

though she wasn't sure if she was more freaked out that he had caught her talking to a strange ghostlike guy who could turn into an owl or that he was outside on his crutches when his doctor had quite clearly told him that, for the first week, he should keep his leg elevated as much as possible and use his crutches only on even surfaces.

"I was worried about you. You've been out here for at least half an hour, and I could hear voices," her dad said before catching sight of the overturned recycling bin. "Don't tell me that the neighbor's cat has been at it again."

"What?" She was blank for a moment as she followed her dad's gaze past where Thomas was standing, still as a statue, his face pale, apart from the angry scar running down his check. She let out a little gasp. *Her dad couldn't see Thomas.* Then she realized he was waiting for an answer, and so she dropped to her knees and started to shovel the plastic bottles and papers back into the bin before dragging it back into an upright position. "Yeah, it was the cat. I'll just finish cleaning up out here, but you need to go back inside and put your leg up."

"Remember that chat we had about your not being overprotective?" he asked in a mild voice, before turning and carefully maneuvering himself with his crutches back inside. Once he was gone, she got to her feet and headed to the gate. Her fingers trembled as she unlatched it, but finally it was open and she began to drag the recycling bin and the trash can out to the curb for tomorrow's collection. As she moved, adrenaline pounded through her body. She had no idea what was going on, but she knew that it wasn't something she could get involved in. Not if it meant her dad would risk his recovery just to check up on her. She left the cans on the curb and made her way back inside the gate. Thomas was still waiting there, but she ignored him.

"Where are you going?" Thomas demanded, his face still leached of color.

"I'm going inside. Where I belong."

Then, without another word, she walked straight through the apparition that was Thomas. For a moment his mismatched eyes widened in disbelief, but instead of doing anything, he suddenly disappeared altogether, leaving only a single feather in his place. She locked the back door as soon as she was inside. She waited a moment until her heart rate had returned to normal before going to check on her dad. She had no idea what had just happened, but she was 100 percent sure that she didn't want it to happen again.

EIGHT

"This is extraordinary," Nash said two hours later as he carefully turned the page of the book and pointed to a diagram, his excitement so palpable that he was almost bouncing off the bed. "Do you realize what this is? A genuine grimoire. Here. In my hands. I should've figured it out by the diagrams, but they're just so rare that it never occurred to me. And now, not only do we have it, but *you* can *read* it." His pale blue eyes were alight with awe.

"Shhhhhh." Cassidy held a finger up to her mouth as she glanced toward the bedroom door. It was only ten at night, and even though her mother *still* hadn't come home from the office, her dad had gone to bed an hour ago, which was about the same time Nash had arrived in answer to Cassidy's desperate text message. He'd been saying "This is extraordinary" ever since.

"Sorry." He instantly lowered his voice, his gaze never leaving the book in front of him. "But honestly, it is amazing.

I can understand only about one word in ten, and yet all of a sudden, you can read it like it's a magazine. I wish it would choose to accept my touch so that I could read it, too. Tell me what this one says. Is it a spell or an instruction? Oh, I bet that it's a—"

"I think you're missing the point," Cassidy cut in while trying to avoid looking at the grimoire, since, unlike Nash, she found it more than a little disturbing that it was no longer a blurry mess of confusion but rather was completely legible. Mainly because if that part of what Thomas had told her was true, then it might mean that— No! She slammed the lid shut on that particular thought, since no good could come of thinking it.

Nash regretfully shut the grimoire. "You're right, I'm sorry. It's just hard not to get carried away. The implications this could have are unprecedented. And this Black Rose that he talked about. You do realize that he's referring to immortality. The fifth element: spirit. The unknown factor that every scientist, philosopher, and alchemist has searched for, since . . . Aren't you curious?"

"Not even a little bit," she was quick to assure him.

Nash heroically seemed to swallow his disappointment while trying not to look like a scientist who had just had his lab equipment taken away. Then he perked up a bit. "So if this Thomas of yours comes back, perhaps you could just ask him a few questions for me?"

"He's not *my* Thomas," Cassidy quickly protested. "And you're forgetting that I don't want to see him again. Ever.

Ever, ever, ever. That's why I've got to figure out a way to make sure he doesn't come back again, since one run-in with a freakish knight is enough to last me a lifetime."

"Do you really think he will?" Nash studied her face.

"He was pretty intense—you know that crazy look Mr. Kirkland used to get in his eyes when he talked about dung beetles? It's like that but doubled. I get the feeling that he's not the kind of guy who likes taking no for an answer." As she spoke she glanced over to Nash's silver Zippo, which he had left on her desk. He didn't smoke and as far as she knew he didn't have any major pyro tendencies, but he often did his best thinking when staring into the flame of the lighter. She suddenly wondered how well it would burn through leather book binding.

"Okay, okay." Nash suddenly stood up and pocketed the Zippo, as if somehow reading her mind. Then he headed for the window. "I'll help you, as long as you promise not to do anything dumb. Let me go see Howard. You know, my antiquarian friend. He's an insomniac who owes me a favor or two. Hopefully, he'll let me do some research on grimoires and the best way to deactivate them."

"Thank you." Cassidy gratefully followed him over to the window and watched as he effortlessly swung his long legs over the ledge and dropped out into the garden of the one-story house.

"Don't mention it. And try to get some sleep. You look exhausted," he advised before he disappeared out into the night and started to jog the three blocks back to his own house. Once he was gone, Cassidy crawled into bed and closed her eyes, but regardless of how tired she felt, her mind refused to shut down. Instead, it went over and over her disturbing encounter with Thomas. And no matter how much she tried to block it from her mind, it just kept coming back. In despair, she finally pushed back her comforter to turn some music on, in the hope that it would take her mind off everything.

The wooden floor was cool beneath her feet as she thumbed through her MP3 player searching for a song, but before she could put it into the docking station she caught sight of the grimoire, at the far end of the desk. The MP3 player fell from her hands as she saw a pair of swirling amber eyes staring out at her from the cover. They were there for only a second, and then they disappeared.

Cassidy had to clamp her hand over her mouth to stop herself from screaming as her heart pounded in her chest. They were the same eyes she had seen last time she looked in the grimoire. The same eyes that she'd seen on the owl. Thomas had told her that he'd been using the owl to seek her out, but now she wondered if he was looking at her through the grimoire as well.

However, as she stared at the book, her panic was replaced by anger. She was *so* sick of people telling her what to do. First her mother and now Thomas. Why didn't anyone seem to understand that no meant no? Then she froze as something else occurred to her. If the book didn't exist, then Thomas would no longer be able to find her.

If the book didn't exist . . .

That was it, and before she could change her mind, she reached for a pair of scissors and dug them deep into the leather cover. After all the drama the book had put her through, she almost expected it to make some kind of noise and perhaps ooze some black sticky goo, but apart from the sound of the blade slicing through the leather, there was nothing.

Cassidy stabbed at it again, this time making sure she ripped the pages as well, until all that was left was enough shredding to keep a hamster happy for a month. She gathered up the disemboweled tome and scooped it all into a plastic bag, quickly making her way to the front door.

Her nerves jangled at the idea of being outside, but the thought of having the grimoire in the house for another minute, even in its slashed state, made her stomach churn, and she forced herself to step out into the inky night. The sharp October weather prickled her skin, but she ignored it as she cautiously checked that no one was around—and by no one she meant owls or apparitions of sullen knights with blazing, mismatched eyes. However, apart from a cat howling somewhere up the street, there was nothing. Her heart hammered as she hurried to the curb and quickly threw the grimoire into the garbage can. Then she hurried inside and back down the hallway, so scared that she could barely breathe and—

"Cassidy, is that you?" asked a voice from the kitchen, and Cassidy froze as she realized that her mom must've come home. She reluctantly peered in to where her mom was standing next to the microwave, clutching a sharp knife in her hand.

"I-I didn't hear you come in," she stammered.

"I did call, but when there was no answer, I thought you were asleep. What were you doing out there?" Her mom looked confused as she put the knife back down on the bench.

"Um, I was just getting some fresh air." Cassidy crossed her fingers and tried not to look as if she'd just been disposing of a mutilated ancient book that a time-traveling, demon-fighting knight who was now dead had given her.

"Fresh air? But it's freezing out—" her mom started to say before glancing over to where the articles she'd left had once been sitting. "Oh, let me guess. You were throwing away the information I got for you before the trash gets collected tomorrow."

No, Cassidy started to protest before remembering that she had, in fact, thrown it away earlier, but before she could say anything her mom opened up a nearby drawer and pulled out another bunch of papers.

"I guess it was lucky that I made duplicates."

"You what?" Cassidy bristled. "So you thought that since I didn't want to read them once, it would be good to give me a second copy? Especially when I've already told you that I'm not doing the school play. Why can't you respect my decisions?"

"Because you don't know what you want," her mom said as she neatly placed the articles on the bench as the microwave began to ding. "You never have. I bet if I asked what your favorite candy bar was, you wouldn't be able to tell me."

"Of course I can," Cassidy replied. *It was Snickers . . . no, Mars Bar . . . no, Chunky Kit Kat, or . . .* Then she shook her head and narrowed her eyes. "But that's not the point. This isn't about chocolate bars, it's about—"

"What's going on?" Her dad suddenly appeared, leaning forward on his crutches, sleep still crusting his eyes. Cassidy felt guilty.

"Nothing." She shook her head and was surprised to see her mom give her a grateful look. Not that Cassidy was doing it for her. She was doing it for her dad. Then she yawned. "Anyway, I'm going to bed now. Try and get some rest, Dad," she said, before hurrying back to her bedroom. Then she crawled into bed and fell into a dreamless sleep.

NINE

Feeble rays of light pushed in through Cassidy's white drapes, and she was just about to roll over and go back to sleep when she suddenly remembered what had happened yesterday. The owl. The knight called Thomas. The grimoire.

A chill went through her, and she sat up with a start. But as she glanced around the room, there was nothing but the flickering morning sun bouncing off the scissors that she'd used to destroy the book. More important, the eerie sensation that had been her constant companion since she'd discovered the book was no longer with her. She had been right. No book, therefore no stalker knight following her every move.

She pushed aside the drapes and peered out the window to where the trash cans were standing, their tops flipped back like they always were after they'd been emptied. Which meant that not only had she destroyed the grimoire, but it was now sitting in a pile of potato peelings and moldy bread in the back of a stinky truck somewhere.

It was over.

Then she looked at the tattoo on her arm. It no longer burned, but it was stupid to take any chances; she reached for her nail polish remover and vigorously scrubbed it off until her skin was pink and raw. Then she realized that if she was going to get rid of her tattoo, she should get rid of her dad's as well, just to be on the safe side. She grabbed the remover and hurried to his bedroom, where he was sitting on the bed, fully dressed, with a large pot of tea on the nearby dresser.

"Do you want a cup?" He nodded at the pot, and Cassidy pulled a face. She pretty much loved everything about her dad, but it was going to be a cold day in hell before she drank tea.

"Er, no thanks." She sat down on the side of the bed, careful not to disturb his knee. "So how are you? Did you sleep okay?"

"Actually, I did," he said. "By the way, your mom's gone down to the bakery to grab some croissants, because hey, nothing says Halloween like croissants."

"Well, the chocolate-filled ones can be pretty scary," she joked as she fiddled with the nail polish remover. "But I'm pleased you're feeling better. I was worried that you might have overdone it last night."

"And I'm wondering why you're holding a bottle of nail polish remover. Is this going to be like the time you set up a beauty salon and made me have my nails painted?"

"I was ten," Cassidy reminded him as she opened up the

bottle. "I just noticed last night that your tattoo is starting to fade and look ratty, so I thought it was time to take it off."

"What's going on?" He looked at her in surprise before noticing that her own tattoo was gone. "Cassidy, are you still worried? Because I thought that we had—"

"No, I promise, this isn't because I'm worried. I just realized that it was a bit dumb of me to expect you to wear a stupid fake tattoo that came from the mall," she said in a bright voice while quickly pouring the remover onto a cotton pad and reaching for his arm. "I mean, what will your physical therapists think when they come to visit?"

"I'm pretty sure that they won't have an opinion on the matter," he assured her, but all the same he let her scrub his arm clean. She was just screwing the lid back onto the bottle when the doorbell rang. Reluctantly, she got to her feet.

"That will be Nash. Is there anything I can get you before I go?"

"Actually, you could tell me what you're going to wear to the Halloween party tonight," her dad said.

"How did you know about that?" Cassidy narrowed her eyes.

"Nash sent me a text message. He said you were worried about me and wanted to stay home to help me with my leg exercises. Which is very nice, but completely unnecessary. Besides, if you *do* stay at home, you know that your mom will make you open the door and greet all of the trick-or-treaters."

"Having knee surgery makes you play dirty," Cassidy

answered, while making a private note to kill Nash in a slow and very painful manner for mentioning the party to her dad. "I can't promise that I will go to the party, but I will think about it. Happy?"

"Yes, thank you." He gave her a smile as she leaned forward and gave him a kiss on the brow. Then she said her good-byes and went out to where Nash was waiting for her by the door. Today he was wearing a pair of heavy gray army-surplus trousers and a long coat that wouldn't have looked out of place on a highwayman.

"I thought I would come in to see how your dad is. Plus, I wanted to look at the grimoire and cross-reference it with what I've found."

Cassidy winced. She was pretty sure that once Nash found out what she'd done to the grimoire, he would be crazy-mad—with emphasis on the crazy-mad part—which was why she needed to distract him.

"He's feeling much better, but the chances of your seeing him are slim to none," Cassidy said in a light voice as she crossed her fingers, hoping that her distraction worked. "Thanks to the fact that *someone* told him about a certain Halloween party. Oh, and in case you didn't get it, the *someone* that I'm referring to is you, Nash Peterson."

"Oh." Nash had the good grace to look guilty before he shot Cassidy a curious look. "So did it work? I told him to explain to you that science proves teenagers are wired to take risks and move away from their tribe so that they can keep the gene pool expanding. And that it was, therefore, unnatural of you to want to stay at home."

"Strangely enough, he didn't lead with that argument," Cassidy retorted as they finally reached his car. "And I'm not going to change my mind."

"Fine." He shrugged. "Now, back to my research. If you won't let me come in the house, do you at least have the grimoire with you? Because I have found out that—"

"Actually, before we get into that, d-did you notice the night sky last night? There was this amazing constellation, and I was wondering if you knew what it was called, since you think astronomy is so much fun."

"Astronomy *is* fun," he corrected before coming to a halt and narrowing his eyes. "And since when do you care about the stars—especially when you're in the middle of a crisis. Cassidy Carter-Lewis, what's going on?"

She took a deep breath. "Okay, so don't freak out, but I got rid of the grimoire last night."

"What do you mean 'got rid of it'? How did you get rid of it?" Nash folded his arms, his voice dangerously low.

"I cut it up and threw it out in the trash, which was collected this morning," she said in a rush as Nash's face went completely still, like one of the marble statues that he admired so much. He made a grunting noise before he suddenly walked away from her, his voluminous coat billowing out behind him. Cassidy watched him circle her front yard three times before finally coming back to where she was standing next to his mom's car.

Then he let out a breath. "Cass, my sweets, I love you like

the sister that I, thankfully, never had, but I'm struggling with this. I mean, that grimoire was a *relic*. An *artifact*. It was completely unique, and its existence might've helped us to change our entire perception of how the world really works. *And you destroyed it?* How could you have done something like that?"

Cassidy was sensing that he didn't want a blow-by-blow account of her scissors attack, so she took a deep breath and tried again. "I'm sorry, but I had to. It was like something was trying to claw at me from inside out. It felt wrong. *It felt evil.* And it was all because of the grimoire. Thomas told me that's how he found me, and I saw on the book the same eyes as were on the owl. The guy might be a knight, but he definitely doesn't have any shining armor. I just needed to get him and his creepiness away from me. And more important, get it away from my dad. Please don't be mad at me."

Nash filled his cheeks with air for a moment before slowly releasing it. Then he sighed. "I'm not mad. Just shocked and, if I'm honest, confused."

"What do you mean?"

"I mean, I went back to Howard's. He has an extensive collection of occult books, and he owes me a favor or two, so he let me spend the entire night researching grimoires, and one of the many interesting facts I learned was that they're imbued with magic, and, as a rule, magic books aren't that easy to destroy."

"Well, this one was," Cassidy assured him. "Not only did it look like confetti by the time I finished with it, but

I can tell it's gone just by the fact that I no longer have the unsettling feeling in my stomach that I'm being watched," she explained. "It's over."

"Yes, but—" However, before he could finish, her mom's car pulled into the driveway, back from her Halloween croissant run. Cassidy immediately hurried around to the passenger's side of Nash's car and nodded for him to get moving. Thankfully, he merely scooped his books off the roof, and while his face didn't quite lose its strained expression, he got in, fired up the engine, and pulled away before the electronic garage door had even opened.

✢   ✢   ✢   ✢   ✢

Thanks to the fact that Nash was a certified brainiac who did advanced everything, Cassidy, with her B-minus average, didn't see much of him for the rest of the day. She knew he was still pissed at her about destroying the grimoire, but he would come around eventually; he always did.

She rounded the corner as the final bell rang, trying to decide what movie she and her dad should watch tonight, when a backpack slammed into her chest, knocking the wind out of her. She doubled over as tears of pain stung her eyes.

"Watch it," snapped a large guy wearing deck shoes, as if Cassidy's chest had somehow damaged his precious backpack. Cassidy vaguely recognized him as Scott Wilson, a senior jock and a full-time conceited idiot.

"I think you're the one who should watch it, buddy," someone said, and Cassidy managed to unbend herself enough to see the new guy, Travis, standing next to her, wearing a pair of impossibly faded Levi's and a well-loved gray T-shirt, while his tangled hair was carelessly pushed back from his smooth brow so that she could feel the full impact of his warm brown eyes.

Scott turned back around and stared at Travis, a look of disbelief spreading across his face. "Seriously, are you talking to *me*?"

"That's right," Travis agreed in a pleasant voice. "It just seems like you forgot to offer"—he paused for a moment and turned to Cassidy—"what's your name?"

"Cassidy," she found herself replying in a breathy voice, too surprised to do anything else.

"Thanks." He grinned at her for a moment before turning back to the other guy, his eyes narrow and intense. "Anyway, it seems that you forgot to offer my good friend Cassidy here an apology."

"What the—" Scott puffed out his chest like some kind of predator from Animal Planet before suddenly looking at Travis and freezing. There was nothing aggressive or intimidating about Travis, but whatever mojo he had going on, it seemed to be working; Scott suddenly nodded. "Er, right. Yeah, look, I'm sorry about that," he mumbled before scampering off. The moment he was gone, Travis turned to her.

"Are you okay?"

"Um, y-yeah, I'm fine," she stammered, still feeling the lingering sting where the backpack had hit her and wondering whether her cheeks were blotchy. "And thanks."

"Don't mention it. That guy was a jerk for doing it in the first place."

"Definitely," Cassidy agreed as she glanced around the hallway to where all the other students were getting jostled and pushed around by the seniors. "And by the way, welcome to Raiser Heights High. Land of the jerks. So how did you get him to apologize anyway?"

"I guess I appealed to his better self?" Travis gave a modest shrug before glancing at the time on his cell phone. "Anyway, if you're okay, I'd better go. I need to get to the library before it shuts to get a copy of *To Kill a Mockingbird*. Turns out that being new doesn't get you out of doing the book report that's due on Monday."

"Oh." Cassidy shook her head in surprise while wondering what sort of school he'd gone to before. "You won't have any luck. The library has only two copies, and they probably won't be returned until some time next term."

"Really?" Surprise crossed his face. "Well, that will make the report more interesting to do."

"Just don't try to lift anything from the Internet, because Mrs. Webster has one of those programs that can tell," Cassidy warned before she nodded for him to follow her. "Look, you can borrow my copy if you want."

"You want to give me your book?" He immediately frowned, which somehow made him even better looking. "What are you going to do?"

"Don't worry, I've got Nash," Cassidy assured him as they reached her locker and she punched in her code, only then remembering that her locker was stuffed full of various belts, necklaces, and cardigans that she'd worn and then halfway through the day decided were stupid and ended up taking off. If he saw that mess, he would run a mile.

"Nash?" Travis knitted his brows as Cassidy tried her best to block her locker and grab the book for him at the same time. "What's a Nash?"

Cassidy found herself laughing. "Nash is a person. He's my friend, and he also happens to be a genius. Very handy when it comes to book reports."

"I can imagine." Travis grinned as Cassidy held out the battered copy that was her dad's from when he was in school. Travis gave a reverent nod as he took it, somehow seeming to understand that it was important to her.

"Thank you. You are very kind, Cassidy." As he spoke, his dark eyes caught hers, and Cassidy felt her face start to heat up. But before she could say anything else Celeste Gilbert and a group of her friends walked past, and when they saw Travis, they immediately beelined toward him.

"Travis, there you are," another senior, Rachel Brett, squealed as she possessively hooked her arm under his. "Mrs. Jenkins from the office wants to see you. She had a question about your transfer papers, and she wants to get it sorted out today."

"And since we're not doing anything else," Celeste added,

once again ignoring Cassidy, "we told her that we would escort you there."

"Oh." Travis politely nodded his head. "Sure, I guess."

"Good, come on then." Rachel began to drag him off. As he went Travis rolled his eyes and mouthed good-bye in a pained way, clutching at the book she'd given him as if it was a life raft. Of course, considering that Travis had managed to get Scott Wilson to apologize, Cassidy was pretty sure that he could have avoided being dragged off by Celeste and Rachel if he'd really wanted to. But still, she couldn't help smiling at the thought that he was holding her book. Then she heard Rachel's voice ringing out in the distance.

"By the way, Travis, you still haven't told me what you're wearing to Cade Taylor's Halloween party tonight."

Before Cassidy could hear his answer, Nash appeared. "There you are. I've been waiting outside for ages," he started to say, before suddenly noticing something. He narrowed his eyes. "You look like you've just won the lottery. Why are you smiling?"

TEN

Cassidy stared into the mirror. An Audrey Hepburn zombie stared back at her. She readjusted her tiara and tried to decide if she'd overdone the fake blood, which was covering her chin. Would anyone even think that she *was* a zombie? Perhaps she just looked like Courtney Love on a bad makeup day, which definitely wasn't the look she was going for. Especially since Travis was going to be there.

Travis was going to be there!

Just thinking his name caused a stab of indecision to go racing through her, and she hurried over to her bed and studied the other costumes that were lying there. She picked up the Lara Croft one. She'd almost worn that last year before Nash convinced her they should go as Bonnie and Clyde. But at least no one would mistake her for a crazy person if she was wearing it. Then she turned to the giant Angry Bird outfit, which she'd spent far too much money on, but decided red wasn't her color. She chewed at her fake-blood-stained lip, but before she could make up her mind, she heard Nash's car pull up, so she grabbed the Lara Croft costume and stuffed it into her oversize handbag. At least her choice was now between just two.

As she raced down the hallway, she caught sight of her dad sitting up in his bed, his knee elevated, just as the doctor had ordered. She poked her head in.

"Hey, I just thought I would say good-bye," she said, walking over to his bedside.

"Wow, you look great. Though I'm not sure I'll ever be able to watch *Breakfast at Tiffany's* again without thinking of blood." Her dad smiled as he put his book aside. "I'm pleased that you're going out tonight. What made you change your mind?"

"Nothing," she said a little bit too quickly, trying not to think about her run-in with Travis this afternoon.

"Is that code for *boy*?" her dad asked with interest, and Cassidy let out an embarrassed groan.

"Yes, but you know what? I think I'm just going to cancel, because—"

"Because nothing," he cut her off. "Cass, we've been through this. I'm feeling much better, so I want you to go to this party, eat lots of brains, and then come home and tell me all about it."

"Thanks, Dad." Cassidy hugged him, careful not to let her zombie makeup smear on his shirt, and then headed out to where Nash was waiting. He was wearing tightly fitted pantaloons and a velvet jacket with ruffles of lace hanging down over his wrists, while his normally dark hair was covered with a stark white judge-style wig, à la the Scarlet Pimpernel.

He also seemed to be having a boring conversation about particle physics with her mom, which caused Cassidy to roll her eyes before she grabbed his hand and dragged him away with a quick good-bye.

They hurried down the path, only just avoiding a group of trick-or-treaters who were swinging their pumpkin-shaped candy bags and complaining about being given oranges by one of the other houses.

"After you, Ms. Hepburn," Nash deadpanned, holding open the car door. "And can I just say that you look very fetching for a living-dead person."

"Thank you, and you look very dashing as well." She grinned back at him and then suddenly shot him a hopeful look. "So does this mean that you've forgiven me?"

Nash pushed back one of his stiff white curls and reluctantly nodded. "Yes. Apart from the fact that you destroyed a once-in-a-lifetime opportunity to learn more about a quantifiable link between science and spirit, which up until this point in time has only been conjecture, I've made my peace with your decision."

"Well, that means a lot to me—even if I did only understand one word in three of what you just said. Now let's get going before I freeze to death." She got in and waited for Nash to start the car and pull away from the curb.

Cade Taylor lived only about ten blocks away, but the

temperature had dropped, plus neither of them wanted to walk past all the hyped-up kids who were crawling all over the neighborhood. A few moments later they were there, and Cassidy looked up at the house. It backed onto the woods, but the spooky factor was lost, given all the lights that lined the brickwork.

The party was in full swing when they walked in, and they were accosted by drunken seniors all dressed up and dancing to loud music. Thankfully, Cassidy had been to enough parties with Nash to know that he had an uncanny ability to find where the real party was happening, and so she obediently trailed after him until they reached a second living room. Sure enough, everyone in there was less drunk and started their sentences with words that didn't include "Oh, my God" and "Get stuffed, douche bag." They were even playing Kings of Leon, as opposed to the trance music that had first greeted them.

"See." Nash sank down into a nearby couch and stretched his long legs out in front of him, causing a nearby Cleopatra to let out a dreamy sigh. "I told you it wouldn't suck."

"Well, not yet, anyway," Cassidy conceded as she realized that pretty much everyone was dressed up as zombies. There were Cheerios cheerleading zombies, panda zombies, Snow White zombies, and she was pretty sure that, over in the corner, she could even see a zombie nun. Too late, she realized she should've worn the Lara Croft costume after all.

She turned to Nash, but before she could speak, a senior dressed as a Super Mario zombie wandered over and asked

Nash his thoughts on the last biotech symposium; Cassidy contented herself with scanning the room for Travis.

There was no sign of him, but unfortunately, she did manage to see Reuben, who was wearing a Renfield-style straitjacket. He was chatting up some girl, popping candy flies into his mouth as he swayed drunkenly. Oh, and she was pretty sure she heard him use the Dracula's-thrall-is-nothing-compared-to-the-thrall-you-have-over-me line.

"Is that guy eating flies?" a soft voice asked in her ear, and she turned to see that Travis, dressed as James Dean, had joined her on the couch. His dark hair was slicked back, and his plain white T-shirt clung to his chest and seemed to make his dazzling smile more dazzling than ever.

"I don't think they're real," Cassidy assured him, while trying to ignore the fact his leg was so close to hers, it was almost touching. "Anyway, nice costume, James."

"Pardon?" He shot her a blank look.

"James Dean," Cassidy explained. "Your costume."

"Oh." Travis shot her a rueful smile that transformed his face and made him look like a sunbeam. "Should I confess that I've never heard of him? I just went to the store, and the woman thought this would suit me."

"She was right," Cassidy couldn't help replying as she fiddled with her tiara to try to hide her nerves.

"Thank you. I like your costume, too, though where is the tattoo you had on your arm the other day? I thought that was really cool."

"Oh." She unconsciously dropped her arm back down

to her side, surprised that he had even noticed it, let alone remembered it. Not that she was going to tell him why it was gone, since appearing like a weirdo wasn't in her how-to-talk-to-cute-boys handbook. "It was only a temporary one. I got it when my dad was going into the hospital, but now that he's better, I took it off."

"I hope it was nothing serious?"

"As he keeps telling me on a regular basis, it was just a small operation and he's feeling much better," Cassidy assured him, touched by his concern. "But thanks for asking."

"I'm pleased to hear that. Though it's a pity about the tattoo. I liked it," he said before giving her a boyish grin. "So I was wondering if you could tell me what the situation is with the school play. I was thinking of auditioning but didn't want to step into a land mine."

"Sorry, I'm not much of a drama person," Cassidy admitted—though for the first time since her mom had mentioned it, she *was* genuinely sorry.

"Really?" Travis sounded surprised as he arched an eyebrow. "That's too bad, because I think you would be pretty amazing up on the stage."

"If, by amazing, you mean shaking violently and forgetting my own name, then yes, you might be right," she quipped before she could stop herself, but instead of looking at her as if she was stupid, he gave her a reassuring smile.

"Stage fright can happen to the best of us," he said, his gorgeous eyes catching hers. Before she could reply, his cell phone rang. For a moment he just stared at the pocket of his leather jacket, seemingly unsure whether to answer it or not. Cassidy nodded to let him know that she didn't mind, while privately impressed that he'd even considered it might be rude.

She watched him answer it in a low voice. He didn't say much, but as the conversation continued his face darkened until he finally shoved the phone back in his pocket and rubbed his full lower lip.

"Is there a problem?"

"Not exactly, but there is something I have to take care of." He let out a frustrated sigh before shooting her a curious look. "Seriously, is it just my family, or does every family have one person in it who drives you crazy?"

"Oh, you definitely don't have the franchise on crazy family members," Cassidy assured him as she thought of her mom. Who wasn't so much crazy as overpowering, detached, and selfish—but hey; tomato, tamahto.

Travis looked at her with interest. "Sounds like we'll have to compare notes one day."

"I-I'd like that," Cassidy said, surprised at just how disappointed she was that he was leaving so soon.

"Anyway, Cassidy, I'd better go and sort this thing out, but hey, it was nice to see you, and thanks again for the book."

"What book?" Nash suddenly turned to her, his conversation with the Super Mario zombie finished. Cassidy waited until Travis had finally disappeared from sight altogether before turning to Nash and letting out her own dreamy sigh.

"Harper Lee. I lent him my copy. Can you believe he thought he might find a copy in the library?"

"Good-looking and innocent?" Nash reflected. "He's going to get eaten alive at this school."

"I don't know." Cassidy shook her head as she told him about what happened with Scott in the hallway earlier. "He obviously has some kind of mojo that he uses."

"So I'm discovering." Nash raised his eyebrows, causing her to flush. At the same time Reuben's fake laugh floated over, and they could both hear him tell the very boring story of how he once got kicked out of a concert for wearing the wrong footwear.

"Could your ex be any more of a jerk?" Nash rolled his eyes as he pulled her to her feet and led her out through sliding glass doors to the large patio. There were two large coal patio heaters to ward off the chilly weather, and pumpkin-shaped lights were dotted across the lawn below, stopped only by the shadowy darkness of the surrounding woods. As far as spook factor went, it was definitely an A-plus.

"I didn't think it was possible, but he does seem to be doing his best to prove us wrong." Cassidy shivered, since thanks to the groups of people huddled around the braziers, not much of the warmth was reaching her. Nash immediately slipped off his Scarlet Pimpernel jacket and draped it over her shoulders.

"Here you go. You already look ghoulish enough with the zombie face paint, I don't think you need to turn blue."

"Thanks." Cassidy slipped her arms through the sleeves.

It was miles too big for her, but it smelled of Nash, and it was warm. She was just about to ask him what his thoughts were on helping her with the book report due Monday when she was hit with an overwhelming smell of perfume and Baileys Irish Cream. She looked over to see Celeste Gilbert walking toward them, dressed as a slightly drunk Marilyn Monroe.

"Nash," the senior squealed in delight as she grabbed at his arm to stop herself from wobbling on her high heels. As usual, she completely ignored Cassidy. "I was hoping you'd be here."

"Really? Because I was hoping you were going to be at Abbott Thornton's party." Nash neatly removed Celeste's hand from his arm. "In fact, I'm certain that's where you told me you were going."

"I could say the same about you," Celeste scolded with a mock pout. "Didn't you say you'd be there?"

"I did? My mistake," Nash said in an innocent voice, which Cassidy knew all too well. "Anyway, it was nice to see you, but Cassidy and I were just leaving."

"Oh, I am as well." Celeste clapped her hands like it was some amazing coincidence. "Perhaps you could give me a lift and we could discuss the play? Remember that auditions are Monday."

"Actually"—Cassidy coughed as she caught sight of Nash's pained expression and decided to take pity on him— "Nash isn't going home. He's off to pick up some dead rats. He feeds them to his pet snake, Hamish. And while it's normally great to have someone in the backseat who can deal with the smell and hold the dead rats, there won't be much room because Hamish will be traveling with us. What are your thoughts on pet snakes and dead rats, Celeste?"

Cassidy blinked and turned to Nash. "Did anyone ever tell you that your friend is weird? I've got no idea what she's talking about. Why would you have a pet snake or a—"

But whatever Celeste was going to say next was cut off by a loud crashing noise coming from the edge of the woods. They all turned to see an enormous creature smashing through the tree line and tearing across the dew-laden lawn toward the patio, its large silhouette illuminated by the moon, which had pushed through the clouds.

As it got closer to the patio, Cassidy could see it was at least six feet tall. Its red, scarred face was twisted into a distorted mask of fury, complete with sharp yellow teeth and long horns that ran back behind its skull, while its hulking body was thick with roped muscles. But the things that clearly stood out were the vile stench of blood and decay that hit her nose and the pair of familiar, amber-colored swirling eyes, so bright that they cut through the air like laser beams.

Cassidy felt ill.

"Jeez, would you look at how drunk that demon dude is?" Celeste stopped her Marilyn pouting and wrinkled her nose at the trail of carnage the creature was leaving behind it. "I mean, it's a great costume, but you can't go around knocking stuff over like that. Or waving a sword in the air. Whoever he is, I think Cade should ask him to leave, because—"

But Cassidy hardly heard as she stared in fascinated horror as the creature paused for a moment, completely indifferent to everyone around it.

"Cass," Nash said in a low whisper as his hand reached out and grabbed hers. "Please tell me that it isn't what I think it is."

"I-I don't know," she croaked as bile rose in her throat. This encounter was *nothing* like her run-in with Thomas the previous night. But, she reminded herself, Thomas was human, and whatever this thing in front of her was, it definitely wasn't.

That was another thing she'd been wrong about. She'd thought it was the owl/Thomas who had been watching her through the grimoire, but the familiar fear that had been clawing at her chest for three days now was even more intense than ever, and it told her everything she needed to know.

This was the creature that had been watching her.

This was the thing she'd been scared of.

The skin on her arm where the tattoo had been began to tingle as the creature turned to them, its dreadful eyes locking firmly in on them like a heat missile. Then it charged. It moved at incredible speed, racing toward them, completely indifferent to the moans and screams of the people it knocked out of its way. A small fire erupted as it kicked over the patio heater, but still it didn't stop until it reached them, its fetid breath and decayed yellow teeth just inches from them.

Celeste let out an ear-piercing scream and darted behind a surprised Nash, just as the creature lunged. Cassidy was thrust out the way and she was forced to watch, in slow-motion horror, as the creature used a giant foot to slam into Nash's chest, sending him stumbling back onto the patio floor, where he landed with a sickening thump.

"No!" Her scream echoed around the now-silent patio. The blood thumped in her temples as the creature raised the sword and was just about to bring it crashing down into Nash's exposed chest. She had to get up. She had to move her legs. But before she could move, the creature suddenly doubled over in pain. It lowered its sword, then turned and tore back across the lawn and into the dark night.

As soon as it was gone, the silence was broken as dozens of voices all seemed to be talking at once. Someone was debating whether to call an ambulance, and someone else was frantically trying to put out the small blaze that had been started by the knocked-over brazier, but she didn't pay any attention as she dropped down to Nash's side.

She grabbed his hand and studied his face. His brow was covered in a fine layer of sweat. Next to them Celeste was still screaming hysterically, even though, from what Cassidy could see, the only thing that had happened to her was that she'd ripped her Marilyn dress.

Nash tightened his grip on her hand, and his eyes flickered open. "Hey."

"Hey, yourself." Her voice quivered, and she noticed that

some color was returning to his face. Her heart pounded in relief. "H-how do you feel?"

"Like I've just had my coccyx kicked," he retorted in a weak voice.

"What's a coccyx? Is it bad?" The words caught in her throat.

He gave a slight shake of his head as he cautiously moved his arm. "Sore ass. I'm just a bit stiff, but I should make a full recovery."

Cassidy let out her breath, almost faint with relief. "Are you sure? Perhaps we should go to the emergency room just in case?"

"God, no." Nash looked at her in horror as he gingerly managed to get up into a sitting position and paused for a moment as if to double-check he really was okay. "Have you ever seen the emergency room on Halloween? Nightmare. Besides, I'll get my dad to check me out when I get home."

Cassidy chewed her lip, still undecided if she should try to convince him to go to the hospital. However, since he was the genius and she wasn't, she supposed she should take his word for it.

"Fine, but make sure you do. Can I get you anything? An ice pack? Water?"

"No, I'm good. Just give me a minute or two, and I might even be able to stand up," he said before lowering his voice and catching her eye. "But Cass, that thing wasn't wearing a costume, was it?"

"I-I don't think so," she started to say, just as she heard a familiar scraping noise and looked across the patio into the dark night. The lawn was now ripped up from where the creature had crossed it, and some of the Halloween lights were flickering, unsure whether they should be working or not. But just on the edge of the woods, Cassidy could see a familiar pair of amber eyes. They were somber and intense and seemed to be staring directly at her.

These eyes didn't belong to the demon that had just attacked them; they belonged to the owl. *To Thomas.* The thing that was responsible for all of this. Rage and annoyance bubbled away inside her.

"Cass. You're hurting my hand," Nash croaked, looking at her in alarm. "What's wrong? Is it coming back? Because I know I was playing tough guy before, but I don't think I'm quite ready for round two with a demon knight yet."

"No." She instantly loosened her grip. "But will you be okay here? There's something I've got to do."

"What?" He looked at her in alarm, as if reading her mind. "Because if what you want to do involves going into the woods, then I have to say that I think it's a very bad idea. A terrible one. In fact, now I think about it, I should definitely go to the hospital."

"I promise I won't do anything stupid, I just really need to sort something out. Wait here, okay?" She jumped to her feet and scanned the patio, looking for someone who could keep an eye on Nash, but it was a sea of unfamiliar faces apart from . . .

Reuben. She let out a soft groan. He was standing by himself, idly playing with the long straps that dangled from his straitjacket. There was no sign of the girl he'd been talking to earlier, and Cassidy had the feeling he hadn't gotten lucky. He was also hardly her first choice, but there was no way she was leaving Nash on his own, so she raced over to him and dragged him to where Nash was still sitting.

"Cass, you know I love it when you turn all alpha on me," Reuben slurred as he tried to wink at her. Cassidy ignored him.

"Okay, I need you to stay with Nash until I come back. Do you understand?"

"What?" Reuben blinked, obviously not quite getting the response that he was after.

"Stay. With. Nash," Cassidy repeated with a growl. "As in, don't leave his side, even for a second. And if you do desert him, then I'll tell everyone what I caught you doing that time at—"

"Hey, whoa. No need to go there. I'm in, okay? I'll stay with Nash until you get back," Reuben interrupted. Cassidy didn't even bother to look at him. Instead, she crouched next to Nash, pushed his white wig back off his damp forehead, and squeezed his hands.

"I'll be back soon. I promise." She gave him one final nod and then got to her feet and ran.

E L E V E N

Branches scraped and prickled against her arms, but Cassidy hardly noticed as she went flying into the woods. Thankfully, she had decided to wear her Dr. Martens instead of the high heels that her mom had suggested.

"Thomas," she called out, her eyes frantically searching for any sign of the bird, but there was only darkness and trees and the sound of her own heart hammering frantically in her chest. "Thomas," she repeated, but there was still no answer, and Cassidy felt her annoyance grow as she finally stumbled into a small clearing.

It was dark with only thin slivers of moonlight pushing down through the canopy of the overhanging trees. She had no idea where she was, but for some reason it felt like the place she should stop. Anger pounded in her veins as she fumbled around in the pocket of Nash's jacket until she found his ever-present Zippo lighter. Never had she been so thankful to see the stupid thing. She quickly held it up to give herself a better idea of where she was.

"Thomas," she called again. "I know you're here somewhere. I can feel it. I want answers. Was this your doing? Was it?"

Silence answered, and she was about to start retracing her steps back down the trail when there was a rustle of feathers and the owl appeared, its sleek feathers casting a radiant light.

"Ah, so you're finally ready to show yourself," Cassidy snapped, her annoyance lending her strength. "Did you make that *thing* attack my best friend and terrify all of those other people? Well? Did you? Thomas, answer me."

"Non." The owl disappeared, and Thomas was once again standing before her. Tonight his coarse brown shirt was covered in heavy chain mail that glinted and gleamed from the moonlight and only served to make his angry red scar stand out even more against his pale, sullen face. He didn't exactly look happy to see her.

"And why should I believe you?" She started to pace around the small clearing, suddenly conscious of the fact that she was out in the middle of the woods with only a Zippo to protect her. "How do I know you're telling me the truth? Just because you say you're a knight doesn't mean that you're honorable."

"Honor?" Thomas spat in disgust, his words a disturbing contrast to the mail he wore. "There's no such thing as honor. There is only duty. However, in this case I do not mislead you. That attack was not of my doing."

For a moment Cassidy blinked, taken aback by his response. "Yes, well, why did that . . . did that—"

"Demon," Thomas supplied in his cool, blunt voice as he folded his arms tightly in front of his chain mail. His jawline was taut and grim, reminding Cassidy just how infuriating it was to try to talk to him. "It was a demon."

Cassidy glared at him. "So why did this *demon* come into a Halloween party and attack so many people? Including my friend. What did it want?"

"It wants what we all want. The Black Rose."

"Are you seriously telling me that some virginal vessel was at Cade Taylor's Halloween party? So who was it?"

"I-I don't know who it was." A flicker of frustration crossed his face, as if it pained him to admit any weakness. "Being in this world . . . drains me. All my strength went toward trying to stop the demon."

"That was you?" Some of the fight drained away from her as she realized that while the demon had tried to kill Nash, it was Thomas who had saved him. "How?"

"How is not important now." His voice was still tight. "What matters is that it will keep happening. The demons will come after you, your family, your friends, and they won't stop until they get what they want. No one will be safe. Now do you see why I need your help?"

"My family?" The words caught in her throat. "Wh-why would the demons come after them?"

"Because you are the guardian, and the grimoire leads a trail that ends at your door. The demons will follow it, and they won't let anything stand in their way." Despite the darkness, his mismatched eyes were blazing with such intensity that Cassidy struggled to believe he wasn't really standing next to her.

Her throat tightened.

What if the demon she had just seen tried to attack her father?

What if Thomas wasn't there to stop it like he had done this time? It had been easy to refuse him the first time. But now that she knew what it was capable of, knew what it had done to Nash and might do to her family, saying no wasn't quite as simple.

Indecision clawed at her chest. Then she remembered something else.

"Please don't get mad, but there's something I need to tell you. About the grimoire. I sort of destroyed it," she confessed, not quite looking at him.

"One mortal cannot destroy the grimoire," he corrected. "You only *tried* to destroy it. Look in the sack on your shoulder, and you will find it there."

"What?" Cassidy stared at him for a moment before she fumbled with the top of her purse and opened it up. Indeed, in among the clutter she could clearly see the corner of the leather-bound book. Her hands shook as she inspected it, but its faded leather showed no signs of being hacked into small pieces, nor did it smell of garbage or Dumpster. It was as it had always been.

Then she felt a tingling sensation on her arm, and she

pushed back her sleeve to discover two black roses, their stems twisting and twining up her skin, exactly where the temporary tattoo had been before she had scrubbed it away.

"How is any of this possible?" Her voice little above a whisper.

"You are the guardian. The mark of the Brotherhood belongs on your arm and the grimoire belongs in your possession," Thomas informed her, sending a chilly wave of panic down her spine as the truth of it hit home.

It was real. All of it was freaking real. The owl. Thomas. The demon that had just attacked an entire party of people looking for the essence of eternal life, and somehow she had managed to get stuck in the middle of it all. *Somehow she was meant to stop it?*

Then the book began to glow, and Cassidy dropped it in horror. "Why's it doing that?"

Thomas's face darkened. "The demon is returning. If I could fight it, I would. But I can't. I"—he paused for a moment and gritted his teeth—"please, I need your help."

She stared at the fake zombie blood, which was now smeared on her fingers. If she didn't do anything, the blood might soon be real. And not just hers. Nash, her dad, even her mom were all at risk. She swallowed her indecision and nodded.

"Tell me what to do."

"Open up the grimoire to the middle page," Thomas instructed, and without questioning him Cassidy dropped to her knees and picked up the book. Despite the glowing light, it was cool to her touch, and she felt the tattoo on her arm burn and tingle. "Lay it flat on the ground and press both of your hands into the pages, palms down. Good. Now repeat after me: 'I pledge myself to protecting the Black Rose.' You need to say it three times."

What? Half of her wanted to protest that this was the most ridiculous thing she'd ever heard of, but her fears were waylaid by the thunderous sound of the demon knight as it charged through the trees, obviously indifferent to pain and obstructions. Judging by the way the crickets and other nocturnal sounds of the woods had faded away into unearthly silence, she knew there wasn't much time.

She took a deep breath and did as Thomas instructed. The tattoo on her arm tingled as a surge of white light came racing up from the page and through her fingers, consuming her whole body with energy and vibrating atoms. It was. *It was—*

"Prepare," Thomas said, his voice blunt as the demon knight burst into the clearing where she was still kneeling. Instinct made her gather up the grimoire and place it by the base of a tree just as the demon let out a bloodcurdling wail. It was the sound of despair. The sound of victory. The sound of death. Cassidy suddenly felt her will slipping away from her as she fumbled around for Nash's Zippo.

She flipped it open, the flame only serving to show her just how truly hideous the demon was. Fear rose in her chest as it lunged at her, and it took all of Cassidy's willpower not to scream. Instead, she threw the Zippo over to one side, managing to distract the creature long enough to dart out of its way.

She heard the demon's blade slice through the bark of a tree like it was butter, and panic surged up in her again. The creature spun around, the huge muscles on its neck bulging with annoyance. She scanned around, looking for some kind of weapon, while trying not to regret her decision to wear the Audrey Hepburn dress instead of the Lara Croft, which had a weapon—even if it was a fake one. However, all she had was a tiara, which she whipped from her head and threw at him.

It bounced off his chest like a fly, and Cassidy turned and darted out of its way again onto a pile of stones that crunched under her boots. Stones. Definitely not her first choice, but since that was all she could think of, she quickly dropped to her knees and grabbed a handful as the creature once again came charging at her. The smell of blood and herbs and decomposition caught in her nostrils, but she ignored it as she took aim and threw the small stones into the gleaming amber eyes before once again darting out of the way.

"*Non, non, non!* Do you have a death wish?" Thomas gave a savage snarl.

"Yes," she snapped as rage and fear simultaneously welled up inside her. "Death wishes are my favorite pastime, didn't you know?"

"Then your wish is about to be fulfilled," Thomas retorted coolly. The creature let out a howl, which Cassidy reasoned had more to do with the appearance of Thomas than with her feeble attempt to throw stones at it. "Take the sword."

There was a sword? What sword?

Cassidy blinked as a long, gleaming sword suddenly appeared at her feet. The creature saw it at the same time and increased its pace. Fear drenched her, and she found herself helpless to do anything other than just stand there and wait for—

"You need to thrust upward, directly under his ribs. The sword will do the rest," Thomas hissed, his fury so palpable that it had the power to snap her out of her daze, forcing her to drop to her knees and grab the weapon.

The handle felt warm and familiar in her hands, and her fingers wrapped around it as if it were an Xbox controller. She used both hands to lift the sword vertically and thrust it under the creature's ribs, ripping through its flesh until there was a painful scraping of bone. The creature let out a curdled wail, and Cassidy only just managed to roll out of the way before it went crashing forward, impaling itself completely on the sword. Then everything was silent.

TWELVE

"Is it dead?" The stench was making her head spin, while unwanted adrenaline coursed through her body until she was unsure whether she should be laughing, crying, or collapsing into a heap.

"It is, but it won't stay that way for long unless we burn it. And since I doubt you'll be so lucky the next time you fight, we need to act with haste."

"Lucky?" she spluttered, as the horrors of what had just happened started to catch up with her. Her shoulders ached from holding the sword, her dress was ripped, and she was pretty sure that the dark stuff on her arm was demon ooze. "You call this *lucky*? That thing tried to kill me. Like, for real." But when he didn't answer, she just let out a sigh. "Okay, fine. I'm acting with haste."

She bit back her nausea and grabbed one of the arms of the dead demon so that she could roll it over, but the thing weighed a ton, and it wasn't until her third attempt that she managed finally to half push, half pull it onto its back.

Her muscles screamed with pain at the exertion, but she knew better than to complain to Thomas. Up close the demon was even more hideous, almost like it was standing in a distorted mirror at the fair, with grotesque muscles making the reddish-black, decaying skin bulge like they had outgrown the body in which they were meant to serve. Then she caught Thomas's impatient look, and she reached for the sword, which was still buried deep in the demon's chest. Her fingers curled around the hilt and . . . *ouch*.

Pain enveloped her skull, and she instantly released her grip on the sword, clutching her ears as she dropped to her knees. But nothing could stop the vision of chaos that suddenly slammed through her mind.

A thousand screams.

House after house was burning. Person after person was bleeding. Crying, terrified, dead. And above them all was one person. Its face distorted, eyes filled with madness. And in the distance was a voice calling out to her: Pick me. Pick me.

"Cassidy." Thomas's voice dragged her out of the terrifying abyss, and she turned, surprised to see that his whole expression had softened so that even the angry scar didn't seem quite so red. "You saw it, didn't you?"

"I-I don't know," Cassidy said in a shaky breath as the tattoo on her arm prickled her skin. "I saw something. There was blood. So much blood. *Wh-what was it?*"

"Paris. The year 1151," he said, the words sounding flat and dull as he uttered them. "A returning Crusader brought home something that he shouldn't have. The Black Rose. He pulled it away from its guardians, and once he discovered its secrets, he inhaled the essence to become immortal. The guardians followed him, but they were too late and he killed them and almost destroyed Paris, which, as you saw, became ash and blood."

"That was real? It happened?" Cassidy was overwhelmed with horror. "How did I see it?"

For a moment Thomas was silent; he clicked his jaw several times before he finally spoke. "I don't know. I-I get visions. Some of them are what's happened in the past. Some are what might happen in the future. All of them have the potential to be real. I didn't expect you to get them as well," he added before he once again stiffened. "Please. Our time is short. You must retrieve the sword, cleanse the blade, and burn the demon. *Now.*"

Cassidy was too perturbed by the vision to protest. Instead, she got to her feet and gingerly reached for the sword. She caught her breath as her fingers wrapped around the hilt, but this time there was nothing but the feel of rough, bound leather that had been crudely wrapped around the handle. Relief flooded through her, but after catching Thomas's glare she refocused and used all of her strength to pull it out through the demon's thick skin.

Once it was free, she threw it down to one side before she reluctantly searched for Nash's lighter. Thankfully, the silver casing made it easy to find, and she walked back to the corpse, getting just close enough to set it alight. Then she waited until the flames danced and licked their way along the hideous body. She watched as they sparked higher and higher into the night sky, her eyes trapped like a hypnotic lure.

She wasn't sure how long she had been standing there when the flickering fire suddenly sucked back in on itself, like a DVD being played in reverse. Then both body and fire were gone, as if they had never existed.

"And now the blade. You must run the fire along the blade to cleanse it of the demon filth," Thomas said in a tight voice.

Of course she must. However, she couldn't be bothered to argue, so she merely held the lighter up to the metal blade and watched as the flame went racing along the steel, turning a violent green color before disappearing. Leaving behind a blade that was clean of the blood that had been covering it only seconds earlier.

"Someone comes." Thomas broke the reverie, and Cassidy once again held the sword up in the air just as Nash came crashing through the trees, holding a flashlight, his annoyance highlighted by the beam of light. She quickly lowered the blade before he noticed it.

"Cass, where the hell have you been?" he demanded. "Are you insane to go racing off after a freaking demon?"

"You shouldn't be here." She shielded her eyes from the flashlight to stop it from blinding her. "I told Reuben to keep an eye on you."

"Yeah, well, Reuben's a douche. Now come on, we need

to get out of here . . . and what's that smell? Have you been burning something?"

"Um." She looked at him helplessly before turning to Thomas, who was still standing there, his impassive gaze as unflinching as ever.

"Do *not* say anything," the knight warned.

"Who said that?" Nash waved the flashlight around the clearing, but despite the fact the beam landed directly on Thomas, he didn't even blink. Then he turned back to Cassidy, confusion written all over his face. "Cass, seriously, what's going on? *Is Thomas here?* Is that who was just speaking?"

"You can hear him?" Cassidy asked in surprise as she once again turned to Thomas. "How is that possible? My dad looked straight through you the other night and couldn't hear you at all, so why can Nash?"

"He shouldn't be able to." Thomas folded his arms, looking dangerous. "The only way it is possible is if he's touched the—"

"The grimoire," Nash finished off, as his flashlight focused on the discarded book. He hurried toward it and bundled it up as if it was a small child. "It's here. It's not destroyed?"

"He knows about the grimoire?" Thomas hissed. "You have allowed *a nobody* to touch our most ancient relic?"

"Hey!" Cassidy was stung into retorting as everything started to catch up with her. "Nash isn't a nobody, and since he cares about the stupid book more than I do, I think you should watch what you're saying. Now you might as well show yourself to him. And figure out a way to let him read the grimoire, too. Nash is a lot smarter than I am, so if I'm going to have any chance of doing this thing, I'll need his help."

Thomas glared at her, but instead of speaking he bowed his head and began to chant something she couldn't understand. When he looked up, Nash let out a small gasp, and she realized that her friend could now see the bad-tempered knight. She was guessing that he could now read his beloved grimoire as well.

"Thank you," Cassidy grudgingly said to Thomas before she quickly filled Nash in on everything that had happened. From the sword through to the burning corpse that had disappeared from sight. By the time she finished, Nash was rubbing his jaw in fascination, his eyes bright with excitement.

"So it's all true then?" He stared directly at Thomas. "There really is an elixir of eternal life? An essence?"

The muscles of Thomas's face flinched. "The Black Rose gives eternal life, but it can also bring death and destruction to many. And as you have seen, the demons will stop at nothing to get it."

"S-so how many demons are we talking?" Cassidy croaked, as the blazing amber eyes and fetid breath of the creature she'd just fought came crashing back into her consciousness.

"We're talking more. There are *always* more, and they

will keep on coming until they get what they want," Thomas replied in a weary voice that sent a shudder through her spine.

Nash frowned. "I'm still not quite clear on how that all works. If the demons use blood magic to time travel, then how did you send the sword through?"

"These questions are not relevant," Thomas snapped in annoyance before realizing that they weren't going to let it go. "With earth magic we can still send inanimate objects through time. Though it is . . . draining," he said, and Cassidy suddenly noticed that except for the angry scar on his face, his skin was pale and pinched.

"And the grimoire?" Cassidy demanded as she realized that she hadn't asked nearly enough questions. "How did it get back into my purse? I—"

"The same way. Once the grimoire restored itself, we used earth magic to guide it back to your sack. But enough of this idle conversation, we need to concentrate on the Black Rose," Thomas growled. "You are the guardian, which means you must return to the feast and identify the vessel."

"That could be a problem"—Nash coughed—"since the party is over. Everyone thought the demon knight was some drunk college guy who was dressed up and looking for a fight. Unfortunately, someone called the police, and suddenly everyone disappeared quicker than when Mrs. Webster calls for volunteers to work on the school blog. Still, on the bright side, we know that it was someone who was there, so once we get a list of everyone who attended the party, it shouldn't take too long to figure it out."

"And what happens in the meantime?" Cassidy wanted to know.

"You need to get some sleep," Thomas retorted after he had finished cursing under his breath. "Because I will be back here when the lauds bells ring to start your training. We have a lot to do." Then without another word he was gone, and there was only a faint rustle of feathers to let them know he had ever been there. Nash opened his mouth to speak, but Cassidy shook her head.

"If you say, 'This is extraordinary,' I will scream," she warned him as she stalked around the small clearing. "Don't think I won't."

"Sorry. And hey, you did the right thing." Nash wrapped his arms around her in a comforting hug.

"I hope so," she said in a muffled voice. "I mean, it's one thing to say no when a crazy guy turns up near my recycling bin, but it's a bit harder to ignore it when my best friend is attacked by a freaking demon knight in the middle of a Halloween party. Plus, turns out that now I'm linked to the grimoire, I'm like a demon beacon. That means they won't just come after me, they might come after my family and friends. Everyone's at risk."

"All the more reason to stop them," Nash said as Cassidy finally stopped her pacing. She retrieved her purse and then dropped to her knees to where the sword was. She paused for a moment and took a deep breath before wrapping her fingers around it.

Thankfully, there were no visions, and since she was

fairly sure that walking out of the woods with a lethal weapon probably wasn't the best idea, she quickly slipped Nash's jacket off and wrapped it around the sword. Then she glanced around and realized that she didn't have a clue where they were.

"I don't suppose you left any bread crumbs on your way in here?" she asked as Nash swung the flashlight around until he finally found a small pathway. Then he turned the light off for a moment and checked the stars before nodding for her to follow him.

"Who needs bread crumbs when we've got Orion marching across the sky?" Nash grinned as he shone the light down the trail. Cassidy knew better than to question him. Instead, she eagerly grabbed his waist, suddenly longing to get away from the suffocating feeling of the trees and scrub. Five minutes later they burst through the branches and skirted around the side of Cade Taylor's now-quiet house to where Nash's car was parked. Then she turned to Nash and wrinkled her nose. "By the way, what time do the lauds bells ring?"

THIRTEEN

Cassidy wasn't sure what to expect the following morning as the pale pink sun finally decided to push some weak tendrils through the overhanging canopy of the woods, but it certainly wasn't this.

"Don't drop your shoulder," Thomas barked as Cassidy threw a slim, sharp knife at him. Unfortunately, she had recently discovered that not only were her knife-throwing skills less than stellar, but throwing things at an apparition was completely pointless. Thomas seemed indifferent to her mental turmoil. "Now try it again. And this time concentrate."

"I *am* concentrating." She gritted her teeth and pressed the blade into her leather-gloved hand so that the point was facing her. Then she drew back her arm before throwing it forward. Once she released it, the metal blade spun as it flew through the air before landing harmlessly on the sodden leaves that covered the dark, damp dirt, nowhere near the apparition of Thomas.

"Well, concentrate better," he retorted in an unyielding voice. Today his coarse brown shirt was rolled up to his arms. Cassidy could clearly see a tattoo similar to hers running up his forearm; all around it were crisscrossing scars. And though they paled in comparison to the angry red welt that ran down his face, she was sure each of the cuts would've hurt. However, whatever suffering he had been through seemed long over, and his face and mismatched eyes were an impassive mask.

He had been waiting for her and Nash in the woods, and it was obvious from the scattered feathers that he wasn't happy about it. Even though, as it turned out, lauds bells rang at five thirty in the morning, so the fact that Cassidy was even awake was a minor miracle.

However, it wasn't just having to get up early and sneak out of her bedroom window. Once she and Nash had pushed their way through the tangle of creepers and low-lying bushes to reach the clearing, they had discovered that, as well as a knife, a small shield, and some leather gloves that smelled of sweat and looked like the bottom of someone's foot, Thomas had also sent forward a shirt of heavy chain mail that he called a hauberk.

The mail was a dull metallic color, covered in tiny spots of rust. The undershirt that he insisted would protect her skin was hot and prickly and the most uncomfortable thing she had ever worn. Worse was to come when Nash had helped lift the hauberk over her head and onto her body.

It fell almost to her knees, but despite its length, the arms were too short, making Cassidy think it must've originally been made for someone younger than herself. She had felt sorry for any child who was thrust into battle. But that thought, and all others, left her head the moment the full weight pressed down on her shoulders and chest, like she was buried under a pile of stone, leaving her gasping and short of breath.

Cassidy marched over to retrieve the knife, the hauberk making it almost impossible to bend. Sweat beaded her brow from the exertion. She gritted her teeth as she tried to walk back, the heavy steel rubbing harshly against her skin despite the prickly undershirt. Then she turned and tried throwing again. Her shoulder immediately dropped, causing the knife to land in the pile of leaves with a thud.

"This is useless," Thomas growled.

"I know." Cassidy ignored the knife and sighed. She longed to wipe the sweat from her brow, but the heavy gauntlet made it difficult. Instead, despite the discomfort, she waved her arms in frustration. "Perhaps we could practice without all of this mail?"

"*Non,*" Thomas corrected. "We could not. The demons you will be fighting are stronger than you and better shielded. The only reason I didn't bring you more is because, even with the added power of the grimoire, you would never be able to bear the weight."

"People wear *more* mail than this?" Cassidy groaned, wishing she could sit down but not sure if she would ever be able to stand up again. "Okay, so the mail stays, but didn't you say that the grimoire had given me extra strength, and if you're with me, then you can just tell me what to do, right? I mean, it worked last night, and—"

"Last night you were lucky; you can't expect it a second time. The demons you will be fighting are all fueled by rage, strength, and insanity." He clenched his fists, and Cassidy noticed that his hands were as heavily scarred as his arm.

"He's got a point," Nash piped up from the large fallen log where he was sitting, reverently studying the grimoire. His dark hair was casually tousled, and his pale blue eyes were lively with curiosity. It was easy to see that, despite being attacked last night, he was actually dealing a lot better than she was. Then he caught Cassidy's beady glare and flushed. "Sorry, I just meant that I've found a section in the grimoire that talks about the demons. It says that they are highly trained warriors who will fight to the death to reach the Black Rose."

"It does?" Cassidy suddenly felt the full weight of the metal shirt pressing down on her shoulders.

Nash nodded. "It does. And speaking of the Black Rose, I've just gone on Cade Taylor's Facebook page to try to get an idea of who was at the party last night."

"What are they saying about the demon attack?" Cassidy pulled off one of the gloves and wiped away the layer of sweat from her brow.

"Just that some smacked-out, sword-wielding college guy crashed the party. So far, I've got a list of fifty people, and all but three go to Raiser Heights High. The thing is, I was thinking about it. What if *I'm* the vessel for the Black Rose? After all, I was the one the demon attacked," he reminded them. "And I'm most definitely a virgin. In fact, I would've thought that Cassidy and I were the only two virgins there. Me, because of my complete lack of interest, and Cassidy, because it was a better alternative than hooking up with Reuben. Plus, it would hardly be fair if Cass was both the vessel *and* the guardian. That's just bad logic."

"Nash." Cassidy glared at him as she felt her cheeks start to flame.

"What? You don't want me to talk about this in front of Thomas?" Nash asked in surprise. "Because I'm pretty sure he has no opinion at all on if we do or don't hook up with anyone."

"That's hardly the point," Cassidy retorted, still annoyed at him. However, when she looked at Thomas, it was obvious that Nash was right: the not-really-there knight looked completely indifferent to what they were discussing.

"You're not the vessel that houses the Black Rose," Thomas merely said, and if Cassidy hadn't known better, she would have said that Nash actually looked disappointed.

"How can you be so sure?"

"Because I am a guardian, and when I see the Black Rose, even encased within its human vessel, it glows. Radiating out with a bright but terrible beauty. It will be the same for you."

"Are you seri—?" Cassidy started to say before breaking off, since it hadn't taken her long to realize that Thomas was *always* serious. "So now that Nash has a list of people who were at the party, I need to walk around and see who 'glows' at me?"

"That is correct. Now that you have said the oath and become a guardian, you will be able to see the Black Rose." Thomas nodded before reluctantly sighing. "Unfortunately, with their blood magic, all the demons can *also* see the Black Rose, which is why it's so important to protect the vessel."

"Hey." Nash looked up in excitement. "I was just reading about that in the grimoire. There's an amulet you can make so that, when the vessel wears it, it makes them invisible to any demons, no matter how much magic they're using." Then he turned to Thomas. "Is this something that we could do?"

"It is possible," Thomas admitted, but before Nash could begin to look too happy, he narrowed his eyes. "*However*. For the ritual to be done correctly, everything you use must be consecrated. You will find another chapter on that. If you master that, then you will master the protective amulet."

"I'm on it." Nash immediately turned the pages of the grimoire to find the chapter Thomas was referring to.

"So what about me?" Cassidy asked in a hopeful voice as she looked longingly at the water bottle that was sitting over by Nash. "Can I have a break?"

"*Non.*" He shook his head. "You can pick up the knife and try it again. *And this time, don't drop your shoulder. . . .*"

✣   ✣   ✣   ✣   ✣

By three o'clock on Sunday, there was no part of Cassidy that didn't hurt. Even her eyelids felt as if they'd been working out. At least she'd found it surprisingly easy to slip in and out of the house all weekend—her mom had been in her home office, and her dad had been either doing his exercises or talking to a legion of visitors who wanted to see how he was doing. Unfortunately, Nash hadn't been so lucky and had been forced to go to a family lunch, which meant that Cassidy had been on her own. Then she realized that Thomas was looking at her expectantly, and she forced herself to concentrate.

"If you've stopped daydreaming, we can start working with the sword."

"Really?" Cassidy was surprised, since so far everything they'd done had been with the knife. Thomas had said she would have a better chance of surviving if she could kill her enemies from afar, and so, after she had finally managed to hit the makeshift target, he'd drilled her in how to roll, kick, and duck—all while wearing the horrible bulky mail. She dropped down next to the sports bag that she had been using to store all the equipment in and looked at the sword. Ever since she'd had the vision of Paris burning, she had been scared to touch it, and so she sat there, staring at it with uncertainty.

"It won't hurt you," Thomas said, as if reading her mind. "Just because you got the vision, it doesn't mean it's your enemy. That sword has been my faithful companion."

"It's *your* sword?" Cassidy couldn't hide her surprise.

"*Oui.*"

"But why did you send me your own sword? I don't understand. What if you need it?"

For a moment he clenched his jaw before relenting. "The sword is . . . unique. It was a gift from my father. I sent it to you because what I ask of you is difficult. I can't be there to fight myself, but my sword can. *It will help you.*"

"Is that why I got the vision the other night?" Cassidy's voice was only a little above a whisper, despite the fact that she had only birds and insects for company.

"It is possible," he admitted, his harsh features softening, making him look almost handsome in a brutal way, though his mismatched eyes were still laden with pain. Suddenly, she had the most overwhelming urge to reach out and touch his savaged face. "I feel . . . shame about that. I did not wish to pass on that particular burden."

Cassidy managed to resist the urge to touch him and instead she solemnly nodded. "I'll take care of it. It must mean a lot."

"I do not value sentiment. My true father was not the one who raised me; my foster father did, and he taught me better than to worship before an inanimate object. The sword holds value to me only because of the power it affords me. Nothing else," he said as the softness was replaced by a fierce expression, which rolled in like a storm. Cassidy shuddered at the mercurial change in his demeanor before she busied herself unsheathing the sword.

On Friday night it had been dark and her mind had been too filled with the smells of death and blood to pay any attention to it, but now in the cold afternoon light she could study it properly for the first time. Underneath the leather binding, she could see that the handle was the color of dull brass, with a circle at the top; at the bottom of the handle there was a flat bar, which Cassidy could only figure was to stop her hand from accidentally slipping onto the blade. Not something she was eager to do. She turned her attention to the blade itself. The metal was pitted with small nicks and imperfections, while down the center were a series of symbols that Thomas had told her were runes.

"That one is for strength, that one is for protection, and that one is for courage." Thomas was suddenly next to her, his face carrying a more even expression, which Cassidy could only assume was his version of an apology. "My father carved them himself. If I'm not around to assist you, you must trust the sword. It will help you. The first thing we will work on is your stance, next blocking, and finally attack. Normally, you would spar with someone, but since you are alone, you will have to practice with me."

"How will I know if I've hit you when you're only air?"

"You will not hit me," he assured her in a blunt voice. "I fear that your sword skills will be as poor as your knife-throwing skills. Now, let us commence."

Cassidy, guessing that the moment was over, reluctantly got to her feet and put her heavy leather gloves back on. She winced as Thomas proceeded to bark out orders, urging her to bend her knees lower and hold the sword higher, making sure that the tension in her arms was stronger.

It was going to be a long afternoon.

FOURTEEN

Cassidy tentatively opened one eye on Monday morning as a weak beam of sunshine slipped into her room and she groggily realized that she hadn't drawn her curtains properly last night. She groaned and tried to pull a pillow over her head to block out the light, but the effort of moving her arms caused her to wince in pain. She hurt. A lot.

Then she let out an even longer groan as she recalled exactly why she hurt. Turned out that knife throwing was a picnic compared to sword fighting, and after drilling and yelling at her for an hour on how to block a weapon, Thomas had made her spar with him. And despite the fact he wasn't even really there, he kept pressing forward so much that she had found herself falling backward over the log Nash had been sitting on the previous day. As if she needed any more bruises.

It was also why, when Thomas had suggested another training session this morning, Cassidy had been quick to insist that she needed a chance to recover. She ignored her aching body and scrambled to her feet, hoping that a shower might relieve some of her aches and pains, but after letting hot water sluice over her bruised, cut skin, she felt worse than ever and limped back to her room, only to discover that there were already three text messages waiting for her.

Two were from Reuben, which she deleted. Apparently, in Crazy Reuben World, her asking him to keep an eye on Nash on Friday night was tantamount to her saying that she wanted to get back together with him. The third was from Nash, reminding her that he would be around to collect her in half an hour.

Cassidy felt remotely better at the idea of not catching the bus, and she quickly got dressed, trying to ignore the black Audrey Hepburn dress that was balled up in a plastic bag at the back of her closet. It was ruined beyond all recognition, and she would have to throw it out when she had the chance. Once she was finished dressing, she pushed her comforter from the side of the bed so that she could pull her sports bag out from underneath, the steel chain mail making a dragging sound against the wooden floorboards.

Thomas had tried to convince her that she needed to wear her mail at all times, but she had quickly assured him that that would most definitely *not* be happening. Even carrying it to school with her wasn't ideal, but after recognizing the stubborn set of his full mouth, she realized that he would not concede that point. At least the sports bag didn't seem as heavy as it had on Saturday, and Cassidy could only assume that whatever superpowers the grimoire had bestowed upon her were finally kicking in.

She silently made her way down the hallway, trying to hold the sports bag so that it didn't clink as she walked. It was probably the earliest that she'd ever gone to school, but she and Nash had decided last night that the sooner they could start looking out for a virginal vessel who glowed with a bright but deadly beauty, the better.

The plan was to grab some breakfast and get out of the house before her parents were up, since she had hardly been home all weekend, and right now she didn't really feel like explaining—

"You're awake early."

Cassidy let out a groan as her mom poked her head out of the spare bedroom, which she had taken to using as a home office. So much for her plan to slip out of the house before anyone was up.

"I've got some things to do before school with Nash," she said in her most casual voice.

"At seven thirty in the morning?" Her mom raised an eyebrow.

"Pots and kettles, Mom," Cassidy retorted as she glanced back into the spare bedroom at the desk, which was covered with documents and a laptop that was all fired up and displaying a spreadsheet on its screen.

"No need to get so defensive, Cass." A flash of hurt flashed across her mom's face. Then she narrowed her shrewd eyes. "Why are you limping?"

That would be the intense pain that comes from learning how to hold a sword and throw a knife for the last two days, Cassidy wanted to say, but instead she tightened her grip on the sports bag. "It's no big deal. I just got hurt in PE. Volleyball. Anyway, I'd better get going. Nash will be here in a moment."

"Hey, not so fast." Her mom held up her hand. "I hardly saw you over the weekend, and you never told me how the party was on Friday night."

Cassidy imagined that her mom was getting her confused with some other teenage daughter, since the number of times that the two of them had sat down and talked about parties was, er, *never*. However, her mom didn't seem bothered when Cassidy didn't answer and instead just smiled.

"Thankfully, Reuben came around yesterday afternoon while you were out and told me all about it."

"He did *what?*" Cassidy exploded in fury before remembering her dad was still asleep. She lowered her voice. "What was he doing here?"

"He came to see you, of course," her mom said in surprise. "Apparently, he'd been trying to text you all weekend, and you hadn't been replying. He was worried, Cass. He said you suddenly disappeared from the party and didn't come back."

"Did he also tell you that the party got shut down by the police?" Cassidy retorted, while at the same time wondering if she would be allowed to use Thomas's sword to inflict on Reuben slow, torturous pain. "So since the party was over, Nash and I left. Now I've got to go, but please don't let

Reuben think it's okay to come around to the house, because it's not."

For a moment it looked as if her mom was going to say something, but she finally just nodded her head and shrugged. "Fine, if you don't want my help or advice, then I'll keep it to myself."

If only. However, before she could reply, she heard Nash's car pulling up, so she mumbled an annoyed good-bye and hurried outside.

"Whoa. You look like you've just poured sour milk on your Frosted Flakes," Nash said as Cassidy put her sports bag in the backseat and climbed in beside him. "What happened?"

"Just the normal *interfering-mother* stuff. Apparently, Reuben came by yesterday, and now my mom thinks that he's a lovely guy, which just proves how little she knows about anything."

"Ouch." Nash pulled a face as he drove down the street. "But I think I have something that will make you feel better." He nodded to indicate a brown paper bag in the backseat.

Cassidy, who had been so annoyed with her mom that she'd forgotten to grab breakfast, reached for the bag, her stomach churning in anticipation. It probably wouldn't be a doughnut, because Nash was too healthy for that, but perhaps it would be a bagel or a . . . *bunch of parsley?*

Cassidy raised an eyebrow. "I'm sure there's a reason for this, but I'm too tired and sore to figure out what it is."

"It's for the amulet ritual that I was talking about with Thomas on Saturday. . . . The one in the grimoire," Nash elaborated, no doubt in case Cassidy got it confused with another amulet ritual. "I've figured out how to consecrate all the instruments, which means that we can try to do it tonight. Do you know what this will mean if it works?"

"That parsley's a very versatile herb?" Cassidy suggested in a dry voice.

"That we will have a concrete way to prove that science and mysticism are linked," Nash corrected in a stern voice as he pulled into the half-deserted parking lot. When they got out, Nash reached into the backseat to pick up her sports bag, his handsome face almost turning puce in protest as he tried to lift it. Then his eyes widened as Cassidy grinned and plucked it up like it was filled with feathers. "That's incredible," he said.

"I know, right?" she agreed. "Yesterday afternoon I hardly even noticed I was wearing the mail, apart from how difficult it was to get it on by myself. But I seem to be getting stronger. However, instead of being pleased, Thomas merely retorted that it was lucky, since my fighting skills were that of a babe in arms," she added, her face darkening.

Nash, who had already heard all about the sword fighting, gave her a sympathetic look. "You know he's just frustrated that he can't be here to protect the Black Rose himself."

"Humph," Cassidy snorted as her aching muscles howled in protest. She ignored the pain as they made their way down the deserted hallway so that Cassidy could drop the sports bag off before anyone decided to question her about what was in it. Especially since some kid had been suspended last month for carrying a switchblade with him. She dreaded to think what would happen if she got busted with a sword and a knife. Definitely not something that would look good on those precious college applications that her mom kept going on about.

As soon as she shut her locker, Nash pulled out a piece of paper and passed it over to her. "Okay, according to Cade's Facebook page, this is a list who was at the party; it may not be complete, but at least it's a start. Look, there's Sam Ridgeway. He was definitely there. Is he glowing?"

Cassidy swung around, but all she saw was a tall jock with overly groomed hair and an attitude. She shook her head. "Nope."

"Oh, well, there are still a lot more names to go through. Let's head over to the C-block lockers. There are more seniors there. I'm sure that we'll find the Black Rose soon."

However, for probably the first time in his life, Nash was wrong, and despite their prowling the hallways in between their morning classes, there was no sign of any virginal vessels.

✢ ✢ ✢ ✢ ✢

By the time the lunch bell rang Cassidy reluctantly headed for the cafeteria. As if she hadn't suffered enough. It didn't take her long to make her way into the overcrowded room. Her nose twitched in protest at the greasy smells that clung in the air as she began to scan the crowd.

There was no sign of anyone glowing at her with a bright but terrible beauty; however, she did manage to catch sight of

Nash, who was sitting on the far side of the room right next to three big open-topped trash cans, his long legs crammed under the table and a miserable look on his face. She made her way over and joined him.

"Why are you sitting so far away from everyone?"

"Remember how we hate coming in here?" He pushed away the homemade fruit salad he had been picking at, and Cassidy nodded. "Well, there's a very good reason for that. It's because the cafeteria's full of jerkwads who take their social hierarchy *very* seriously, so I guess we're stuck over here in Siberia for now. Still," he added in a thoughtful voice, glancing at the nearby trash cans that were already overflowing with oil-laden scraps, "if the vessel doesn't like the taste of today's spaghetti, then we might be in luck."

"Oh." Cassidy pulled an old apple out of her purse and dusted off the fluff before biting into it. "Well—"

But before she could continue, there was a loud crashing noise behind them. The apple fell from her hand and bounced onto the floor as she grabbed the plastic knife that Nash had been using. She jumped to her feet, while trying to remember everything that Thomas had taught her. But as she spun around, instead of seeing a demon knight looming down on them, all she could see was a ninth grader picking up his lunch tray; suddenly, Cassidy realized that she was standing up in the middle of the cafeteria wielding a plastic knife.

Earth, please, swallow me now.

The ninth grader looked at her like she was a weirdo, and Cassidy sat back down and felt the color rise in her cheeks. Then she wiped her brow as a surge of unnecessary adrenaline pumped through her body, reminding her just how unprepared she was for any of this.

"Are you okay?" Nash looked at her in concern.

"Not really," she admitted. What if that *had* been a demon knight instead of some random kid? Would she have fought it in the cafeteria in front of everyone? Was that how these things worked? Because if so, she suddenly had a new appreciation for superheroes, who made the whole saving-society thing look so easy. Her throat felt dry as she turned to Nash in horror. "I really don't think I can do this. It's—"

"Going to be tough? It's going to hurt? You're going to get demon goo on your favorite preloved nana dress?" Nash asked, his calm, familiar voice anchoring her and pushing away the last of her panic. "Yeah, I think so, too. But Cass, for whatever reason, you're the one who has to do it."

For a moment Cassidy stared at him before letting out a groan. "You're just saying that because you want to keep reading the grimoire and talking to Thomas about what it's like in the fourteenth century."

"Well, yes, that is true," Nash ruefully agreed as he squeezed her hand. "But it doesn't mean I'm not right. You can do this. Trust me, I'm a genius. We will find the Black Rose, and you will do all of your fancy fighting stuff, and it will be fine."

"What will be fine?" a voice asked, and they both looked up to see Reuben dragging a chair back from the table and slipping his thin frame into it. Today his emo hair was poking up in six chunky spikes, and he had his favorite chain belt on, the one he saved for special occasions. He smiled at them both as if they'd been expecting him.

"Reuben? What are you doing here?" Cassidy blinked.

"What do you mean? I've been texting you all day to say I would meet you here, and since you *are* here instead of outside in the freezing cold where you and loser-boy normally sit, then that can only mean one thing. That you feel the same way I do."

"Um, no, I don't. Now can you please go away?" she said, staring at him as she tried to figure out where all of his delusions came from. Then she decided that she really didn't care.

"And by go away, she means leave," Nash added in a pointed voice, but Reuben only shrugged as he got to his feet.

"Fine, but you'll come around," he said in a confident voice. "After all, how will you be able to resist me when we're working together every day at lunchtime, not to mention every afternoon and on weekends?"

"Reuben, for the last time I'm not getting back together with you. I can barely handle being in the same biology class, so there's no way I'm going to hang out with you after school."

"Of course you are," Reuben insisted. "When I was around at your house yesterday, your mom was telling me all about how you were auditioning for *Romeo and Juliet*, and hello, I'm stage manager. We'll be seeing each other all the time. Don't try to tell me it's a coincidence," he said as he waggled a finger at her and then sauntered away, his chain belt rattling as he went.

The minute he was gone, Cassidy shook her head. "Seriously, what is it with my mom? How many times does she need to be told that I'm not going to do the school play? She has to stop thinking that she can make my decisions for me, and—"

"Nash, there you are." Celeste Gilbert suddenly appeared, and this time it was Nash's turn to let out a long groan, which Celeste ignored as she sat down and patted her fitted T-shirt. "Can you believe how crazy Friday night was, with that maniac attacking us like that? By the way, what happened to you afterward? We all went to Eric's house. I was hoping that you would be there. Okay, and why is your friend staring at me like that, because I've got to be honest, it's freaking me out big-time."

"What?" Nash asked in confusion, but Cassidy couldn't bring herself to reply as she stared at the soft white tendrils of light that radiated from Celeste Gilbert, shimmering and undulating in an ethereal dance that was like nothing she had ever seen before. But suddenly, the soft strands sharpened and narrowed as an angry black line formed around the pale, pure glow, and Cassidy gasped in horror as she realized that what she was seeing was a bright and terrible beauty.

Oh, crap.

FIFTEEN

"Celeste Gilbert is the Black Rose? *Celeste Gilbert is a virgin?*" Nash repeated ten minutes later as they stood in a huddle at the side of the cafeteria, his normally clever face looking totally confused. "Are you sure?"

"I'm sure... well, I'm sure about the Black Rose part, so I guess that makes her a virgin. She's glowing like a Christmas light." Cassidy took another glance over to where Celeste and her friends were now sitting, the searing white light so dazzling but at the same time tinged with a dark edge that Cassidy couldn't quite describe. It was unnerving.

"I did not expect this." Nash ran a hand through his shaggy hair, and a group of nearby girls sighed in appreciation.

"That makes two of us." Cassidy finally gave in to her urge and began to pace up and down the greasy cafeteria ignoring the strange looks that people were shooting them. "I mean, it's obvious that Thomas, while being an expert on weapons and fighting, is a complete fail when it comes to high school, because there's no way that I can follow Celeste around everywhere."

Nash thoughtfully chewed his lip for a moment. "Okay, so we've already started getting everything together to make the protective amulet, which will stop her from going all Glow Girl to demons. And if we get a copy of her schedule from the office, we'll at least know where she is during the day."

"You can get a copy of her schedule?" Cassidy asked in surprise since, at the start of the term, she'd had problems getting a copy of her *own* schedule.

"Hey, I'm practically a shoo-in for Harvard. I can handle this," Nash assured her as he squeezed her hand. "Don't worry, I've got your back."

✤ ✤ ✤ ✤ ✤

By the end of the school day, Cassidy realized that they'd completely underestimated what was involved in protecting Celeste Gilbert. For a start, Celeste's classes were all over the place, and even worse, it turned out that she was selective with regard to which classes she bothered to attend. And none of it was helped by the fact that Celeste now seemed to think that Cassidy was bona fide crazy.

"What possessed you to tell her that I had a snake called Hamish that ate dead rats?" Nash asked as the pair of them reluctantly made their way to the auditorium.

"I was trying to turn her off you, and that was the first thing that came into my mind. Of course, that was before

I realized that I needed to follow her every move. This is a disaster," Cassidy wailed as they reached the auditorium for the dreaded auditions.

"You do realize that I wouldn't step foot in this place for anyone else but you," Nash complained as they squeezed past all the would-be thespians nervously hovering outside the auditorium, reciting the balcony scene. "If Celeste sees me, then she's going to think I'm auditioning."

"And if Reuben sees me, then he's going to think that I want to get back together with him," Cassidy said in an equally appalled voice as they finally managed to make their way to the main stage, where a frazzled Mrs. Davis, the drama teacher, was standing with a clipboard and a general look of panic. "But we really don't have much of a choice."

"I know." He let out a pained sigh as he nodded toward the far side, where Celeste was glowing so brightly that Cassidy had to shade her eyes to stop herself from squinting. Then he ducked as Celeste glanced over. "Okay, so how about you keep an eye on her and I'll wait down in the seats to make sure that no demons come in. Oh, and while you're following her, there is one other small little thing that we need to do before we can make the protective amulet tonight."

"What is it?" Cassidy said in a cautious voice.

"In addition to the parsley, I need a strand of her hair." Nash coughed as he took a step back from her.

"What?" Cassidy stared at him for a moment, waiting for the punch line, but when it wasn't forthcoming, she quickly shook her head. "Sorry. It's bad enough that I have to try to follow her around at a distance—but now you want me to get a strand of hair?"

"Did I mention that I really need two strands?" Nash admitted before giving her a supportive pat on the arm.

"Nash, that's ridiculous. She can barely stand to look at me—how am I going to get within hair-stealing distance? Anyway, why can't you do it? At least she likes you."

"Yes, that's the problem, and I can't do anything to encourage her or she might get the wrong idea. Then I'll be forced to move to Australia to escape her. Besides," he said in a coaxing voice, "it'll be easy."

"Nothing about this is easy," Cassidy reminded him. "And why are you only telling me about this now?"

"So you wouldn't have time to wriggle out of it, of course."

"Fine. I'll do my best to get two strands of Celeste Gilbert's hair. But I warn you, if she catches me, I'm going to tell her they're for you."

"*Australia,*" he reminded her in a singsong voice, knowing that she wouldn't go through with her threat. Then he scuttled away before she could change her mind. Cassidy let out a sigh and climbed up to the stage. As soon as she got there, Celeste darted behind the heavy curtain, and Cassidy was forced to trail after her, privately wondering if someone was having a laugh at her expense.

She was just making her way past the leftover props from last year's production of *Cats* when Celeste came to an abrupt halt to read a text message, giving Cassidy only a moment to scramble out of sight behind a fake boulder.

She watched as Celeste thumbed a reply to someone, and a moment later she held the cell phone up to her ear and began a loud, angry conversation about a pink dress. Whatever the problem was, Celeste wasn't happy, and she began to pace around the backstage area, waving her free hand in annoyance.

Cassidy ducked even lower behind the fake boulder and ignored her cramping muscles as she glanced at her watch. Was this what it was going to be like until the solstice? Because if so, then she was going to have a problem, and she was just deciding if she should try to find Thomas to discuss it with him when she heard a rustling noise from over by some dismantled lighting equipment.

Someone—or something—was over there.

Panic flared in her chest as Celeste, oblivious to any danger, continued to argue into her cell phone. Cassidy took a deep breath and tried to remember all of Thomas's instructions, but unfortunately, all she could think of was rule number one: *Never go anywhere without your sword.*

The rustling noise increased, and Cassidy looked around for a potential weapon, adrenaline surging through her veins. Then she caught sight of an umbrella. It wasn't quite a sword, but it was still a weapon, and she tightened her grip on it just as Celeste suddenly finished her call and angrily marched back out through the heavy curtains.

The moment she had gone, Cassidy jumped out from behind the boulder toward the lighting equipment. As she went, she centered her energy and lifted the umbrella in front of her, so that she could—

"Cassidy?" Travis asked as he walked out from behind an old spotlight and looked at the umbrella in surprise. "What's going on?"

"Travis?" She lowered the umbrella and swallowed a groan. Now that he wasn't dressed as James Dean, his dark curls once again fell around his face and he was chewing his full lower lip, which made him look even more gorgeous than ever. Unfortunately, while he looked gorgeous, she probably just looked crazy. "Wh-what are you doing back here?"

"I'm here for the auditions, so I was trying to meditate first. It makes me feel centered," he admitted, still looking with confusion at the umbrella in her hand. "What are *you* doing backstage?"

"Um." Cassidy could feel her cheeks going bright red, since she could hardly tell him that she was trying to protect a virginal vessel from being ripped apart by a demon. "I was looking for Nash and thought that I saw a mouse. I really hate mice." Then she groaned. What was it with her and all the reptiles and vermin? Next time she told a lie it was only going to involve unicorns and happy animals.

"Obviously." Travis raised an eyebrow before grinning. "Still, it works out well for me, since I was hoping to see you today."

"You were?" she asked, all thoughts of Celeste forgotten

as she self-consciously smoothed down her green silk dress. She'd teamed it with some boots and one of her dad's old vests, and while this morning it had seemed cool, now it just seemed dumb, and she wished she was wearing something from the Gap like a normal person.

"Yeah, I felt really bad that I had to bail on you at the party. It sounds like I missed all the action. Did some crazy guy really go racing through there with a sword?"

"Yeah. They think he might've been a college guy who'd had a little bit too much of . . . well . . . too much of something," Cassidy said, merely repeating the rumor that the rest of the school had been buzzing with all day. It certainly made more sense than the truth.

"I hope you weren't near him."

"Actually," Cassidy confessed, "he did come right up to us, and Nash ended up getting knocked over. But don't worry"—she added hastily, noticing that Travis's face had drained of color—"he's fine. Just some bruising in an embarrassing place."

"So what happened to the guy? Did the police come or anything?" Travis asked, and Cassidy felt a flood of memories come racing back. The stench of the demon as she had thrust the sword through its distorted flesh. The flames as its body burned. *The vision she'd shared with Thomas.* She felt her face go pale, and she jammed her nails into the flesh of her palm to bring her back to the present.

"He ran off before anyone could stop him," she said in

what she hoped was a casual voice just as Mrs. Davis called for everyone's attention. Cassidy immediately lowered her voice. "Okay, I think that's my cue to go. But good luck with the audition."

"And good luck to you, too. I'm pleased you changed your mind."

For a moment Cassidy looked at him blankly before realizing what he meant. She went to shake her head to explain that it would be a cold day in hell before she ever auditioned, but before she could open her mouth Travis reached for her hand and pressed something into her palm. The feel of his fingers on hers sent an electric shock racing around her body.

"What's this?" Cassidy asked as she uncurled her fingers to see a crystal. It was a ruddy orange color, with speckles of black running through it, hanging off a thin piece of leather.

"It's a good-luck charm," he explained. "I normally use it when I audition, but after what you were saying about your stage fright, I thought it might help you."

"But—" Cassidy again tried to explain that she wasn't going to audition, but Travis cut her off with a shake of his head. She watched in fascination as his dark curls spread across his brow, perfectly framing his eyes.

"It's okay. I know you don't think you're going to audition, but just in case you change your mind, I would like you to have it." He smiled, his perfect white teeth dazzling against his smooth tanned skin. Before Cassidy could reply he slipped away and headed over to the rest of the group, leaving Cassidy clutching the crystal necklace tightly in her hand.

Had any of that really just happened?

However, as much as she longed to stand there, she suddenly realized that not only should she be keeping an eye on Celeste (no matter how little she deserved it), but she wanted to see Travis audition, and so she quickly hurried out to the front where Nash was sitting, his long frame sunk low into one of the seats.

"Okay, so you look happy." Nash studied her face, an amused expression tugging at his lips. "Does that mean you got the strands of hair?"

"Not exactly," Cassidy admitted before smiling again. "But I have been talking to Travis. Can you believe he was totally bummed that he had to leave early on Friday night?"

"Did you explain that you were otherwise engaged with a demon?" Nash wanted to know.

"Of course I did, because all the magazines say that you should talk about demons when hanging out with your crush," she deadpanned before relenting. "Okay, so I actually just told him that I didn't stay long. And get a load of this, not only did he say he wanted to see me again, but he also gave me this for good luck in case I was going to audition for the play. Isn't it gorgeous?"

Nash studied it for a moment. "It looks like a carnelian. Not worth much, but as far as a healing stone goes, it offers strength and helps give a person confidence in her decision making. Which is actually very fitting for you."

"Not to mention that it's a token of how pleased Travis is that he's met me." Cassidy let out a happy sigh as she took it back from Nash and slipped it over her neck so that it was hanging just to the right of her heart. She grinned some more, and Nash rolled his eyes.

"Yes, this mineral was formed over hundreds and thousands of years just to help you get a date. And while of course I'm thrilled for you, may I look at the grimoire now? These auditions are going to go on for ages, and I figured that I might as well start reading up on how to make the amulet. Assuming that you can get the hair," he said, but Cassidy hardly heard as she craned her neck so that she could watch Travis move fluidly across the stage, so gorgeous and powerful.

"Grimoire," Nash repeated, this time with a nudge, and Cassidy vaguely thrust her purse toward him, still not taking her eyes off Travis. As she watched, her fingers clutched at the necklace, making her feel somehow connected to him.

He was alone in the middle of the stage now. A haunted expression replaced his normal easy smile, while his soaring voice rang out. He was doing the scene at the end of the play when Romeo has woken up to discover Juliet was dead. Cassidy watched in mounting admiration as his haunted look made way for bone-searing grief.

Suddenly, the whole auditorium was silent as Travis fell to his knees, his despair so palpable that Cassidy longed to race up and ease away the deep lines that were now running across his brow, but instead she just sat there, glued to the spot, mesmerized by his compelling performance. Finally it was over, and one by one, students everywhere spontaneously applauded. Cassidy joined them, completely fixated on Travis's face, still so raw with emotion.

"Er, Cass." Nash's voice suddenly rang in her ear. "I-I think you'd better look in your purse."

"My purse?" Cassidy reluctantly dragged her gaze away from Travis and narrowed her eyes. "Is this one of those jokes about it being like a black hole?"

"No." Nash quickly shook his head, his hands shaking with panic. "This isn't a joke. You need to look in your purse. *Right now.*"

"Okay—" she started to say, but the rest of the words died on her lips as she saw the grimoire burning with such intensity it could only mean one thing.

That somewhere close by there was a demon.

SIXTEEN

The noise backstage faded away so that all Cassidy was conscious of was the blood pounding through her temples and the screaming cries of people being burned alive. All the demon knight had to do was race in and see Celeste standing there, glowing like a beacon, and it would rip the Black Rose from her flesh. It would be Paris all over again.

Innocent people being killed. Their crucified flesh. Their blood. Their—

"Cass." Nash's urgent voice dragged her back into reality. She gave him a grateful look and quickly peered around, but wherever the demon knight was, it wasn't backstage. Her heart hammered in her chest.

"I've to go and find it." She took a deep breath and tried to focus herself.

"It might not even be in the school," Nash tried to protest, though it was obvious by the way his face was drained of color that he was just as worried as she was.

"It's here," she said in a croaky voice. "Look at the grimoire. It wasn't even that red when I fought the one in the woods." Then she took a deep breath and pulled the book out of her purse. Despite its fiery appearance, it was cool to the touch. "I've got to find it."

"You know, I'm having second thoughts about all of this," he said as he reached out to hold her hand, his knuckles white. "Perhaps—"

"It's okay," she lied as she squeezed his fingers in reassurance. "That whole speech you gave me before? Well, you were right. I've got to do this. Especially after seeing Thomas's vision. But you need to stay here and make sure that Celeste is okay, and if you see *anything*, you text me right away. Okay?"

"But—"

"Nash," she cut him off as she caught his gaze in hers. "Please."

"Fine." He nodded, and she slipped away before she could change her mind. She was vaguely aware of Reuben waving to her, but she ignored him and hurried off to her locker, while trying not to think of just how badly this might end. Her fingers fumbled with the code, but finally she opened it and pulled out the large sports bag, then grabbed her coat for the bracing autumn weather.

There was still no sign of any demon, so she quickly made her way outside to the empty courtyard.

"Thomas," she hissed in a low voice as she scanned the sky for an owl, but there was nothing. She cautiously started to jog around the outside of the school, hoping that that the grimoire would show her where to go. She stopped at the deserted table where she and Nash normally ate lunch and pulled the grimoire and the small knife out of her purse. Then she looked at the heavy mail.

The last thing she wanted to do was to get caught wearing it, but then she remembered just how brutal her sparring had been with Thomas, who was just an apparition. She reluctantly shrugged off her coat and pulled the horrible, itchy undershirt on over her green dress (which, on reflection, wasn't ideal demon fighting attire) before she wriggled her way into the awkward chain mail.

Now she understood why old-fashioned knights had squires to help them dress. However, she finally managed to get it on, and then she slipped her coat back over the top so that she didn't look any more freakish than she needed to. Then she tied the belt around her waist and slipped her knife into it. As soon as it was done, she hurried toward the back of the main building, where the Dumpsters were kept.

The wind had picked up now, blowing leaves around in mini whirlpools, causing them to spiral up in the air before dropping them back down. A plastic bag had caught on the side of the brickwork and was being pressed in like a kiss. However, there was still no sign of any demon. Cassidy shivered and was trying to decide where to look next when her nostrils were assaulted by an overwhelming smell of putrid blood.

She gagged as she forced herself to pull the heavy leather

gloves on, and then she slipped the shield onto her left forearm before picking up the sword. Despite the gray weather, the blade suddenly burst into a myriad of colors as the runes lit up, so dazzling that Cassidy was momentarily blinded by it. Finally, she dragged her gaze away and spun around, but instead of seeing just one demon, there were six of them, all racing toward her as one.

Six.

There were *six* demons.

Fear tore at her throat as they raced toward her. Her horror mounted at the way their distorted muscles seemed to pulsate under their skin. Their sharp teeth glistened with slobber. Then a feather fell in front of her and she let out a strangled cry of relief. *Thomas.*

"Move." His voice rung out in her ear. "You need to move. Now."

Cassidy didn't need to look at him to know that his face would be pinched with frustration at not being able to fight them himself. Instead, she did as he said, darting away just as the first of the demons reached her, amazed at the extra strength she felt just from knowing he was there.

"Thrust," he commanded, and she plunged the sword deep into the demon's chest, sending it through the thick leathery skin until it crashed into flesh and bone. The runes on the sword blazed with energy, and the demon fell away from her like she had swatted a fly. Thomas had said they held special power, but she had no idea it would be this much. Before she could consider it further, the stench of the dead demon rose up to choke her. She forced herself to ignore it as a second demon came racing toward her. She lifted her shield to block a blow and was just about to thrust forward with her sword when Thomas stopped her.

"Wait," he instructed, and despite her natural desire to press forward, Cassidy's fingers tightened around the hilt. Her heart pounded against her ribs, and the wind swirled around them in eddies. She didn't even realize that she was holding her breath until Thomas finally commanded her to strike. The moment she did, a burst of energy ran along her arm, and again the runes on the sword blazed with power. As soon as the blade touched the demon's distorted flesh, it fell to the ground.

"Jeez," Nash's voice came from somewhere behind her. "Are you kidding me with that? That was like something from *Star Wars*."

"Nash, I thought the plan was that you stayed inside," Cassidy panted, her eyes never leaving the next demon that was charging her.

"Yeah, well, it's lucky that I didn't," he retorted as he dropped to his knees and used his Zippo to set both dead demons on fire. Then Thomas's voice rang out in her ear, once again barking instructions to her.

"Drop your elbow and bring your sword in close to your body. Closer. You need to aim for the point between his collar and his neck. Now."

She obediently followed his command, and instead of feeling a familiar ache in her muscles, it was almost exhilarating as the third demon fell at her feet. Without being told, she nimbly jumped out of the way as the fourth demon reached her.

This time she dropped her shield and put both hands on her sword to use it like a baseball bat. Blood spurted everywhere as the blade cut through the creature's thickened neck like it was a Thanksgiving turkey. As soon as it had fallen, Nash was beside it with his Zippo, the flames quickly engulfing the creature before being sucked inward and the whole body vanishing from sight.

Cassidy repositioned herself as the fifth demon charged toward her. She tightened her grip on the hilt of the sword, but at the last moment the creature turned sideways and headed directly for Nash, who was still down on his knees next to the space where the dead demon had been only seconds earlier. For a split second Cassidy just stared in mute horror, her sword dangling hopelessly in her arm before Thomas's blunt voice brought her crashing back to earth.

"Use your knife," he hissed, "and aim for the spinal cord at the top of the neck. If you don't make an exact hit, then your friend is dead."

Fear pounded in her ears as her leather-clad hands clumsily fumbled for the knife that was hitched into her belt. Finally she had it out, the blade looking blunt and ineffective. She closed her eyes for a moment and tried to remember everything that Thomas had taught her. She took aim, careful to keep her shoulder up, and released the knife. It seemed to move in slow motion as it rotated through the air before finally embedding itself in the demon's neck. The creature immediately toppled, but as it fell, its blade made a wide arc and sliced through Nash's arm.

Cassidy hardly noticed as Nash fell to the ground with a sickening thud, a pool of blood flowing out from his injured arm.

"No." The word was ripped from her throat and the sword fell with a clatter as she raced over to him, trying to avoid the demon lying next to him, its distorted, misshapen body still looking threatening, despite the knife that was plunged into its main artery.

Cassidy wanted to move Nash away from such an abomination, but she didn't dare do anything to make his condition worse. Instead, she dropped to her knees and forced herself not to cry. His brow was the color of chalk and covered in a fine layer of sweat. Blood was pouring freely out of his arm, and she quickly stripped off her jacket to help stanch the flow while ignoring the chill air prickling her skin.

"I need to get him to a hospital," Cassidy said in a tight voice, desperately trying to think where her cell phone was. Before she could stand up to look for her purse, Thomas was beside her.

"First you need to dispose of the dead demons and cleanse your blades."

"What?" Cassidy glared at him as she continued to press the jacket into Nash's arm while trying not to notice his blood seeping onto her hands. "No, I need to call an ambulance."

Thomas opened his mouth to speak, but then, as if

catching her stubborn expression, he let out an exasperated sigh. "The boy is not fatally wounded. I will ensure that he is healed. But first we need to burn the corpse."

"You can save him?"

"I told you, he's not dying, and therefore he doesn't need to be saved. However, I can heal him a lot faster, *after you dispose of the demon*." Once again the muscles around his jaw flickered, and Cassidy reluctantly laid Nash's arm across his chest and reached for the Zippo that was lying on the ground beside him.

She tried to ignore the stench of decay that was rising up from the demons as she set fire to the coarse garments they were wearing and watched the flames encase their entire bodies, until, as before, the flames were sucked inward. Soon there was no sign that the demons had even been there. Then she retrieved the sword and her knife and ran the Zippo flame along them until the brilliant green flame made way for a more natural color and finally faded away to nothing. As soon as it was done she turned her attention back to Nash.

"So?" She glared at Thomas, demanding that he keep his word. He nodded to the grimoire that was lying on the ground, still glowing faintly despite the fact that the demons were gone. Cassidy scampered to pick it up while trying to ignore Nash's shallow breathing. "I've got it. Now what? Is it something in the grimoire that I need?"

He shook his head. "You don't yet have the skills. But if you put one hand on the grimoire and the other hand on the boy's chest, I will transfer the power."

Cassidy raised an eyebrow curiously, but had learned enough about Thomas to know that he didn't joke. Instead, she slid one hand over the leather-bound book and rested her other hand on the tattered sleeve of Nash's white shirt. His breathing was low and shallow, and Cassidy just hoped that Thomas really would be true to his word.

"Okay, no matter what happens, don't remove your hands," he instructed. Then without waiting for an answer he suddenly disappeared from sight. Cassidy felt a stab of fear go racing through her. He hadn't kept his—

But the rest of her thoughts were lost as she felt a surge of energy come up from the grimoire, move along her arm, and flow down into Nash's chest. The tattoo on her arm heated up and prickled her skin as the energy continued to pour through her. She kept her hand on Nash's chest until his breathing slowly returned to normal. Thomas reappeared, his mismatched eyes unnaturally dull.

"It is done," he said simply, but Cassidy didn't answer. She was too busy pulling away her blood-soaked jacket and inspecting Nash's arm. The deep gash that moments before had been gushing with blood was gone, and in its place was a small pink line. She stared at Thomas, unable to think of what to say. Then Nash groggily opened his eyes and blinked several times before cautiously wriggling up into a sitting position. The minute he did so, Cassidy immediately threw herself at him and hugged him.

"You're okay. I was so worried. How do you feel?" she demanded, her hysteria giving way to relief.

"I . . . I actually feel amazing, but I'm not sure why. The last thing I remember was the demon charging at me and—" he said, then paused and twisted his neck to better inspect his arm. When he caught sight of the drenched jacket and Cassidy's bloodied hands, he let out an astonished gasp. "I felt the knife slice through my arm. There was blood, and then I fell backward. I must have fainted." As he spoke, his hand flew to the back of his head as if checking for lumps and bumps.

"It's the grimoire," Cassidy quickly told him as she reached out and clasped his hand. "Thomas did . . . something . . . through the grimoire to help you. Anyway, are you sure you really feel okay?"

"I am. I really, really am." He stood up, still flexing his arm as he stared at the pale pink scar that only moments ago had been open and bloody. Then he turned to Thomas. "That's some trick you've got there."

"It's not a trick," the knight retorted in a tight voice, his face chalky pale. "And it's not something I do on a regular basis, so make sure you don't get cut again."

"You're preaching to the choir on that one," Nash assured him with a shudder. "Being on the receiving end of two demons is enough for me. Anyone would think that they didn't like me."

"They don't like anyone," Thomas snapped, his eyes burning like embers against his pale skin. "And you would both do well to remember that."

"Er, okay," Nash said before he turned back to Cassidy. "That was some fight. You were amazing. How many demons did you kill?"

"I killed five—" Cassidy started to say before her throat tightened and she let out a strangled gasp. *"But there were six to begin with.* Which means that there's still another—"

"It's gone," Thomas cut her off. "Look at the grimoire and see for yourself. It's no longer glowing intensely, which means that the immediate danger has passed."

Cassidy looked down to where the book was lying and sank to her knees as she reached out and skimmed the leather with her fingertips, still bloody from Nash's wound. It was cool to the touch despite the faint glow that lingered. "S-so what happens now? Do we go after it?"

"Non."

"What? But we can't just sit back and do nothing. It could be out there getting more recruits."

"Guardians do *not* chase demons," he said through clenched teeth, his jaw so tight that Cassidy thought something might snap. "They protect the Black Rose. That is all. Have you found the vessel yet?"

"Unfortunately, yes." Cassidy was immediately distracted. "And I think we're going to have a problem because the Black Rose is Celeste Gilbert."

"It doesn't matter who the vessel is, you need to do your duty. You need to follow the Black Rose and protect it. Everything else is irrelevant."

"You're not listening to me. Celeste is a senior. Following her everywhere isn't going to be easy. I was thinking that we should tell her what's happening."

"Non." He gave a definitive shake of his head. "That is not an option. You must find a way to protect her."

"Fine. *I'll find a way,*" Cassidy mimicked in annoyance as the mail pressed down on her shoulders. She tried to wriggle out of it, but instead managed to get her hair tangled up in the tiny steel links. Pain raced down her neck before Nash hurried over and helped ease the cumbersome metal cloth over her head. Cassidy panted in relief and quickly slipped off the equally uncomfortable undershirt. "But I still don't see why—"

"Where did you get that?" Thomas suddenly cut her off as his eyes narrowed in on the carnelian necklace that had swung free now that her armor was off.

"A friend gave it to me," she said in surprise, before adding, "Why? Is there some stupid rule to say that I can't wear jewelry while I'm fighting?"

"No, but would you take it off if I asked you to?" he suddenly asked, his voice as uncompromising as the red scar on his cheek that shimmered and throbbed with anger.

"Why, what's going on?" Cassidy studied his face, since up until now Thomas hadn't shown any interest in anything that wasn't the Black Rose. Her fingers tightened around the necklace, unsure whether she should take it off or not.

"Nothing." He shook his head. "I-I must go. Follow the vessel. Make the protective amulet and ensure that the

Black Rose is safe. That is your only mission. I will return tomorrow when the lauds bells ring for your training. Your stance during the battle was not acceptable."

Then he was gone, and Cassidy and Nash were left sitting in the empty courtyard with only the sword and a couple of feathers to let them know that there had ever been a fight. But despite the fact the dead demons were gone, she could still feel their presence everywhere. Like acid burning through her skin, covering her clothes, clogging her nostrils so that she could barely breathe. And her hands. Stained with Nash's blood.

"Okay, so that was abrupt even by his standards. And what was with the necklace?" Nash complained before suddenly pausing and studying her face. "Hey, are you okay?"

"No." Cassidy tried not to look at her hands. "Not really. I mean, there were six of those demons, and Thomas wouldn't even listen to me when I tried to explain how hard it's going to be to follow Celeste. Nash, those demons: that was real. You could've been killed."

"You could've been killed, too," Nash said in a soft voice. "And Celeste still could be."

"I know." She tried to ignore the way her body was now shaking. "Wh-what are we going to do? What if I can't stop them?"

"We'll just need to make sure that we do," Nash said firmly.

"Thank you," she said in a choked voice. Nash had always been there for her, but she was certain that this went far beyond the normal job description of best friend.

"Don't thank me too soon," Nash warned as he rubbed his arm where the demon's sword had slashed him. "Because there's one other thing we can do, but I'm not sure you're going to like it."

"There's a lot of this that I don't like," Cassidy said, still refusing to look at her bloodstained hands. "But that doesn't mean I won't do it. What are you thinking?"

"You could audition for *Romeo and Juliet*, and then you would be able to spend all the time you want with Celeste. Whether she likes it or not."

What?

Cassidy opened her mouth to protest, since not only did she hate acting but the idea of standing onstage made her feel physically sick. But then she closed her mouth and looked at where the five demons had been slain, already knowing that this was one more decision that she didn't have a choice about.

"Fine." She slowly got to her feet and looked for somewhere to wash her hands. "I guess we'd better get going if I don't want to miss the auditions."

SEVENTEEN

Cassidy stepped out of the shower and studied her hands. Despite scrubbing them for the last twenty minutes, she could still see Nash's blood running down her fingers and onto her calloused palms. Was it always going to be like this? Then she caught sight of her tattoo. Ever since she had let Thomas heal Nash through her, the tattoo had felt like it was dancing under her skin.

She could ask Thomas what that meant, but right now she was still too mad at him. Not only because of his disappearing act but because he made her burn the demon and cleanse the swords before letting her attend to her best friend. Duty first.

Even thinking about it made her furious, and she bit into the fleshy part of her lip as she hurried back to her bedroom, where the green dress had been condemned to the back of the closet along with the black one. At this rate she would have no clothes left by the end of the week. She grabbed some old jeans and the Snoopy hoodie that her mom kept trying to get rid of, and finished getting dressed while trying to ignore her aching muscles. All she really wanted was to sleep and pretend that none of it had happened. But she'd arranged to go over to Nash's house to make the amulet.

She just hoped it worked.

Especially since it turned out that trying to audition for *Romeo and Juliet* after killing five demon knights wasn't such a bright idea. It was bad enough that she'd been forced to grab the longest jacket she could find from the collection of discarded clothes in her locker to try to cover the worst of the blood, but then there was the whole trying-to-speak-in-front-of-an-audience thing to get over.

Nash had tried to convince her that it wasn't so bad, but Cassidy knew that even with the help of Travis's lucky charm, she'd be lucky if she managed to get cast as a tree. The only small consolation was that when they'd gone back into the auditorium, there had been no sign of Travis, something that she was very grateful for, since embarrassing herself in front of cute guys wasn't her favorite thing in the world.

At least while Cassidy had been auditioning Nash had broken into Celeste's locker and found her hairbrush, which meant that they had all the hair they needed. After that they had followed an annoyed-looking Celeste out to her car and trailed her all the way back to her house, before deciding that the sooner they made the amulet, the better.

Which was why she needed to get moving.

She slung her sports bag out the window so that her parents wouldn't see it and then left the bedroom. As she walked down the hallway she could hear her mom in the kitchen, but she continued on to the living room, where her dad was sitting on the couch, his leg stretched out in front of him. He was no longer wearing the protective brace, and his cheeks were flushed from doing his exercises. Despite the crutches that were still lying nearby, he was looking happier than he had in ages.

"Let me guess, more homework with Nash?" her dad said as he turned down the volume on the television. "Or are you going to celebrate your good news?"

"Wh-what good news?" Cassidy asked in a cautious voice, since she was fairly sure he wasn't talking about her killing five demon knights this afternoon.

"The play. According to Colin Thompson, you were at the *Romeo and Juliet* auditions," her dad said before frowning. "But Cass, tell me the truth, did you audition because you wanted to or because your mom thought it would be a good idea?"

Cassidy groaned. It was one thing to audition so that she could get close to Celeste Gilbert, but it was another thing entirely for her mom to think that she was following her advice. Then she realized her dad was still waiting for an answer, so she let out a reluctant sigh.

"It just seemed like it would be fun. But it was only an audition, and I don't even know if I'll get a part yet," she said. "In fact, considering that I had the lousiest audition ever, I doubt it."

"Nonsense, everyone can act, even you. You just need to tap into your emotions," her dad said, and for a moment Cassidy thought of Travis and his haunting performance. What emotions had he been tapping into? Then she thought of the way he seemed to have eyes only for her, and her face heated up. "Besides, *Romeo and Juliet* is my favorite Shakespeare play, and I would love to see my daughter up onstage."

"It is?" Cassidy instantly forgot about Travis as she looked at him in surprise. Her mom had mentioned that the other day, but Cassidy hadn't believed her.

"Sure. Family feuding? Star-crossed lovers? Teenage angst? What's not to like?" His navy eyes twinkled. "And when you get a part, I'll help you learn your lines."

Cassidy was pretty sure that she wouldn't get any part, based on her bad audition, but the idea of spending more time with her dad—not to mention Travis—was definitely appealing, and she nodded her head. "I'll be taking you up on that. Anyway, I guess I'd better go, since I can't put this homework off."

"Words that every parent longs to hear." He grinned as Cassidy gave him a grateful hug before racing to the front door. She stopped to yell a cursory good-bye to her mom and then scooted around the house to retrieve her sports bag.

The night air stung at her cheeks, and the sounds of the evening traffic and the low hum of voices from some joggers who were braving the cold weather hung in the air. She thrust her hands deep into the pockets of her coat while she hurried the three blocks to Nash's house.

He'd also changed out of his ripped clothing and was now wearing his favorite Smiths T-shirt under a black buttoned-up vest and some heavy gray surplus trousers. His parents weren't home, so they went straight to his room. Cassidy had once dubbed it the Old Curiosity Shop because it looked like it had come straight out of a Dickens novel and was filled to overflowing with ancient books and paintings, as well as a giant floor-standing globe over by his bed and an equally giant telescope propped up next to his window. The antiquities were broken up by posters and ticket stubs of his favorite bands, which Nash had hung around the room to remind anyone that, despite his love of history, he still liked to rock out from time to time.

"Okay, so I think I've got everything. Though it's a bit unclear how long I'm supposed to consecrate it all for." Nash chewed his lip. "I wonder if Thomas would know?"

"Probably, but since he disappeared we can't exactly ask him, can we?" Cassidy retorted.

"Look"—Nash put down the river stone he had been holding—"I know that you're pissed off with him."

"Pissed off with him?" Cassidy spluttered as she raised her eyebrows. "He almost let you die, Nash, just so I could burn a couple of demons. Demons that were already dead."

"The cut wasn't life-threatening, so he made a decision based on priorities," Nash corrected her before relenting.

"And I know he can seem a bit high-handed, but try looking at it from his point of view. He's frustrated that he can't be here fighting the demons himself. From what I can gather he's been protecting the Black Rose almost single-handedly for the last three years, so the idea of his having to—"

"Trust a girl?" Cassidy retorted in a dark voice. "Because obviously he's sexist. Oh, and I'm pretty sure he doesn't like my dating, either, because did you see what he was like when he saw this necklace? It was like he knew it came from a guy."

"Cass. I don't think—"

"Stop trying to defend him," she snapped as her fingers curled around the carnelian. "Besides, if he's so concerned, then where is he now? This whole amulet thing would be a lot easier if he hadn't deserted us."

"It would also be a lot easier if you stopped moaning about him," Nash retorted in a dry voice as he turned his attention back to the small mortar and pestle he had been using to grind up the ingredients that he had neatly lined up on his large oak desk.

Suddenly, Cassidy felt guilty. "Sorry, I didn't mean to make things worse. I'm going to forget about Thomas and his lack of social manners. So I guess you need the grimoire?"

"Yes, please." He nodded, and Cassidy unzipped her sports bag and handed it over, trying not to notice that the cool leather was warm under her fingers despite the chilly weather. The more time she spent with the book, the creepier it got. However, Nash didn't seem to notice as he carefully turned the pages until he reached the one he wanted, his head bent in concentration. Cassidy knew better than to try to interrupt him when he was working, so she silently sat on the floor until he eventually looked up and ran a distracted hand through his dark hair.

"I was thinking that instead of just doing an amulet that Celeste can wear, we could do a second one for her house. That way she'll be safe when she's there and it will save us a lot of time camping out in the car."

"Anything that reduces the number of hours we have to be protecting her is fine by me," Cassidy agreed as Nash got to work.

"Now, the parsley, rosemary, two strands of burned hair, and a cup of soil are all here, and I've ground them into a fine paste," he said as he checked off his list. "We have river stones that have been cleansed with salt and two small cotton bags to put them in. One we can tie around her wrist and the other we'll put by her house. Oh, and I've got a piece of paper and have used a consecrated pen to write out the words: *No matter if demons shall touch, see, or smell the vessel. Keep her invisible to all of them.*"

"Catchy," Cassidy giggled before catching Nash's stern glance. "Sorry. So what now?"

"Now I need your sword."

"I thought we were making an amulet, so why do we need the sword?" Cassidy frowned as she carefully got it out of her bag and put it down on the desk for him while trying to shake the memory of her latest fight from her mind.

"The sword represents that protection," he explained as he unsheathed it with almost as much reverence as he used when handling the grimoire. He let out a long breath as he studied the runes that ran down the pitted blade. "It's extraordinary to think that these runes can give you so much extra power. The strength of the sword should never be underestimated. I mean, you should've seen the way you were slicing through those guys, and . . . hey, there's something written on the quillon. *'As above.'* I don't suppose Thomas told you what that means?" he asked, his natural curiosity once again surfacing.

Actually, Cassidy didn't even know what a quillon was until she followed the direction of Nash's finger to where there was a tiny inscription that ran along the horizontal bar that stopped her hand from slipping down onto the blade. Then she realized Nash was waiting for an answer.

"Sorry, I don't have a clue. Not that it's really a surprise since, in my experience, Thomas isn't the chattiest of people. He normally prefers to grunt and growl. All I know is that his father gave the sword to him and that it's special, but I've got no idea what the inscription means."

"Perhaps it's a family motto?" Nash pondered for a moment, but before Cassidy could answer, her cell phone beeped and she gratefully reached for it, since talking about

Thomas's sword was the last thing she wanted to do. She was half expecting the text to be from her mom, but instead it was from a number she didn't recognize. She clicked on the message.

```
Heard you auditioned. I wish I'd
stayed 2 c it. Bet u were amazing ~
Travis.
```

Cassidy stared at the screen for a moment before it sank in that Travis was sending her a text message. Suddenly, the ugliness of the last few hours receded in her mind as she traced her finger over the screen. Travis Lenoir had taken the time to get her digits. She quickly saved his number into her contacts and then sent him a reply.

```
No I wasn't but YOU were. I swear
that Mrs. Davis fainted with
excitement.
```

She grinned before realizing that Nash was staring at her expectantly. She flushed.

"Sorry, that was Travis. He heard that I auditioned," she apologized, the smile never leaving her face. "So where were we?"

"We were just about to do the ritual to make the amulet. If that's okay with Travis?"

"I'm sure he would be fine with it," Cassidy assured Nash, choosing to ignore his sarcasm. She put her cell phone away and watched as he took the sword and beckoned for her to join him over at the desk.

"Okay." He took a deep breath, and then he seemed to slip into a trance. Cassidy felt a shudder go racing up her arm as she watched. Without speaking, he lifted up the piece of paper that he had written on earlier, put it in the mortar, and set it on fire with his Zippo. When it had burned to ash, he used the pestle to grind it into the rest of the paste and carefully rubbed the stone in it before placing it in the small lunch box filled with dirt, explaining that it was important to keep the amulet grounded. The small pouches were tucked next to it, presumably to slip the stones into once they were ready. He then repeated the ritual with a smaller stone and picked up the sword.

Cassidy watched him stand up so that he could lower the blade and press it onto the tops of both the stones. Then he slipped a glove onto his hand and carefully put the stones into two separate pouches and then back into the dirt before shutting the lunch box. Finally, he looked up at her. "That should do it."

"Thank you." Cassidy's fingers tightened around the necklace Travis had given her. Suddenly, she had the desire to laugh, as some of the weight that had been pressing down on her shoulders was lifted. Her dad was happy, Travis had sent her a text message, and they now had amulets to stop the demons from finding Celeste and possibly ripping her to shreds. Suddenly, she felt as if the glass was half full.

EIGHTEEN

The following day Cassidy was having second thoughts about her glass-half-full theory. Especially since her day wasn't going as planned. She had woken up at five o'clock and jogged through the frosty predawn to meet Thomas in the woods for a training session, only to discover he wasn't there. Her mood had improved slightly as she pictured him while she practiced her knife-throwing skills, and then she'd jogged home and showered before meeting Nash so that they could keep an eye on Celeste.

The good news was that they'd managed to hide an amulet in a rosebush at the front of Celeste's house, and the moment they'd done so, the whole place took on a shimmering glow that Cassidy figured made it a demon-no-go zone. The bad news was that trying to slip the other amulet onto Celeste's wrist was proving much more complicated, and despite following her to school, it was impossible to get within touching distance of her—let alone amulet-tying distance.

It had been the same all morning, which was why she was now standing outside the girls' locker room clutching the lunch box Nash had put the amulet in. She turned to him.

"Do you really think it will work?"

"Of course it will." Nash leaned against the wall and gave Cass an encouraging nod. "It's a locker room, so there's lots going on. I'm sure you can get the bracelet on without too much trouble. And according to everything that I've read in the grimoire, once it's on, she won't even be able to tell it's there. Now, off you go."

"Fine," Cassidy muttered, though she was fairly sure that Nash was overestimating how easy it would be. And he had better be right about it being invisible once it was on, or they would all be in trouble. She grasped the lunch box that the amulet was in and walked inside, and was instantly greeted by the smell of hairspray and perfume. Cassidy resisted the urge to gag as she searched for Celeste. It didn't take long since, thanks to the Black Rose, she was still glowing with a bright but terrible light.

If Thomas were here, he would probably stalk over in his brutal fashion and slap the amulet around Celeste's wrist without saying a word before marching off. However, Thomas didn't have to go to high school every day and Cassidy did, so she was going to need a bit more finesse.

Thankfully, Celeste's sports locker was at the end of the row, and she was facing inward, having an animated conversation about some kind of hair-related crisis, which gave Cassidy the chance to slip behind her. She pressed her back into the side of the locker and hoped that her years of being invisible at high school would finally pay off.

She took the small pouch out of the lunch box and waited, her stomach churning with nerves. Celeste was still talking, and while she was waving one hand in the air, the other was resting down at her side.

This was her chance. She loosened the thin ties of the pouch and lowered herself down so that she was now at wrist level. Celeste still hadn't noticed her, so Cassidy angled her hands as she tried to get the amulet around Celeste's wrist without her knowing. As she worked, her finger brushed Celeste's skin, and Cassidy immediately whipped her hand back as a wave of pain slammed into her chest and the smell of burning flesh filled her nostrils. Her throat tightened as an unwanted vision flashed through her mind.

Celeste lying limply in the dirt, her normal perma-tanned face leached of color. A large sword protruding from her chest was keeping her pinned down like a specimen in the biology lab, and blood was seeping down her chest and pooling on the dirt around her. Hovering over her was a demon, oblivious to everything but the curling plume of smoke that was rising up from Celeste's crushed body in the shape of a rose—

"Seriously, you've got to be kidding me." A voice dragged Cassidy out of the tangled scene in her mind, and she looked up to see Celeste's disdainful glare. It was amplified by the white tendrils of the Black Rose, which were flickering around her head like Medusa. So much for being invisible.

"Um, hi." Cassidy gulped as her fingers closed around

the amulet, and she quickly stuffed it into the pocket of her jeans, praying that Celeste hadn't noticed anything.

"Oh, no. Don't you dare try to 'hi' me," Celeste retorted. "Instead, you can answer me a question. Why is it that every time I turn around, there you are?"

"Because you're lucky?" Cassidy tried to shake the last of the vision from her mind as she slowly got to her feet and smoothed down her jeans, as if it was totally normal for her to be there.

"Lucky to see you and your weird clothes every day?" Celeste gave an unladylike snort. "I don't think so. In fact, if you ask me, I'd say that you were stalking me."

"S-stalking you? That's crazy. Why would I do that?" Cassidy stammered, while letting out an inward groan, since pissing Celeste off wasn't part of the plan. Why did this have to be so hard?

"Please, I can read girls like you in my sleep. It's because you're secretly in love with Nash, and you're jealous at the obvious animal magnetism that we share. So now you're doing everything to keep us apart. Like at lunch yesterday, when he was desperate to sit with me and you kept dragging him away. And as for all of that rambling about a snake at Cade's party, that was just embarrassing. Why can't you just accept that Nash has feelings for me?"

Because it's not true, Cassidy longed to scream at her, but she stopped when the image of Celeste lying on the ground, a sword piercing her chest, flashed into her mind. Regardless of how much she detested Celeste, there was no way she wanted to see her dead. Which meant that she had to figure out a way to get the amulet onto her.

"Look, Celeste, I'm sorry if you think that I don't like you, because I do," Cassidy tried again, but it was no good, and instead of warming up, Celeste just narrowed her eyes.

"Of course you do, because I'm awesome. However, that doesn't mean that *I* like *you*, so if you know what's good for you, you will keep your distance," Celeste informed her before she marched away, her friends all falling in line behind her.

Cassidy groaned as she watched them leave before she slowly made her way out to where Nash was waiting for her.

"So?" Nash pounced on her. "How did it go? Did you manage it?"

"Not exactly," Cassidy confessed as she transferred the amulet back into the lunch box, burying it deep into the dirt. "I almost had it, but the moment I touched her wrist I had a vision."

Nash's face went pale. "What was it about?"

"It basically involved Celeste and a lot of blood. It was pretty horrible." She shook her head as the smell of burned skin and blood flared in her nose, causing the panic once again to rise in her chest. "What are we going to do? How are we going to protect her? I mean, I don't like her. At all. But it was bad enough seeing her die in my mind. I don't want to see it happen for real."

"Cass, it's going to be okay," Nash said, but she just shook her head.

"You're only saying that because you want it to be true. It doesn't mean that it *will* be true. And after what happened in the locker room, I doubt I'll be able to get within ten feet of her. Oh, and by the way, the reason she dislikes me so much is because she thinks that I'm jealous of the obvious animal magnetism that you both share."

"What?" Nash looked at her in horror. "Please tell me that she didn't say those exact words."

"Verbatim," Cassidy assured him before sighing. "I hate to say it, but I think you're going to have to do it."

"What? No, no, no. That's a bad idea. A very bad idea."

"I know it's not ideal," she said as she pressed the lunch box into his hands. "But you know it makes sense. Plus, I heard her say she's going to be in the library all lunchtime, which is loads better than having to go into the cafeteria."

"Can you at least come with me?" He reluctantly took the lunch box.

"I would," Cassidy assured him, "but she'll be in a lot better mood if she doesn't see me again today. I think she's about a second away from taking out a restraining order against me. I'll just go and get my lunch and then wait nearby with the grimoire to make sure that there are no demons around."

"Fine." He let out a pained sigh as he slumped his shoulders and turned in the direction of the library. "But you owe me for this. Big-time."

"Just get the amulet on her," Cassidy said as he disappeared around the corner. She headed for her locker to grab her brown-bagged lunch, but decided to leave the sword in the locker, because even looking at it made her shudder and the blisters on her palms prickle. *Besides, hopefully Nash would get the amulet on and she wouldn't have to fight any more demons and—*

"Hey," a soft voice suddenly said in her ear, and she turned around to see Travis leaning against the locker next to hers. Today his dark hair was falling into his eyes, and Cassidy longed to reach up and push it to one side.

"Travis." Cassidy suddenly forgot about her aching muscles and the problems associated with trying to slip the amulet onto Celeste's skinny wrist as she basked in his gorgeousness.

"I was hoping that I'd find you here. Have you eaten lunch yet?"

"Not yet," she said as she waved her brown paper bag in the air. "But this feast awaits me."

"Hmm, let's see," Travis said as he plucked the bag out of her hand and peered into it. "A squashed piece of bread and some brown things?"

"Not brown things, raisins." Cassidy laughed while holding her hands up in protest. "And I know it looks odd, but I was in a hurry this morning. *Hey, what are you doing?*" she yelped as he balled the bag up and gracefully lobbed it into a nearby trash can. "You can't just throw away my lunch."

"It's not lunch," he corrected in a stern voice. "It's rabbit food. And not very nice rabbit food, either. I've got a much better idea. Lunch. With me. To celebrate."

"Celebrate what?" Cassidy knitted her brow in confusion, but instead of answering Travis grabbed her hand and began to tug her arm gently in the direction of the stairs. Part of her thought of Nash and Celeste at the library and how she was meant to be watching the grimoire to make sure that no demon knights turned up, but the other half of her was too intrigued. "Where are we going?"

"Has anyone ever told you that you ask a lot of questions, Cassidy Carter-Lewis?" he asked, giving her another one of his disarming smiles as they climbed the stairs. When they reached the top floor, he let go of her hand and fumbled around in the pocket of his Levi's for a key. Before she could even protest that students weren't allowed up on the roof, he'd pushed the door open to where a red picnic blanket was spread out and a large wicker basket was sitting in the middle of it. He led her toward it. "So? Is that a yes for lunch?"

"Um, do I have a choice?" she said as he flipped open the basket and began to lift out container after container of food.

"You *always* have a choice," he said in a serious voice before he suddenly grinned. "Which is lucky, since I had no idea what you would like, so I got a bit of everything."

"I'll say you did," Cassidy agreed as he pulled out a jar of pickles followed by pastrami, pâté, some runny cheese, crackers, and about a zillion other things, most of which she didn't even recognize. She wrinkled her nose. "And you still haven't told me what this is about."

"Does it have to be about anything?" He opened up a bag

of tiny red apples and offered her one. She shook her head.

"I guess not, but Travis, in case you hadn't noticed, this isn't exactly normal behavior at our high school," she said, her heart pounding in excitement.

"Well, it's not my fault there are a lot of unsophisticated heathens about the place." He slowly bit into an apple, and Cassidy found herself hypnotized by the way his teeth cut through the bright red skin into the pale white flesh underneath. Then, as if realizing that he was being studied, he quickly tossed the apple core across the roof. "But there is actually a reason that I brought you up here. It's so we can celebrate that we're both in the school play." His warm eyes met hers.

"What?" Cassidy's jaw dropped in confusion. "But Mrs. Davis isn't announcing anything until tomorrow."

"Let's just say that a little bird told me." He toyed with the corner of the hamper for a moment. "I'm going to be Romeo, and you're to be Juliet's understudy."

"That's impossible." Cassidy shook her head in disbelief. "I'm the understudy? Are you sure?"

"I know. I was disappointed, too. Personally, I found Celeste's performance a bit over the top for my liking. I think you would've brought a lot more true emotion to the role."

"No. That's not what I meant." Cassidy quickly shook her head. "I meant that I was terrible. How could I possibly be . . . *It was you, wasn't it?* Did you say something to Mrs. Davis?"

"Of course not," Travis said a little bit too quickly, his eyes not quite meeting hers. Then he grinned. "Perhaps the crystal worked? I see you're still wearing it."

"Of course. I love it."

"Good. Anyway, I predict that I will need a lot of help learning my lines for this play, and since I'm sure Celeste will be far too busy, perhaps her understudy will take pity on me?"

"I guess I could. For the sake of the play," she said.

"For the sake of the play," he agreed, before he suddenly reached for her arm and carefully rolled back the sleeve of her denim jacket to reveal her tattoo. His face was pale and his voice hoarse. "You got another one? Don't tell me something else has happened to your father?"

"What?" Cassidy asked in surprise. "What do you mean?"

"Nothing." He shook his head as he carefully traced the tip of his finger around the roses and up to where the two vines twined, causing a herd of elephants to stampede in her stomach. Then, as if noticing her confusion, he gently put her arm back in her lap and coughed.

"Travis." Cassidy was alarmed at how his sunny mood had faded away. "What's going on?"

"Sorry. It's just, you told me at Cade's party that you had the tattoo because your dad was sick and that when he got better you got rid of it. I was just being stupid. Forgive me."

"There's nothing to forgive. I just decided to put on another one, but not because my dad is sick again. He's fine," she assured him, since she couldn't very well tell him that the tattoo had magically reappeared after she had bonded with a mystical book. But it still didn't explain his reaction. "Why did it freak you out so much?"

He studied his hands silently for a moment before he finally looked up. "I lost my father. It happened a while ago, but it's still pretty raw. I guess when I saw the tattoo and what you had told me about getting it, I put two and two together and came up with idiot."

Cassidy gasped as her eyes widened in horror. "I-I didn't know. I'm so sorry."

"Oh, no, don't be sorry. I didn't mean even to say anything. It's not something I normally talk about," he admitted, a confused expression still on his face. "And please don't feel sad. I'm just glad your dad's okay."

"What happened?" Cassidy asked him in a small voice.

"It was an accident," he said, his eyes suddenly looking up to the sky, lost in another world. "A terrible accident that could've been avoided. I relive it every day and wish that it had been different. I keep asking myself if there was something else I could've done to change it."

"You can't blame yourself," Cassidy cried, before shyly threading her fingers through his. She then watched in delight as his face transformed from one of haunted pain to one of happiness.

"Thank you." He tightened his grip and looked at her hand as if it was the most precious thing he'd ever seen. "It's been a long time since anyone cared about how I feel. It means a lot."

Then, before Cassidy quite knew what was happening, his mouth was on hers. Kissing her with an infinite gentleness that sent wisps of happiness racing through her entire body. It wasn't a long kiss or a deep one, but it was more than physical, and she melted into his chest as he kissed her again. Then, too soon it was over, and there was once again space between them, though his fingers were still woven into hers. He gave her a sheepish grin.

"Well, that was unexpected. But I believe I promised you some lunch. What would you like? I have brie from France, olives from Italy. And for the purists among us, there are Pringles. Of course, if you can't choose, you could just have a bit of everything. After all, there's no rule to say that we can't have it all."

Cassidy, who could hardly decide what to eat at the best of times, let alone after such a mind-blowing kiss, gave him a grateful smile as she took the plate he had prepared for her. She could definitely get used to this.

NINETEEN

"Okay, you can stop smiling now," Nash complained as he merged into the afternoon traffic and followed Celeste's bright pink SUV, which unfortunately seemed to be heading in the direction of the mall.

"Sorry." Cassidy put her hands over her mouth to try to hide her grin, but it was impossible not to be happy. Nash had managed to slip the amulet onto Celeste's wrist at lunchtime, and while to Cassidy she still glowed like an electric substation, there was a more subtle shimmer around her as well, which hopefully meant that the demons could no longer see her at all. Also, now that Cassidy was in the school play, it would make following her a lot easier. *And then there was Travis.*

Despite the fact that her fingers were pressed against her mouth, she could feel the smile pushing its way back onto her lips. Lunch had been a blur of delicious food and sunshine, and Cassidy was pretty sure that she had floated back down the stairs when the fifth-period bell had rung, conscious only of the feel of Travis's fingers on her hand as he'd held it.

"No, you're not sorry," Nash retorted. "Since not only did you force me to spend far too much time with Celeste Gilbert—who, for the record, doesn't seem to understand what the term *asexual* actually means—but then you shimmied off and had an enjoyable lunch with someone who doesn't make you want to gouge your eyeballs out. And you kissed him."

Yes, she had! Cassidy gave up trying not to smile. "I'm really sorry that you had to spend so much time with Celeste. But at least you got the amulet on her wrist and it was obviously successful, since otherwise she would have just taken it off. Hopefully from now on I'll be able to follow her, so your work here is done."

"Stop trying to appease me, I'm far too clever for that," Nash lectured before relenting. "But I guess you're right. And you're also right about Celeste heading to the mall."

"Hopefully, this is her last shopping trip before rehearsals start," Cassidy said as Nash turned his car into the giant parking lot and they both shuddered. If they had to go shopping, it would be nice if it could at least be down in the village, where Cassidy's favorite vintage shops were, rather than in the mall with its miles of overly bright stores full of identical outfits.

"Are you going to be okay without me?" Nash asked as they watched Celeste make three attempts at parking her oversize vehicle. Cassidy nodded her head, since she knew how much Nash loved the art history class he was taking at the local college. He was also taking some advanced physics classes, but apparently they were purely for academic reasons. The art history was to feed his soul. There was no way that Cassidy wanted him to miss class just for her.

"I'll be fine," she assured him as Celeste finally managed to get parked. "If she leaves the mall before you're back I'll just catch the bus home."

Cassidy patiently listened while Nash gave her some last-minute instructions about not doing anything dangerous and that if she was in doubt, she should text him immediately. Finally he was done and she hurried into the mall. Even with the glow, there was no sign of Celeste, so Cassidy quickly pulled out her cell phone and went onto Twitter.

According to Nash, social networking was now leading to a new age in narcissism, during which people thought that their every move was worthy of being documented. Which was probably true, but all Cassidy knew was that it was a lot easier to find someone when they said:

```
going 2 spanglenails 2 get
mani&pedi with @mriley @happykitty
#bliss.
```

Cassidy made her way over to the large floor plan that was on the wall and searched for Spangle Nails. It was on the third floor, and by the time she reached it, she could clearly see Celeste and two other seniors sitting in the bright nail salon, their hands all sticking out like they were about to meet the queen. She glanced at her watch and then looked around for somewhere to get comfortable, since she had no idea how long a "mani&pedi" took. She finally found a spot just behind a pillar, giving her clear sight of the salon without making it obvious she was there.

Ten minutes later Cassidy decided that this following thing wasn't for her. For a start, she was dying for a drink. Would she be a bad guardian if she slipped away to the food court so that she could grab a Diet Coke? Or a slushy? Or a—

"Hey, Cass, fancy seeing you here." Reuben dropped into the seat next to her, oblivious to her look of distaste. At least his aftershave no longer had any effect on her, apart from making her want to gag.

"What are you doing here?" Cassidy glared at him, while careful to make sure that Celeste was still in the nail salon.

"I thought I would make it easy for you to find me, since you're obviously trying to keep track of me." He grinned as he nodded to her cell phone, and Cassidy saw that underneath Celeste's tweet was one from Reuben saying that he was hanging out on the third floor of the mall.

She made a mental note to *un*follow him as she shoved her cell phone into her pocket, but Reuben didn't seem to notice as he leaned forward and did that thing with his mouth that Cassidy used to love but that now just made her wonder when was the last time he had cleaned his teeth. "Besides, if you're nice to me, I'll tell you a secret about the play."

"If it's about my getting the part as Juliet's understudy, I already know," she retorted, pleased to see the smug look on his pasty face falter for a moment.

"What? How do you know?" He pouted as he began to twist one of his thick spikes of hair.

"I have my sources. Now if that's everything, you can go."

"Look, Cass, you can deny it all you want, but there's no way you don't feel it, too. We're meant to get back together. You said you hated acting, and suddenly you're in the play? And now you just happen to be here at the mall? It's a sign."

"Um, no it's not, and I don't know how many different ways I have to tell you that I'm not interested."

"Like Romeo says, 'The lady doth protest too much, methinks,'" Reuben retorted with a smug grin, even though Cassidy was fairly certain that he'd got his plays muddled. But before she could reply, Reuben wrinkled his nose as he stared past her shoulder. "Hey, there's that freak again. I keep seeing him everywhere lately. First at Cade Taylor's party, then hanging out by the old warehouse down on Exeter Street, and now here. Someone needs to tell him to get out of the costume already. Dude, the party's over."

"Wh-what?" Cassidy followed his gaze, her fingers tightening on her purse handles as she caught sight of a demon marching through the mall. Its sword clattered noisily at its side, while its blazing amber eyes swirled in annoyance, as if it was looking for something it couldn't find. It paused for a moment, oblivious to the attention it was receiving from passersby. Cassidy caught her breath as the creature reached the nail salon where Celeste was still sitting. But instead of stopping (and ripping her to shreds), the demon kept going, pausing only to knock someone out of its way as it continued its search.

The good news was that Nash's amulet had definitely worked, but the bad news was that there was a demon at the mall. Adrenaline pounded through her as she reached for the sports bag that she'd tucked under the chair.

"Hey, where are you going?" Reuben scrambled to his feet, his chain belts rattling as he raced after her. "What about us?"

"Reuben, there is no us," she spluttered, not slowing down as she darted between the shoppers, making sure that the demon never left her sight. "But if you want to help me out, you can text Nash and tell him he needs to get over here."

"If I text him, will you go on a date with me?" he persisted in a whiny voice, which made Cassidy want to throttle him. Instead, she slowed her pace for just a moment.

"No date," she snapped, and he held his hands up as if to say he was helpless to do what she wanted. Cassidy clenched her teeth before nodding. "Fine, but it won't be a date. It will be a five-minute discussion. Now can you text him for me?"

"I knew you'd come around." He grinned, but Cassidy hardly noticed as she followed the demon to the mall exit. She picked up her pace and managed to slip through the neighboring door so that by the time the creature had stepped out into the dull afternoon, she was already waiting for it. Then she pulled the glowing grimoire out of her purse and held it up in front of her, hoping that Thomas was right when he said that they were drawn to the grimoire.

"Hey, ugly." She waved the book in the air. The creature came to a halt, its swirling eyes narrowing in on the book. Then it let out a howl and charged directly for her. Cassidy turned on her heels and raced across to the bus stop and around the side of the mall to where all the delivery trucks went.

She willed her feet to accelerate as she slipped in and out between Dumpsters and delivery vans until she finally came to a deserted loading bay. She could hear the demon catching up to her, so she dropped onto her knees and rolled under a nearby truck, giving herself a chance to get out her sword, shield, and knife. Sweat was already pouring into her eyes as the demon's legs came to a halt at the truck and it tried to lower its large body to reach her. For a moment she considered trying to get her mail on, but before she could decide, the demon's hideous foot slipped farther under the truck.

Cassidy leaned over and used both hands to thrust her knife deep into the grotesquely misshapen foot. The demon cried out in fury, and while she knew the injury wasn't fatal, it at least gave her enough time to wriggle out the other side of the truck and tuck the knife into her belt. But no sooner had she done so, the demon limped its way around toward her, its dark face pulsing with rage. Cassidy almost gagged from the stench and from the way the flesh had torn away from its cheekbones, making it look like one of the monsters from the horror movies Reuben used to make her watch.

She held her sword the way Thomas had taught her. And speaking of Thomas, now would be a really great time for him to fly in, but just as during her training session earlier, there was no sign of either owl or man. The demon charged, and Cassidy only just managed to dance out of the way, narrowly avoiding the deadly sharp blade. But she didn't see the packing pallet behind her, and she went crashing backward onto the hard concrete.

The breath was pushed from her chest, and she groaned in pain as the demon pivoted around, its amber eyes gleaming with malice, its sword once again out in front. She scrambled back onto her feet, but the creature had her at a disadvantage; panic slammed into her chest as the stench of the demon reached her. Bitter blood mixed with something else so vile that Cassidy didn't have a name for it. Hope leached out of her body. But just as the creature reached her, Cassidy looked at her own sword. It was humming with energy as the powerful runes blazed along the blade like fire.

Suddenly, Thomas's words came racing back to her. *Trust the sword.*

The moment she thought it, a blast of energy tore through her body. She lashed forward and watched in detached fascination as the sword sliced directly through the demon's chest. The creature was so startled that as it fell, its expression was almost comical. But Cassidy didn't waste any time trying to examine it. Instead, she groped around in her pocket for the spare Zippo Nash had given her and set the creature on fire. She waited until she was sure that the flames had consumed the beast before she turned her attention to her sword and knife and cleansed them just as Nash came hurtling toward her, his face drained of color.

"Holy freak show. What happened? Where's the demon?"

"I killed it," Cassidy said, nodding at the faint pile of charcoal that was left behind. "And get a load of this: I didn't even have Thomas here."

"Are you insane?" Nash demanded as he hurried over to her and began to check her arms and legs for signs of injury. "You ran after a demon with no backup?"

"It's not my fault that Thomas has gone AWOL," Cassidy protested. "And besides, I made sure that Reuben sent you a text. Did you have any problems finding me?"

"No, strangely enough, I just followed the freaked-out shoppers who kept pointing in this direction. Speaking of which, we should get moving in case any of them decided to call the police."

"Of course." Cassidy finished putting her sword away, suddenly feeling bad about the worry lines still imprinted across Nash's face. "Stop looking at me like that. I'm okay, I promise."

Nash seemed to relent as he slung a protective arm around her shoulder, and they began to walk back around to the front of the mall to wait for Celeste. "So tell me what happened, and don't forget to include the part about why I had a text message from Reuben."

It didn't take Cassidy too long to fill him in, and while he wasn't 100 percent happy, by the time Celeste had finished having her nails done and they'd safely followed her home, he grudgingly admitted that it had all turned out okay.

"And don't forget that your amulet totally worked," Cassidy reminded him as he pulled onto her street. "The demon didn't even blink as it walked past the salon. It obviously knew the Black Rose was somewhere, but it couldn't find it."

"Cassidy Carter-Lewis, please don't try to butter me up," he instructed, even though a small smile nudged its way onto his mouth. "Okay, yes, it's cool that the amulet worked. But next time you have to promise that you won't go racing after demon knights on your own."

"Fine, I promise," Cassidy assured him.

"Thank you," he started to say before he slowed the car down and glanced farther down the street toward Cassidy's house. "Oh, dear. That can't be good."

"What?" Cassidy asked, just as she caught sight of the large brown owl circling her house. She might not know much about owls, but she was pretty sure that this one was very pissed off. *Oh, dear, indeed.*

TWENTY

"Are you sure you don't want me to come in with you?" Nash asked, but Cassidy shook her head as she stood on the curb, sports bag in her hand.

"No, it's fine. I'll call you later and tell you what happened," Cassidy assured him, and by the time Nash had driven off down the road, the owl was gone and Thomas stepped out, his arms crossed and his mismatched eyes blazing.

"You fought a demon without me?" His rage was so palpable that, despite his being an apparition, Cassidy took a step backward.

"Um, yes, and in my defense I also killed it," Cassidy was stung into retorting as she glanced toward the front door. "Oh, and for the record, showing up at my house isn't such a great idea. I can't really talk to you here, on account of the fact I don't want my parents to think that I'm crazy."

"The house is empty," Thomas informed her, and Cassidy was momentarily distracted as she glanced at her watch. It was almost six at night, and her mom hadn't mentioned that they were going anywhere. For a moment she stared at him before fumbling with her keys and unlocking the front door.

"Dad? Mom? Hello?" she called out, but there was no answer, which meant Thomas was right. That didn't improve her mood. However, since she didn't exactly want her neighbors seeing her talking to, well, *no one*, she nodded for him to follow her in. He didn't move; instead, the vision disappeared and an owl took its place and flew down the side of the house, presumably toward her bedroom window. Cassidy shut the front door and hurried down the hallway.

She flicked on the light before dropping her sports bag by the desk. At the same time she caught sight of a brand-new copy of *Romeo and Juliet* sitting on her bed and let out a groan as she realized that the news about her getting the part of Juliet's understudy was turning into the worst-kept secret ever. First Travis knew about it, then Reuben, and now, obviously, Mrs. Thompson had found out and told Cassidy's mom.

A pecking noise on the window broke into her thoughts, and Cassidy begrudgingly opened it so that the pissed-off owl could dart through with a rustle of feathers. A moment later Thomas was standing in the far corner, looking around her bedroom with interest.

Cassidy knew that he wasn't even really there, but it still felt strange. Plus, with his coarse woolen shirt and his battle-scarred hands, he looked completely out of place against her calming apricot walls and polished floors. Nothing about

Thomas was calm. He was all anger and fire and duty, and, as he narrowed his eyes at her, Cassidy realized that he hadn't finished yelling yet.

"What were you thinking? You should never have fought the demon on your own. You do not possess the skills."

"How come I managed to kill it then?" Cassidy retorted, her anger from the previous day surging up again. "And why are you so mad at me? I thought I was meant to kill demon knights. That's why you gave me your very sharp sword."

"No." He gave a violent shake of his head. "You are meant to protect the Black Rose, and since the amulet prevented it from finding the vessel, you had no need to fight it. You should've let it pass."

"No need?" Cassidy paced the room to stop herself from throwing something at him. "It was tearing through the mall, knocking people over and causing all kinds of damage. Are you seriously telling me that I should've ignored it?"

"*Oui*. That is exactly what I'm telling you. Or you should make sure that the vessel does not go out in such public places. This is not some game. It's serious."

"We've been through this. Celeste can barely stand the sight of me, so she's hardly going to listen if I tell her not to go to the mall."

"Well, you need to *make* her listen. You need to do whatever it takes to keep her safe. Because your duty is to—"

"*Protect the Black Rose,*" Cassidy mimicked, angrily folding her arms. "So you keep saying. But what about *your* duty? Aren't you meant to be helping me? It's all very well for you to come here and tell me what I should've done, but where were you this morning when we were meant to train? And this afternoon?"

For a moment he didn't speak, as he clenched his jaw and balled his fists. "I had some business to take care of."

"Of course you did." Cassidy was so mad that she marched right up to where he was standing and pushed her face close to his. "And let me guess, you can't possibly tell me what the business is because I'm just a stupid girl whom you don't trust to—"

"Trust you?" Thomas asked in a surprised voice, as his eyes, one as pale as the sky and the other a swirl of browns, fixed on her face. "Perhaps I haven't been clear, Cassidy, but I trust you completely."

"Wh-what?" she stammered, taken aback by his disarming admission. "You do?"

"I do. I-I'm sorry that you would think otherwise. That was never my intention. Forgive me." As he spoke, his eyes flickered for the briefest of moments with something that looked close to pain. Cassidy studied his face like she might a painting, trying to make sense of his mercurial change. But whatever had brought it about was hidden from her.

What made him like that? The need to know burned in her until she found herself reaching up to his face and tracing her finger along the red scar that ran the length of his cheek. Then she gasped. Despite the fact that there was only air where his flesh should've been, Cassidy could almost feel him. Skin to skin. Heartbeat to—

Thomas flinched, and Cassidy dropped her hand as if she'd been bitten. Shame and embarrassment flooded through her. Had she just tried to touch his face? *And had he felt it, too?* Was she insane? Suddenly, she needed to get as far away from him as possible, so she darted to the other side of the room, trying to hide her flaming cheeks.

"Okay, I'm so sorry. I totally didn't mean to do that. It's just, you made me so mad and then you went all nice and . . . Well, I'm sorry."

"No apology is necessary," Thomas said, his voice blunt. "The scars that I bear are not pleasant to look at. I am familiar with the fascination."

"Thomas, no." Shame rushed through her as she took in his controlled expression. "That's not why I tried to touch you. You just seemed . . . in pain. I was stupidly trying to help. Ask Nash, I do stupid things all the time. It's part of my DNA."

Thomas didn't say anything. For a start he probably didn't even know what DNA was, but then he merely shrugged, as if being accosted was all part of his precious duty. Suddenly, Cassidy was grateful for his taciturn manner.

"So." She groped around for a change of subject. "There is something you can tell me. How did you know so much about the fight this afternoon if you weren't there?"

"The remaining guardians of the Black Rose have pooled their earth magic to observe as much as they can." Thomas spoke like nothing had happened, though she couldn't help but notice that he rubbed at his scar. She made a mental note never to try to touch a fourteenth-century apparition again. "However, like me, they find it frustrating to witness the danger yet not be able to prevent it."

"They're watching me?" Cassidy was alarmed. "Are they watching me now?"

"*Non*. To maintain any kind of connection is physically demanding," he explained, and once again Cassidy noticed just how pale his face was, apart from the throbbing red scar that slithered down his face like an angry snake. Then he gave her a rare smile. "They said you fought well and killed the demon cleanly."

"Really?" Cassidy was surprised; Thomas wasn't normally forthcoming with compliments, and she found herself confiding in him. "Actually, it almost ended in disaster, but then I saw the runes blazing on the sword and I remembered what you had told me about trusting it."

Thomas widened his eyes. "I'm impressed. It takes most guardians many years to work as one with their sword. This is . . . unexpected."

"But *good* unexpected, right?" Cassidy asked, and when he nodded his head she found herself grinning. "Well, that's okay then. By the way, Nash wanted me to ask you about the engraving on it."

"I explained the runes to you."

"No. The other engraving," she clarified. "Just above the quillon it says '*As above.*' He was wondering what it did. Does it give strength as well?"

Suddenly, the stoic mask he usually wore was back, and

whatever moment they'd shared was gone. "My father hoped that it would give the sword extra strength, but personally I do not care for it. I will return tomorrow so that we can continue your training in earnest."

"Okay, I guess——" Cassidy started to say, but before she could finish Thomas was gone, and the bird had darted out of the open window, leaving her alone in her bedroom. For a moment she just stared out into the night sky. She was pretty sure that she would never understand Thomas. She would definitely never understand why she had tried to touch his face.

Not that it mattered. After all, according to Nash, the winter solstice was in six weeks, just before Christmas. And assuming that everything went according to plan and she managed to send the Black Rose and the grimoire back to Thomas in his own time, she couldn't see him making any more twenty-first-century drop-ins.

She shut the window and pulled the white drapes as her stomach rumbled. It had been a long time since lunch, and she wandered down the hallway into the kitchen, while trying to figure out just how long her parents would be and if they would come bearing food. As she went, she checked her cell phone, but neither of them had sent her a text message. Not that it was a surprise, since they still treated texting like it was for emergencies only.

She peered into the fridge, but, like always, indecision clawed at her as she looked from the leftover lasagna to the cheesecake that her mom had bought the other day. Then she thought of Travis and his theory that you could have whatever you wanted. Even picturing his face made her smile as she reached in for the lasagna *and* the cheesecake. And to think that she'd spent years and years trying to make decisions when all she'd had to do was pick everything. So simple.

As she ate, she also realized another thing. Thomas was right. If this was going to work, she was going to have to get Celeste to listen to her. Which meant she would have to find a way to become friends with Celeste. This job was getting more impossible by the minute.

TWENTY-ONE

The following afternoon Cassidy walked into the auditorium for the first rehearsal. Nash had refused on pain of death to go anywhere near it, but after the last two demon attacks, Cassidy knew she didn't have a choice. Plus, there was the fact that she was now Celeste's understudy in the play.

It was now becoming second nature to search for Celeste, and she quickly spotted her over on the far side of the stage in an old-fashioned rocking chair that had been used in a previous play. She was having an intense conversation with a girl Cassidy didn't recognize, so she decided to wait until she was on her own before she attempted Operation Become Friends.

Over to the side of the stage was a bunch of props and set decorations, including a rosebush and a fake sword. Without thinking, Cassidy walked over and picked up the sword. She automatically took her stance, unable to hide her distaste at how light it was. There was no way the flimsy blade could pierce demon flesh, that was for sure. Then she realized that a couple of people were looking at her oddly, so she put the sword down and stepped away.

Mrs. Davis stood near the front of the stage, but there was no sign of Travis. Cassidy's entire body tingled as memories of their perfect rooftop lunch yesterday, complete with the kiss, came charging back. They were so strong and overwhelming that they almost felt like a physical bubble surrounding her, separating her from the rest of the world. Making her feel safe, happy, and, most important, *wanted*.

"Hey, there you are." Reuben suddenly appeared at her side, causing her delicious Travis bubble to pop. She turned to face him and tried to ignore how his sludge-colored eyes were ringed with guyliner and his black hair was sticking out in all directions. "I was hoping to see you so we could arrange our date."

"Reuben, there's no date." Cassidy folded her arms. "I said I would talk to you about stuff. It's not the same thing."

"It is to me," he assured her, not remotely put off by her lack of interest. Perhaps she hadn't quite mastered Thomas's glacial glares yet. She would have to work harder on those.

"I'm serious. I'm never going to change my mind about this."

Suddenly, his face darkened. "This is about that Travis guy, isn't it?"

"That's none of your business."

"He's bad news, Cass." Reuben shook his head as he began to tap his backpack with his fingers.

"Why? Is it because he's a nice guy? Or so good-looking? I can see how you would find that disturbing," Cassidy was stung into replying, since Reuben didn't seem to take regular-size hints.

"Fine, but don't say I didn't warn you," he snapped in a high-pitched voice that made Cassidy wonder why he was wasting himself as a stage manager when he had such a flair for drama. But before she could answer, she looked up and saw Celeste disappearing through a red door into the changing rooms. She quickly checked the grimoire, but it wasn't glowing, so that meant there were no demons around. It also meant that it was the perfect time for her to try to befriend Celeste.

"Reuben, I've got to go," Cassidy said, then, not waiting for an answer, she followed Celeste to the changing rooms.

A long mirror ran down one wall, and Celeste stared at her reflection while she unscrewed a tube of mascara. As soon as she saw Cassidy in the mirror, she slammed the mascara down on the table in front of her and glared. "What?"

Cassidy took a deep breath and made a mental note to get an easier hobby, like skydiving or alligator wrestling. Then she stared at Celeste's unflinching face and plastered on a bright smile.

"H-hi, Celeste. The thing is, I'm not sure if you know this, but I'm your understudy."

"Yes, loser, I do know. I also know that Rachel was meant to get that part, so in case you can't tell by my superb acting skills, *I'm not happy*." Celeste folded her arms and poked out her bottom lip, still staring into the mirror.

"I know. I really am sorry. It was as much of a surprise to me as it was to you," Cassidy said in an appeasing voice, wondering if she was going to have to talk to the back of Celeste's head for the entire conversation.

"You think you're so great, don't you?" Celeste bristled as she finally turned around, her blue eyes narrowed. "First, you convince Nash not to be in the play, and then you go and ruin everything with Travis as well. Do you even care that I wanted to put this performance on my reel?"

Cassidy wrinkled her nose in confusion. "What do you mean? Travis *is* in the play. He's going to be Romeo. You can't be pissed at me about that?"

"He *was* going to be Romeo," Celeste corrected in a dark voice. "But yesterday afternoon when I tried to convince him to start practicing lines with me, he just totally ignored me. Like I wasn't even there."

"P-perhaps he had other things on his mind?" Cassidy stammered, secretly wondering if the reason he had ignored Celeste was because he was too busy thinking about their rooftop kiss. "It doesn't mean he doesn't want to be Romeo."

"Actually, it does," Celeste said. "Because he went to see Mrs. Davis this morning, and he's now going to be Tybalt, while I'm stuck with Benjie Western as Romeo. Who, in case you hadn't realized it, is two inches shorter than me. Seriously?"

"What?" For a moment Cassidy thought that Celeste was joking, but then she realized, despite her boasting, she just wasn't a good enough actor to fake it. Which meant it was true. "I don't understand."

"Yes, well, that makes two of us. I mean, Tybalt dies at the beginning of the third act." Celeste shuddered. "And did you not see Travis at the auditions? He was born to play Romeo. *My* Romeo. But for some reason he's changed his mind, and I think it's because of you."

"I swear, it's got nothing to do with me. I saw him audition, and he was—"

"Sublime? Indescribable? Heartbreaking?" Celeste cut in.

"Yes." Cassidy nodded dumbly. "He was all of those things. He was amazing."

"So you really didn't have anything to do with it?" Celeste asked, letting some of her animosity dissolve.

"No." Cassidy shook her head and gave Celeste a hopeful smile. "Though honestly, you're such a great actress, it doesn't matter who plays Romeo—you'll still shine."

"I am pretty amazing, aren't I?" Celeste agreed.

"You are." Cassidy took a deep breath. Here was her chance. "And as your understudy, I'm sure I could learn loads if I was able to study what you did. You know, follow you around and stuff?"

"Well, I suppose for the sake of the play that I should let you. And between you, me, and the wall, Rachel has the tendency to squint when she's onstage. Not that I plan on missing a performance, you understand, so don't get your hopes up," Celeste warned before nodding her head. "However, if I were to miss a performance, it would be much better if you had all of my mannerisms. It could be like a tribute to me."

"Uh, exactly," Cass hesitantly agreed. "And while I doubt I will even get onstage, it would be great for my future roles if you would let me follow you around."

"I guess that's okay," Celeste conceded. "But don't expect me to talk to you or anything."

"Definitely not." Cassidy let out a small sigh of relief, since she had thought this was going to be a lot more difficult. Then she waited until Celeste had touched up her mascara before following her back out to the auditorium. Celeste immediately made a beeline over to Reuben to discuss her lighting requirements, and Cassidy sat down and tried to figure out why Travis had decided to not play Romeo.

Was it really because of her? She fished the carnelian necklace out from under the floral-print dress she was wearing and began to toy with it, as she—

Amber swirling eyes. Pain. A single feather split into two pieces, falling to the ground, and her being forced to watch, helpless to stop them both from landing like an explosion, forever staining the scorched earth with their crimson blood, which flowed like teardrops—

"Hey." Travis suddenly appeared next to her, his dark eyes intense. Today he was wearing jeans and a pale blue T-shirt that showed off his tan. "Are you okay? Has something happened?"

"N-no." She managed to shake her head, as much to push away the last threads of the vision as anything. *How did Thomas deal with such horrific sights and stay sane?* she wondered, before she realized that Travis was still next to her, concern written all over his gorgeous face. She took a deep breath, grateful that his presence was there to center her. "Everything's fine."

"Well, good." He nodded as he leaned forward and began to play with the carnelian that had fallen out of her fingers during the vision. He gave her a dazzling smile that spread across his whole face like liquid sunshine. "You had me worried there."

"Don't be," Cassidy said, touched by his concern, but also eager not to have to explain what had just happened. Not because she wanted to keep secrets from him, but because she had no idea how to explain it or even what it meant. "So I've just been talking to Celeste. She said that you're not playing Romeo anymore. Is that true?"

For a moment Travis was silent as he leaned back in his chair and raised his hands in the air. Then he turned back to her and slowly nodded. "Yeah, it's true."

"But why would you ask to change? I mean, Travis, you were seriously amazing as Romeo. My heart was aching for you."

"Well, right there's a good enough reason not to do it, since I *never* want to make your heart ache, Cass," he said in a light voice before taking a deep breath. "Okay, the real reason was that I just couldn't see myself performing with Celeste. It didn't feel right."

"But to play Tybalt? He's, like, the bad guy," Cassidy protested, unable to hide her confusion.

"I guess it depends on how you look at it," Travis said, a far-off look in his eyes. "Everyone's the hero of his own story. Tybalt just thought he was protecting Juliet's virtue and the family name. And he was willing to die for what he believed in." Then he paused for a moment before grinning at her. "I think I can really bring the role to life."

Cassidy was embarrassed that she'd never considered it from that point of view before. She made a mental note to discuss it with Nash later, since this was more his area of thinking than hers. Then she realized that Travis was almost nervous as he waited for her to respond. She shyly reached out and touched his hand.

"I think you'll be even more amazing than ever."

"Thank you," he said, his voice low and gravelly as his fingers threaded ever tighter through hers, making her stomach contract. "And by the way, I was thinking that perhaps I should meet your dad. Especially if I'm going to date his daughter."

"Y-you want to date me?" Cassidy stammered.

"Well, yeah," he said, as the elusive dimple suddenly

appeared. "Unless, of course, you're in the habit of kissing random guys."

Cassidy giggled as she felt herself getting lost in his warm eyes. "I'd love for you to meet my dad."

"Good." He looked relieved, but before he could say anything else, Mrs. Davis clapped her hands for silence. She then spent the next forty minutes talking about fire exits and the rehearsal schedules until Cassidy thought she might lose the will to live. Finally, it was over, and Mrs. Davis told them that this was going to be an experience they would never forget, before reminding them not to be late for tomorrow's rehearsal.

Cassidy turned to Travis to see if she could spend a few more minutes with him before she had to go back on Celeste duty, and caught sight of Nash hurrying toward her. His face was drained of color, and he was holding his cell phone in his hand. She raced to meet him.

"What's going on? Has something happened?"

"Cass, don't freak, but your mom has been trying to get ahold of you. Your cell phone must be dead. They're at the hospital."

The script she had been holding fell to the ground in a flutter, but she hardly noticed as Nash was suddenly next to her, his arm around her. It took all her willpower to speak. "Wh-what's wrong? Is it my dad?"

"He had problems breathing, so they're running tests now. They're at Greenburg General over on Main Street. The third floor. Come on. We can go there right now." Then, without another word, he ushered her out of the auditorium toward the parking lot. Cassidy was silent. Suddenly, it seemed as if someone had turned out the lights.

✢   ✢   ✢   ✢   ✢

Cassidy was numb. Not only from the shock of finding out her dad was in the hospital but also because of the uncomfortable plastic chair that she'd been sitting on for the last hour. Next to her, Nash was unconsciously tapping his nails against the spine of a book in a repetitive beat.

Dedah. Dedah. Dedah.

Normally, the noise would've driven her crazy, but now she almost found it soothing because it helped her focus on the small things. Reminding her to breathe. Reminding her not to grind her teeth or scream. To stay calm. To have hope. Plus, even if she'd wanted to tell him to stop, she wasn't sure that she could bring herself to speak. So far, they hadn't had any real news, but ten minutes ago the doctor had come out and was now talking with her mom in a room over to the left. It seemed to be taking forever.

Dedah. Dedah. Dedah.

"Are you sure I can't get you a soda?" Nash suddenly stopped his drumming, his pale eyes full of worry, but before she could answer, the door opened, and her mom appeared. Cassidy reached for Nash's hand and squeezed it. Her heart pounded so loudly that she was surprised no one else could hear it.

"Mom?" Her voice was little above a whisper.

"He's got a blood clot in his leg," her mom said in her normal, straightforward way.

"Deep vein thrombosis." Nash let out a gasp as he knitted his brows. "It's always a risk after surgery. Were they not giving him any blood thinners?"

Her mom gave a sigh. "They said he was at low risk, and so they just advised him to take an aspirin every day."

"I don't understand what you're saying. What's wrong with him?" Cassidy felt her own lip start to wobble as a strangled noise escaped her throat. She began to shake, and Nash put his arm around her shoulders.

"For the last two days your father's leg has been hurting," her mom said, "but he thought it was just from all the exercises he was doing. Then today he had problems breathing, so I brought him straight here. They've just done an ultrasound and found a clot at the back of his knee."

"Is he going to be okay?" Cassidy was so cold now that she could hardly feel Nash's arm around her. "Can he come home?"

"They're going to keep him for a couple of days to dissolve the clot, and they'll also do some more tests to see if he has any genetic blood-clotting disorders or if there are any other clots. But the good news is that they discovered it so quickly," her mom said.

"That's right." Nash nodded. "DVT is something that is often misdiagnosed but can be treated once they know it's there, Cass."

"So when can I see him?" she asked, still not sure if any of this was real.

"We can go in now, if you're ready."

Cassidy nodded her head as she followed her mom down the long corridor until they reached a private room. It was similar to the last one he had been in, right down to the pink hospital gown. An IV was sticking out of his arm and his legs were covered in a sheet, but apart from that, he looked just like he always did. Cassidy's face crumpled as she raced over to him.

"Hey, pumpkin." He gave her a weak grin as Cassidy clutched at his hand. "Sorry about the drama."

"That's okay." She sniffed back her shattered emotions, determined not to let him know just how worried she'd been. Then she gave him a watery smile. "But I hope you don't think this is going to get you out of that Halo match you promised me."

"Bring it," he said in a soft voice before shooting her a conspiratorial wink. "Though perhaps don't tell your mom. You know she thinks that Halo is a waste of time."

"Deal." Cassidy grinned back at him while making a mental note to let him win. Not that she cared. All that mattered was that he was okay.

TWENTY-TWO

"Cass, wake up." Reuben was nudging her, and Cassidy shot up in her chair as she fumbled for the knife she'd started carrying in her purse, before suddenly realizing that she didn't have to fight anything, she'd merely fallen asleep in her Health class. *And was that drool on the desk?* The only consolation was that Travis had been called to the office about something, so he wasn't there to witness her little nap.

Of course, in her defense, she hadn't exactly gotten a lot of sleep lately. The last week had been a blur of waking up early to train with Thomas, following Celeste, learning her lines, and spending far too much time on the Internet reading about deep vein thrombosis and pulmonary embolisms. Thankfully, her father's clot hadn't broken off and traveled to his lungs, and even better, all of his tests had been negative, which meant the doctors were confident the clot was an isolated occurrence triggered by his operation, and they had discharged him after two days.

That had been a huge relief, and the weight that had been pressing down on Cassidy's shoulders was lifted when she could see for herself that he really was okay. In fact, apart from the long compression stockings that he now had to wear and the extra medication he had to take, there was no sign anything had been wrong with him.

At the sound of the bell, everyone jumped to their feet, and, as usual, Cassidy headed straight to Celeste's locker and discreetly waited for the senior to finish her after-school ritual of lip gloss refreshing and hair fluffing. Things had definitely been a lot easier since Cassidy had spoken to her, and while they weren't exactly friends, she was no longer on the receiving end of Celeste's death glares. Which was good, because there had been two more demon attacks since that day at the mall, and the idea of not following her every move wasn't viable. At least for the last two attacks Thomas had been with her, and while he had been gruff and abrupt, he hadn't said anything about the weird moment in her bedroom.

There was no rehearsal today, and so she and Nash followed Celeste out to the parking lot. Celeste had almost reached her SUV when she suddenly turned around. In the blink of an eye Nash had slammed himself up against a nearby tree so it would look as if Cassidy was the only one there. She gave Celeste a little half wave, which the senior ignored as she turned and got into her SUV.

"That was way too close," Nash panted as he stepped away from the tree. Today he was wearing a pair of tuxedo pants, his Dr. Martens, and a tattered Smiths T-shirt. "Every time she sees me near her, she thinks it's more proof of our animal magnetism."

"'My ears have not yet drunk a hundred words of that tongue's utterance, yet I know the sound,'" Cassidy idly quoted, to Nash's complete surprise. "Art thou not Nash the hottie that I cannot have?"

"Okay, I'm not sure whether to be impressed that you've started learning your lines, or terrified that I'll never sleep again because of the imagery," Nash retorted.

"Sorry. My dad's getting so bored that he insisted we start learning my lines. I guess some of it must've stuck," she said as they got into Nash's car, and Cassidy reached for her cell phone to check whether Celeste had tweeted about her plans for the afternoon.

"Says here that she's going for a coffee from Haz Beans."

"Well, someone should tell her that she's heading in the wrong direction," Nash said as he swung left onto a leafy street and followed the SUV into a nursing home parking lot. The home was a sprawling place, set out on a large grassy slope, with a small creek running along the bottom. Thankfully, Celeste seemed too involved with parking her SUV to notice them, and once she had finally maneuvered the large vehicle into a spot, they watched her drape a striped uniform over her arm.

Cassidy rubbed her eyes, and even Nash looked

bewildered. "What should we do now? I mean, it's one thing to trail after her at school and at the mall, but I'm not sure we can sneak into a nursing home unnoticed."

"I think we should just stay here. After all, the grimoire will glow if there are any demons close by, and then you can do your thing," Nash said as he undid his seat belt and reached for his iPad.

"Good thinking." Cassidy undid her own seat belt, climbed into the backseat, and got the grimoire out of the sports bag. As normal, the tattoo on her arm tingled every time she touched the book, but she tried to ignore it as best she could as she put the book onto the dashboard so that they could clearly see it. "And I guess in the meantime I could continue learning my lines."

"Or do homework," Nash said, as if he were making an outrageous suggestion. "And speaking of work, I forgot to tell you that while you were following Celeste at lunchtime, I saw Travis in the library. He was working his way through a fairly hefty medical journal. I must say I was pretty impressed."

"He was probably looking up more deep vein thrombosis stuff," Cassidy said as she adjusted the seat so she would have more room to stretch her legs. "This whole thing has really freaked him out. I guess it's reminded him of his own dad." A smile tugged at her lips as she recalled just how upset Travis had been. No wonder he was such a good actor when he wore his emotions so close to the surface. "Actually, he's still really eager to come around and meet my parents, but I keep putting it off."

"Well, I can understand, since it will be hard for him to live up to my awesomeness." Nash grinned, which promptly earned him a slap on the arm.

"Actually, it's because I don't know if my dad would be up for it."

"Cass, your dad is up for anything that stops him from remembering he can't go play tennis and do all the other things he normally does," Nash reminded her. "Just ask him. Have you even told him about Travis?"

"No." She shook her head. "It seemed too frivolous when he's had so much going on. Though I guess you're right," Cassidy grudgingly agreed, since her dad, who was normally superactive, was going stir-crazy. It had been the whole reason he'd had the knee operation in the first place.

"I'm always right," Nash assured her, and they then spent the next hour waiting for Celeste. Nash was having some kind of genius argument on a science forum on his cell phone, and Cassidy was looking at photographs of Travis on hers; it wasn't until the engine on Celeste's SUV started up that they even realized she had finished her shift.

Thankfully, the grimoire still wasn't glowing, so they followed Celeste home. Once she was safely inside, Nash headed to Cassidy's house and arranged to meet her in the morning, after she had trained with Thomas, so that they could follow Celeste to school.

There was no sign of her mom when she walked in, but her dad was in the kitchen cutting up vegetables, his crutches resting on the bench next to him.

"This is your idea of taking it easy?" she quizzed as she hugged him.

"Doctor's orders. I'm allowed to put as much weight on it as I can," he said, tossing a carrot stick at her. Cassidy immediately popped it into her mouth and nodded for him to go sit down while she took over.

"Fine. But in exchange, you can tell me how your day was."

"You really are bored, aren't you?" Cassidy asked as he grabbed his crutches and swung his way over to the long bench that sat under the bay window at the end of the kitchen.

"Pretty much. And unless your teenage angst can keep me entertained, I will need to resort to daytime television."

"Well, my day was pretty normal. Classes, hanging out with Nash." Following Celeste Gilbert to make sure she didn't get attacked by demons.

"Well, you sure are smiling a lot for someone who had such a regular day."

"No, I'm not," she protested, just as her cell phone beeped. She discreetly checked the screen and saw it was from Travis.

```
Is it wrong that I want there to be
a rehearsal every afternoon. Miss
you ~ T
```

"Ah, and now you're doing it again," her dad suddenly

announced. "So you've either just had a text to say that you've won a lifetime supply of Diet Coke, or something's going on."

Cassidy flushed as she tried to bite back her smile, but it was impossible. Besides, while she never talked to her mom about anything, she'd always shared everything with her dad. Even the disaster that had been Reuben. "Okay, fine. The thing is, there's this guy. His name is Travis, and he's new to school, and, well, he's perfect. Mom will love him because he's in the school play. He was going to be Romeo but asked to be Tybalt instead, because he found it a more interesting role. Anyway, he's a sublime actor, and he's going to bring the house down with his performance."

"Ah, so you've been dazzled."

"No." She quickly shook her head. "I mean, yes, he's dazzling as well, but he's more than that," she added, as she thought of how great he had been the day after she'd found out about her dad's blood clot. "I can't explain it, but he really seems to *see me*. Does that sound dumb?"

For a moment her dad didn't say anything before he shook his head. "No, my beautiful girl, it doesn't sound dumb. It sounds like he's someone whom I might like."

Suddenly, Cassidy felt shy. "Actually, he'd really like to meet you."

"He would?" her father asked in surprise. "I didn't think teenage boys did things like that—Nash being the exception, of course."

"Yes, well, Travis isn't exactly your average teenage boy."

Cassidy found herself toying with the carnelian necklace as the memory of their kiss flashed into her mind. When she realized that her dad was still looking at her, she quickly coughed. "So, perhaps he could come over sometime?"

"I'll have to check my schedule, but apart from being waited on hand and foot by my daughter, I'm pretty sure that I can free up some time. What about next Sunday?"

"Time for what?" her mom asked as she walked into the kitchen wearing yet another neat suit and carrying an armful of folders. Her stern face caused Cassidy and her dad to giggle, leaving Cassidy feeling better than she had in weeks.

TWENTY-THREE

"Concentrate," Thomas barked on Monday morning as Cassidy lunged at his apparition. However, before she could reach him, he stepped back and frowned. "More."

"I am doing more," Cassidy wailed. Sweat beaded on her collarbone as the feeble morning sun pushed through the heavy canopy overhead and she felt the fatigue of the last few weeks take over. She put down her sword and folded her arms. "Thomas, please, I need a break. Do you ever stop to think of how much I'm juggling here? As well as following Celeste everywhere—and I mean *everywhere*—I've got my schoolwork, my dad . . ." *Not to mention my boyfriend, who's coming to meet my family next Sunday.*

For a moment Thomas was still, an odd expression on his face. Cassidy found herself thrusting her hands behind her back in case she was overcome with the strange temptation to touch his face once again. Then she braced herself for whatever lecture he was going to give her. But Thomas just studied his hands for a moment before looking back up, his expression almost soft.

"I heard your father has been unwell," he said. "I imagine it must have been troubling for you."

"You know about my dad?" she asked, surprised since she hadn't told him about the blood clot and he had certainly never asked. Then she remembered he and his fellow guardians of the Black Rose liked to keep tabs on her. She shot him a hopeful glance. "So does this mean that I can have a day off from training?"

"Will your arm stay on if a demon slices through it with a rune-strengthened sword?" Thomas inquired in a pleasant voice.

"Er, I don't think so." Cassidy shook her head, not quite sure what he was getting at.

"Then, no. You cannot have a day off from training. Today we are learning how to avoid having your body parts cut off. Now lift up your sword in the high stance that I taught you." Then he paused for a moment as emotion flickered across his face. "But I am truly sorry that your father was unwell. *Now you can begin. . . ."*

✢ ✢ ✢ ✢ ✢

Despite his momentary kindness, Thomas was true to his word, and the training session hadn't been easy. By the time the bell rang at the end of the day, Cassidy was still feeling the effects of it every time she moved. But there was no way she was missing the rehearsal, since she was longing to see

Travis. She hadn't seen him since she had invited him to come meet her dad, but they'd had numerous text messages about it over the weekend. And any chance she'd had of seeing him at lunchtime vanished when Celeste had decided that it would be fun for her and her friends to sneak out for a hamburger, forcing Cassidy and Nash to follow them.

"Are you sure you don't just want to sit at the back of the auditorium?" Cassidy asked as Nash strode along next to her, his long jacket flying out behind him and making him look more like a highwayman than a student. A group of girls stopped and sighed, but as usual he was oblivious to their admiration.

"As much fun as the wonders of high school dramatics sound, I would much rather be in the library doing something useful. And speaking of useful, I had an idea. I know you normally take the grimoire with you to give you a heads-up on any nearby demons, but I figured that since you're probably not actually going to have it with you while you're rehearsing, it makes more sense for me to have it, and then I can come and tell you," he said. Then he suddenly added, "And I must admit that there was a section in there that I wanted to cross-reference with a book I found on the Knights Templar."

"Of course there is." Cassidy resisted the urge to laugh as she reached into her sports bag, pulled out the book, and handed it to him. "But you're right, it does make more sense for you to keep an eye on it."

Then she realized that Nash's fan club was still hovering

behind them, looking at them and the book with interest. Cassidy abruptly spun around and shot them a burning glare, then was surprised to see that the girls immediately scampered away. Perhaps all the time she'd spent with Thomas was starting to pay off.

"Hey, neat trick." Nash nodded his head in approval, then put the grimoire into his own satchel and promised to meet her when the rehearsals were over. Once he was gone, she walked into the auditorium and casually made her way to where Celeste was arguing with Benjie Western over something. Cassidy silently sat down near them so she could keep an eye on Celeste without being intrusive.

There was no sign of Travis, and Cassidy felt a twinge of disappointment go racing through her. She sent him a quick text message, but when there was no answer, she reluctantly put her cell phone away and looked over to where Celeste was now glaring at a ratty-looking bed that was in one corner of the stage. It was obviously meant to be where the death scene was to take place, and Celeste was shaking her head.

"If you think that I'm going to lie down on that thing, you are very much mistaken," Celeste informed them as she marched over to the large shopping bag that was sitting next to her purse and pulled out a crisp cotton sheet.

"Celeste, no. It's meant to be in a tomb. You can't have an Egyptian cotton sheet on it," Reuben said, joining the conversation, but Celeste ignored them as she meticulously spread the sheet over the bed.

"He's right," another senior who was working in props

added. "We were going to paint the bed gray to make it look like stone. And wow, how do you know how to make a bed like that? It looks like something a nurse would do."

Suddenly, Celeste stopped tucking in the sheet as more people gathered around.

"That's because they're hospital corners." Rachel, who had been meant to be Celeste's understudy, suddenly appeared, her eyes sharp and beady like a raven searching for food. "Since when do you even know how to make a bed like that?"

Cassidy knew the answer to that. It was because of the volunteering she did in the nursing home; however, for some reason Celeste seemed at a loss for words.

Which was weird because normally it was impossible to shut her up. Why would she care that people knew she was volunteering at a nursing home?

"Seriously," Rachel continued. "Don't you have three maids at home? What's going on, Celeste? Is there something you're not telling us?"

Cassidy widened her eyes. Unless, of course, Celeste wasn't volunteering. What if she had a part-time job there? Suddenly, her hesitance made a lot more sense. And without stopping to question why, Cassidy coughed.

"I taught her."

"What?" Rachel spun around and looked at Cassidy like she was something that the dog had brought in. "Why would you teach her that?"

"We were rehearsing lines, and I was playing the Nurse.

I guess I got carried away and started making the bed, and Celeste wanted to know how I did it. Any more mysteries that you would like me to solve for you, Sherlock?"

However, before Rachel could reply, Mrs. Davis clapped her hands, and Reuben was forced to hurry away and retrieve his clipboard. Celeste didn't say anything as she walked past Cassidy, but that was probably good, because Cassidy still had no idea why she had bothered to help her out. She was fairly sure that even Thomas wouldn't have expected her to be quite so vigilant in her guardianship duties.

"Right," Mrs. Davis began. "We have a lot to get through, so no interruptions, please—"

"Sorry I'm late, did I miss anything?" Travis suddenly appeared on the stage from behind the curtains, wearing black jeans and a dark shirt. As soon as he spoke the entire cast and crew erupted in laughter, and even Mrs. Davis joined in. A boyish grin escaped his lips. "Okay, so I've got no idea what's so funny, but let's hope I don't do it on the first night, since this isn't meant to be a comedy."

"It's fine, Travis, just sit down," Mrs. Davis said in an indulgent voice as she nodded to a spot nearby. He obediently sat down and stretched out his long denim-clad legs as Mrs. Davis went over the scenes they were going to practice. But Cassidy, who was behind Travis, hardly heard a word as she found herself staring at the back of his head, marveling at how the curls fell just above his shirt.

Finally, the cast split up into groups to practice their lines and staging. Cassidy saw Celeste heading for the restroom and she knew she should follow her, but when Travis gravitated toward her, she couldn't bring herself to leave.

"Hey, you're here," he said, his voice low and gravelly and his gaze hot and steamy.

"H-hey," Cassidy squeaked in delight before inwardly groaning at her lack of coolness. But Travis hardly seemed to notice as he threaded his fingers through hers as if it was the most natural thing in the world. "I didn't think you were coming."

"I know. I totally lost track of time. I was in the library working on something. Thanks for texting me, or I would've been even later," he said. Then he pulled her forward and kissed her.

Cassidy's stomach fluttered as the kiss deepened and her hands tentatively reached up toward his chest, but before they could get there, Travis suddenly captured her hands in his and broke away.

"I-is everything okay?" she asked, her heart still pounding as she tried to adjust to the sensation of no longer kissing him.

"Yeah. It's just, well, it's a little bit crowded here," he said in a rueful voice, and Cassidy realized that he hadn't pulled away because he didn't want to kiss her, but more because he did. She blushed while relishing the feel of her hands in his.

"So my dad's really looking forward to meeting you on Sunday."

"I'm looking forward to meeting him. And your mom," he added. "And actually, there's something I've been meaning to tell you—" Then he suddenly broke off and nodded over to the door of the auditorium. For a moment Cassidy was too lost even to realize what he was doing, but she reluctantly turned around to see Nash urgently waving at her.

"Just ignore him," Cassidy advised as she tightened her grip on his hand, but instead he politely untangled his fingers and shook his head.

"And have your best friend hate me? I'm many things, but crazy isn't one of them," he assured her, his dark eyes locking into hers. "Besides, I'm supposed to be doing a read-through of the first act."

"Okay." Cassidy sighed with happiness as she watched Travis walk over to where the other Capulets were horsing around. He nodded at Nash on his way past, but it wasn't until he'd gone that she hurried over to where Nash was standing, his alabaster brow knitted and serious.

"This had better be amazing, because Travis was just about to tell me something, and he said it was important," she informed him in a tart voice.

"Not exactly amazing. More like disastrous." Nash held his satchel up to her so that she could see the grimoire. It was glowing like a beacon in the middle of a storm. "Where's Celeste?"

"She went to the restroom," Cassidy croaked as she and Nash hurried over toward the girls' room door, just in time to see Celeste emerge, her lip gloss freshly applied and her hair looking perky; she didn't look at all like she'd been attacked by a demon. Relief raced through Cassidy. Not that Celeste seemed to notice; instead, all her attention was on Nash.

"There you are. I've been looking for you everywhere, Nash. Now, despite my disappointment that you didn't audition, there is still something you can do for me. I was hoping that you could give me some insight into what Verona was really like when the play takes place."

"He would love to," Cassidy said, while giving Nash an apologetic look as fear racked through her. There was definitely a demon somewhere in the school, so should she go and look for it, or should she stay with Celeste? The decision was especially tough, considering the brutal speech Thomas had given her.

"Yes, but Cassidy, what about that *other* thing we were going to do?" he asked in a tight voice, his face pale. Not that she could blame him. Twice now he'd been hurt by the demons, and despite his assurance that he was fine, she was sure those attacks were still on his mind.

"Well." Cassidy forced herself to make a decision. "I could always go and look for the *other thing*. And if I need help with it, I could call you. Yes?"

"Yes, but what if—"

"I'll be careful. I promise," she said, and she reached for his satchel so that she could take the grimoire with her. Celeste was staring at her as if she was crazy, but that was probably better than her knowing the truth. Then, when

Nash didn't offer any immediate objections, she hurried off before he could change his mind.

Cassidy slipped out into the first restroom she could find so that she could awkwardly put on the heavy mail before pulling her large black coat over it all, making her seem about three feet wide. Not exactly a great look.

Still, it was better to be safe than sorry, and she headed outside, jogging around the grounds to make sure they were clear. There was no sign of any demons out there, so next she began to search the school, floor by floor. However, by the time she reached the top level, the grimoire had almost stopped glowing altogether. She studied the dull leather cover in confusion. Did that mean the demon had left? Or did it mean that—

Her sports bag fell to the floor as she fumbled for her cell phone.

"Nash," she panted. "Celeste. Is she okay? Is she safe?"

"Safe and now trying to convince Mrs. Davis that Juliet would look good wearing a bikini in the balcony scene," he said in a dry voice before suddenly gulping. "Why? Do you think it's heading back here?"

"No. Yes. Actually, I don't know. The grimoire's stopped glowing, and I suddenly panicked that the reason was because a demon had found her."

"No, definitely not. It seems like the demons can sense that she's around, but thanks to the amulet, they just can't find her." Nash sounded like he was smiling to himself.

"Well, I'm just pleased that it saved me a fight," Cassidy said as she began to jog back down the stairwell. But before she hit the first floor, the grimoire was once again glowing like a fire engine. "Okay, that's weird."

"What's weird?" Nash demanded, a hint of concern lacing his words.

"The grimoire." Cassidy increased her pace and watched it get even brighter. "It keeps changing color. I think the demon's still—"

"Oh, there you are, Cass," a voice suddenly said, and she looked up just as Travis walked around the corner. "I was just looking for you. I forgot to get your address."

But Cassidy hardly noticed. Her eyes were fixed on the grimoire, which burned more brightly with every step Travis took toward her. The book fell from her hands and landed on the floor with a thump.

"No." Her heart pounded in her chest as she tried to make sense of what was happening. The grimoire didn't lie. She knew that. She'd seen it glow every time she'd fought a demon knight. But those demons had been hideous. Monsters who smelled of death and blood and dark magic. Travis was none of those things. He was . . . he was . .

"Cass, talk to me. What's going on?" Nash yelled from the other end of the phone, but Cassidy didn't reply. Instead, she lowered the sports bag to the ground and reached for the sheathed sword, never taking her eyes off Travis's beautiful face.

Cassidy felt sick. She was the girl who couldn't even decide what her favorite candy bar was. How was she meant to figure this one out?

"Okay." Travis took a cautious step toward her, and the grimoire glowed even more brightly. "I know that you're pissed with me, but I did try to tell you. Remember? Before? Then Nash turned up?"

"I thought you were going to tell me that you wanted to go to the movies or something. Not that you're a demon." She unsheathed the sword and tried to ignore the way her hand was shaking.

"Cass." He took another step forward.

"No closer," she commanded as she raised the sword, bracing her knees and holding her arm high, just the way Thomas had taught her.

"If it's any consolation, I was going to ask you to go to the movies as well. Depending on how you took the news. But I'm guessing, from the sword that you're pressing into my neck, that this is not going down well with you," Travis said, his dark eyes never leaving her face.

"What the—" Nash was suddenly racing toward them, then came to an abrupt halt. But Travis didn't even blink as he continued to stare directly at Cassidy.

"Look, I really don't mind if you kill me, but before you do, there's one thing you need to know."

"Wh-what's that?" Cassidy stammered, not sure how she could even be involved in this surreal conversation.

"Just remember. Not all demons are bad."

Then without another word he turned and ran down the hallway. Cassidy raced after him, her breath coming in short, sharp bursts. But by the time she pushed through the large doors that led out of the school, there was no sign of Travis. For a moment she just stood there before she looked up into the sky.

"Thomas!" she screamed. "Get here now. I-I need you."

TWENTY-FOUR

Where was he?

Cassidy marched around the deserted school yard, waiting for the owl that was Thomas to arrive. How could this be happening? It didn't make sense. Travis wasn't a demon. He couldn't be. So why did the grimoire light up like that? *And,* a small voice nudged at the back of her mind, *why did he admit that it was true?*

"No, it's just not possible," she said for the hundredth time as she turned to where Nash was hunched over, frantically studying the grimoire. He was at their favorite table, and though Cassidy was exhausted, she found it impossible to sit down for more than a second for fear that it would sink in and somehow make it seem more real. She marched over to a pile of leaves and kicked them into the air. It didn't make her feel remotely better. "I mean, you saw the other demons. They were revolting. Hideous. Travis isn't hideous. He looks normal. *And where is Thomas?*"

"Perhaps he's asleep?" Nash suggested, his beautiful porcelain brow wrinkled in sympathy. "There is the time difference. Not to mention the seven centuries in between."

"Nash, you're not helping," Cassidy said as Nash continued to flip through the grimoire, past the page where it explained how to make an amulet. "Wait, go back to that page."

"What page?" Nash looked up at her.

"The amulet page," Cassidy said as her mind churned over. The she stared at him in horror. "That's why Travis said he couldn't play Romeo," she gasped. "He actually told me that it was because he couldn't see himself starring with Celeste, but I just thought he meant that he didn't like her. And Celeste had told me that it was like she was invisible to him."

Nash looked slightly stunned that he hadn't figured it out. "You're right. Ever since we put the amulet on her, he literally wouldn't have been able to see her."

Cassidy dropped her head into her hands and groaned. Everything was pointing to the fact that it was true. "But how is it possible?"

"Hang on." Nash feverishly flipped back through the grimoire. "I was reading about demons the other day. According to this, demons aren't born. They're made."

Cassidy looked at him blankly for a moment. "What do you mean? Made from what?"

"Made from humans," Nash said in a low voice as he began to read from the page. "'Demon Lords increase their ranks by turning willing humans into demons for the sole purpose of helping them find the Black Rose. The demons are driven to do so because their demon spirit is too strong for the human flesh in which it is encased. They seek the Black Rose so their bodies may be as eternal as their soul.'"

Cassidy sat down and dropped her head into her hands as she tried to process what he'd just read to her. Not only was Travis a demon, but he'd chosen to be a demon? Then something else occurred to her and she looked at Nash in horror.

"So if those demons were once human, and I've been killing them, then that means—"

"That means that you killed demons." Nash's voice was firm as he nodded for her to come look at the grimoire again. "'When man becomes demon, the only thing remaining is the flesh. Everything else is taken over by the demon, especially their humanity.'"

"Yes, but I'm still not sure that I'm okay with this."

"Well, let me tell you, as someone who has been attacked by those things *twice*, I'm perfectly okay with your killing them. In fact, I'm very grateful that you did," Nash assured her. "Besides, I thought it was my job to tackle all the curly philosophical questions."

Cassidy knew he was right, and besides, right now she wasn't sure that she even had room in her mind for any more crazy stuff. It was all too much.

"Owl approaching at six o'clock," Nash suddenly said

before he scooped up the grimoire and shot her an encouraging glance. "And I really think this is a conversation you should have alone, so I'm going to go and wait in the car. Cass, you text me as soon as you need me. I mean it," he growled. After giving her a fierce hug he marched off, the grimoire clutched firmly in his arms.

Cassidy said good-bye and watched the owl as it flew closer and closer to the ground before landing in front of her. Normally, Thomas changed right away, but today the owl seemed to be studying her for so long that Cassidy began to fidget with the carnelian around her neck. Then she remembered his reaction to the necklace. He'd asked her if she would be willing to take it off. Cassidy felt ill.

"You knew, didn't you?" she asked, her voice so faint that she could hardly hear it. Suddenly, Thomas was there. His normal brown shirt was gone, replaced by a plain white linen one that almost matched the color of his pale face.

"Knew what?"

Knew what?

Cassidy felt hysterical laughter rising up in her throat, and now that he was here, she had no idea where to begin. Did she ask him if it was normal for demons to kiss human girls? Should she see if he knew why some demons had eyes like bottled sunshine and a laugh that could make a girl weep? Finally, she crushed her internal thoughts and turned to him.

"About Travis. You knew *what* he was."

For a moment he was silent, his face pale and unyielding before he finally nodded. "*Oui*. But I didn't know he was here. Not until I saw the stone."

"What's so important about the stone?" Cassidy suddenly yanked at the necklace, eager to get it as far away from her as possible. "Is it some sort of magical amulet like the one that Nash made for Celeste? Has he been doing something to me? Turning me into a demon?" The horror mounted in her throat as she realized just how different the world now was from the world she knew yesterday. Or an hour ago.

Thomas quickly shook his head. "Turning into a demon is a lot more . . . *complicated* than that. The stone is none of those things. It has qualities, yes, but more to do with personal beliefs. Some people might call it a lucky charm."

"That's what Travis said." Cassidy's confusion was mounting. Half of her longed to throw the stone away, but the other half, the half that seemed to be controlling her fingers, remained uncertain. "So what's so special about it then? Why did he give it to me? *Why did you ask me if I'd be willing to take it off?*"

"Because seeing you wearing something that belongs to my worst enemy was painful."

Worst enemy? Cassidy felt sick as her hand flew to her mouth. "So you know him? Have you fought him before?"

"Many times." Thomas nodded, and his finger made its way to his damaged face and slowly traced the length of his scar. "It was he who gave me this."

Cassidy, who was half hypnotized by the way Thomas's finger was touching his face, felt as if she was going to choke as two separate realities crashed into one.

All the stuff with Thomas, the Black Rose, and chasing after Celeste was only supposed to be until the solstice. But Travis was meant to be something else. Something special. Something real. *And now it was all connected?* As she rubbed her brow, Thomas's face softened, transforming his features.

"Perhaps I was wrong not to tell you. It's not easy to explain that a demon can look so—"

"Human?" Cassidy finished, as she looked up and realized how close Thomas was standing to her. Again the urge to reach out and touch him was there. But this time it wasn't because he was in pain, but because she was. Instead, she quickly thrust her hands deep into the pockets of her coat and took a deep breath. "So what's the story? Is he after the Black Rose, too?"

"*All* demons desire the Black Rose," Thomas simply said. "Their flesh is not designed for their souls. It is too flimsy. It cannot contain all that is within. *Flesh pains them.* The Black Rose calls out to them like a siren who promises to soothe them. But in return, they must give away their sanity."

"This is too much for me to cope with right now. I-I know that he saw the grimoire. I heard him admit it, but"— she choked on the words before suddenly remembering the final thing Travis had told her—"he said that not all demons are bad. Is that true?"

For a moment Thomas paused and lowered his head as if he wasn't going to answer her, but after an eternity he looked up and nodded almost reluctantly. "That is true."

Not all demons are bad. Suddenly, Cassidy marched over to her sports bag and then shot Thomas an apologetic look.

"I'm sorry. I need some time to think this all through."

"Oui," he said but she hardly heard him as she hurried to the parking lot where Nash would be waiting for her. *Not all demons are bad.*

✠ ✠ ✠ ✠ ✠

"Cass, is that you?" her mom called as soon as Cassidy walked in the front door an hour later, still feeling weak and overwhelmed by everything she'd learned. Despite what had happened, they'd still had to follow Celeste home to make sure she was safe. Thankfully, Nash had said he would be on Twitter duty if Celeste decided to go out. "I'm in the kitchen. I'm just making some dinner. Are you hungry?"

Cassidy shuddered as she wondered what her chances were of ignoring her mother and sneaking into her bedroom so that she could crawl under the comforter and perhaps stay there for a hundred years. Just until she'd sorted out this mess that she'd found herself in. Then her mom poked her head into the hallway, and Cassidy realized that her chances were slim to none. She discreetly put her purse on the hallway table and tucked her sports bag underneath it. Then she followed her mom's voice into the kitchen.

"Er, sure." She tried to muster up some enthusiasm and

push her conversation with Thomas to the back of her mind. "Can I just go see how Dad is?"

"He's in the shower, he'll be out in a moment, and he seems to be feeling better."

"Oh," Cassidy said. He had been very excited when he was finally allowed to have a proper shower again. Then she suddenly realized that even if her dad wasn't in the shower, it wasn't like she could tell him what was going on. She felt her bottom lip begin to wobble. She glanced away to hide her expression, but it was too late, and her mom's shrewd eyes narrowed.

"Hey, are you okay? What's going on?"

"Nothing." Cassidy quickly shook her head and willed herself not to cry. "I'm just tired."

"Oh." Her mom busied herself with folding and unfolding the cloth in her hands. "Of course. Well, you have been busy lately. Are you sure that you're not overdoing it?"

"That's a good one coming from you," Cassidy said, though her tone was light; instead of getting offended her mom actually gave her a rueful smile.

"Guilty as charged. Cassidy, I know you don't always like my advice, but when it comes to solving problems, I've built a career on it, so perhaps it's something that we could figure out together—"

"It's a boy thing," Cassidy said in a dry voice, knowing that her mom wasn't exactly a fan of dealing with the messy side of life. *When the going gets tough, Mom goes to the office.*

"Oh." Her mom winced, just the way Cassidy knew that

she would. "Travis? The one who's coming around next Sunday?"

"Yeah, him. I've just found out that he's not who I thought he was."

"They never are." Her mom let out a sigh, and Cassidy shuddered; she was closer to the truth than she realized.

"Anyway, the visit is definitely off."

"I'm sorry to hear that. Your father was looking forward to meeting him. So was I." Her mom paused and studied her fingers. "I wish I could help more, but boys aren't really my specialty. Thank goodness I met your father, who was good enough at relationships for both of us. You could say that *Romeo and Juliet* saved me."

"What?" Cassidy looked at her mom, all thoughts of Travis leaving her mind. "You met when Dad was playing Romeo?"

"Yes, I thought you knew that. That's why I thought it would be so nice for you to be in it. It was lucky for your father and me."

"You said you wanted me to do it because it would be good for my college applications," Cassidy reminded her.

"And so it will be," her mom said in a practical voice. "But that doesn't mean it's not a good play."

"Is that how you knew it was Dad's favorite?" Cassidy leaned forward on the counter and really studied her mom's face for the first time in ages. She looked older. And tired. Why had Cassidy never noticed that before?

"Yes. He always loved it," her mom said as her eyes lit up

and a rare smile traced her mouth. "'Did my heart love till now? Forswear it, sight!'"

"'For I ne'er saw true beauty till this night,'" Cassidy finished off in surprise, and then was even more surprised when her pragmatic mother dabbed at her eyes.

"Are you okay?" Cassidy asked in alarm; this was definitely pushing the boundaries of their relationship. Thankfully, before she had to do anything else, her cell phone rang.

"I'm fine," her mom hastily assured her before nodding for Cassidy to answer the call. It was Nash, and so Cassidy quickly slipped back out into the hallway, still not quite sure what had just happened.

"Hey," he said. "What are you doing?"

"Having the weirdest conversation with my mom." Cassidy rubbed her brow. "We were quoting Shakespeare. So what's up? Please don't tell me Celeste's going out again."

"No, I was actually just checking how you're doing."

"I'm fine," she assured him before catching sight of her pale face in the hallway mirror. "Okay, so not fine, but I'll get there," she promised. She just needed to focus on something else. Like breathing. Or not screaming and ripping her hair out. Simple tasks.

"Just try not to keep thinking about it. It's only going to freak you out more."

Too late for that, she thought with a sigh.

Thankfully, the rest of the night was surprisingly calm. Her dad was in a good mood, and when he wasn't declaring that he was going to order compression stockings in all different colors and patterns, he was talking about how tomorrow he had an extra physical therapy session at the outpatient center.

After dinner they'd all gone into the living room to watch an old James Dean movie, and even her mom, who normally had a stack of reports next to her, had sat through all of it without doing any work. In fact, Cassidy couldn't remember when they'd spent a more regular night together.

It was almost eleven when she walked into her bedroom. The light rapping on the window started almost immediately, and for a few moments Cassidy ignored it. She didn't feel like talking to anyone right now. Especially not Thomas. He rapped again, and she reluctantly crossed the floor and pushed back the drapes. But instead of seeing an owl hovering outside her window, it was Travis who stood in the shadows, his beautiful face looking sunken and gray.

"Hey, Cass," he said, his voice still hauntingly the same. "So I was wondering if you were ready to talk?"

For a moment she just stared at him, speechless, before finally nodding her head. "Okay, but not here. There's a park two blocks away. Meet me there in ten minutes. Oh, and Travis, I'll be bringing my sword."

TWENTY-FIVE

Twenty minutes later, Travis looked over at the child's swing that Cassidy was sitting in, the sword resting across her lap. It was dark now, and the moonlight glinted off the blade; from the distance came the thumping bass of a car stereo pounding its way down the road. "You know," Travis said, "I get why you're holding Thomas's sword in case I attack you, but this whole talking-to-each-other thing works a lot better if you actually say something. Do you hate me?"

"Do you care?" She finally lifted her head and dared to look at him, but it was no good. Every time she saw him, her eyes said Travis but her mind said demon.

"How can you ask that?" He joined her on the swings, his long muscular legs looking ridiculous as he tried to make himself fit.

"Well, you're a demon, so how am I to know what you think or how you feel? Or why you even bothered to spend time with me?" She resumed her study of the gravel below her feet. Next to her, Travis leaned back on the swing so that his torso was parallel to the ground. He looked so normal that suddenly the words choked from her throat: "How could you even become one? Nash said that it's a choice. *Why would you choose to be like those things I fought?*"

Travis's normally brown eyes suddenly swirled with amber, so intense and angry that if she'd been in any doubt he truly was a demon, the question was now put to rest. She tightened her grip on the sword in her lap and tried not to flinch.

."You don't need the weapon," he said, but instead of looking at her, he stared up at the night sky, perhaps aware that his eyes had changed. "And for once your clever friend is wrong. Most demons are made. But not all. I was born like this. You talk about choice, but I had none, Cass. *This is my life.* Whether I want it or not."

"You were born like this? I-I didn't realize." Confusion once again descended on her. How was she meant to make sense of anything when the rules kept changing? However, Travis seemed unaware of her turmoil.

"Why would you?" he asked, and when he turned back, his eyes were once again the warm brown that she was used to.

"So is that why you don't look like those other ones?"

He shrugged. "I guess. I never really stopped to ask my true father. He wasn't a hang-around-and-chat kind of guy. I just look the way I look. *I feel the way I feel.*"

"I don't follow what you're saying." Cassidy felt like the confusion was going to choke her.

"That's because you don't understand what it's like to be a demon." He clenched his jaw. "It hurts. All the time. Intense physical pain as the demon inside tries to push out through my flesh like a monster. S-sometimes it's too much. It gets hard to fight it."

"But you *do* fight it. Is that why you told me that not all demons are bad?" Cassidy asked, longing for him to give her a reason to believe in him. Instead, he gave a little bark of laughter.

"I think Nash would remind you that good and bad are variable, depending on where you're standing. I mean, I'm not all good. I did cheat on that book report the other day."

"Travis, can you be serious? I'm trying to understand this," she protested, while forcing herself to ignore just what effect his smile was having on her.

"Okay. Sorry, too soon for humor. In answer to your questions, I'm not always good, but I'm not always bad. And I've done many things that I regret."

"Like what?" Her voice was a little above a croak as she steeled herself for whatever things he had done.

"Like kissing you." He studied his shoe.

"You regret kissing me?" Cassidy's hand flew to her mouth. She was the one who had kissed a demon. Shouldn't she be the one doing the regretting?

"Sorry, that was badly phrased. I don't regret kissing you.

Definitely not. What I meant was that it was selfish of me to kiss you before you knew who I was. You deserve honesty."

"Oh." She flushed, but before she could say anything else he took a deep breath.

"Also, I shouldn't have kissed you because I know that Thomas has feelings for you."

For a moment it seemed like the whole world had gone silent as Travis's words hung between them like physical things that Cassidy could reach out and touch. But as with Thomas, when she stretched out her hand, nothing was there but air.

"I've got no idea what's happened between you and Thomas in the past, but you are wrong about this," she said, but Travis merely laughed. It was rich with just a hint of bitterness in it.

"No I'm not. Thomas and I might be very different, but I know him. *I really know him.* And despite all of that there-is-only-duty claptrap he likes to spout, he has feelings for you."

Cassidy felt her cheeks flame as she jumped up from the swing. This was too much. All of it. Travis. Beautiful Travis, who she now knew was a demon living in constant pain, was telling her that the infinitely less beautiful and much more bad-tempered Thomas, a medieval freaking knight from the fourteenth century, was crushing on her. Then she realized that Travis was curiously studying her reaction, and she walked back to him, still holding on to the sword.

"So you and Thomas have fought, and it was you who

gave him the scar on his cheek," she said. When Travis nodded his head, she continued. "Is that why you kissed me? To piss him off?"

"Nope. That was just an added bonus," Travis confessed before he stood up so that he was just inches from her, his muscular chest so close that it was all she could do not to reach out and touch him. Then he looked down, his dark eyes locking on hers. "And I would kiss you again right now if you'd let me."

"Do I have a choice?" Cassidy was filled with both longing and horror as she realized that if he wanted to kiss her, then she would be unable to resist. But instead of pressing his mouth against hers, Travis stepped back from her and shook his head in annoyance.

"Cass, how many times do I have to tell you? You *always* have a choice." He began to stalk around the playground in powerful strides, looking like an avenging ghost in the darkness. As his stride increased, his fists clenched, and suddenly she wondered if his dark eyes had once again turned to swirling pits of amber. Finally, he turned back to her, his lips twisted in disappointment. "Don't you get it yet? I would never hurt you. It's just not possible."

Cassidy's whole body shook as she longed to cover the distance between them. But she forced herself to stay where she was. "And what about my family? My friends? Celeste? *What about Celeste?* I'm sure you saw her glowing before we put the amulet on her."

"Ah, Celeste. The vessel. Even through her flesh the Black Rose radiated out with a bright but terrible beauty. So golden. So lovely. You have no idea how hard it was to not touch her."

"But you didn't." Hope flooded through her. "Thomas said that all demons desired the Black Rose, but you didn't touch Celeste. So you *are* good."

Travis began to stalk about again, this time kicking the ground as he went. "Thomas is right." His voice echoed around the empty playground. "But then again, he's not often wrong. All demons desire the Black Rose. It's as natural as breathing. We don't think we want it, but rather our broken bodies demand it. It's not goodness that has stopped me from taking the Black Rose. It's a cursed ward that prevents me from getting it. Only a guardian can break it. A guardian like yourself."

"Me?" Horror filled her voice. "Is that why you kissed me? So that I would hand the Black Rose over to you?"

"No. That's why I wanted to meet you, certainly. But Cass, your aura is almost as irresistible as Celeste's. How many times do I have to tell you? I kissed you only because I wanted to."

"I still don't understand this. Travis, I know you're good, so how can you even think of wanting the Black Rose when it's so evil?"

"That's where you're wrong." Travis gave a sharp shake of his head. "Thomas has been filling your head with his lies. The Black Rose isn't designed to be good *or* evil; it just depends on who uses it. There is so much good that can be done with it. It offers immortality and power. Power to heal. Power to fix. Look around you at the world. The wars, natural disasters, disease. The Black Rose can fix them all. Thomas knows this, but he chooses to ignore it and thinks only of what can go wrong."

"No, I've seen what happened in Paris. When I first touched Thomas's sword, I saw the same vision he had. The burning. People dying. *I could hear their cries. I could feel their pain.* Travis, you can't want that?"

"That was a mistake made by a human. A stupid Crusader. His body wasn't strong enough to contain the power of the Black Rose. But demons are different. We're designed for the Black Rose. *The Black Rose is designed for us.*" His dark eyes glittered with passion, his whole face so animated that it was like the sun shining down over her through the darkness. Travis saw her reaction and winced. "I'm sorry, but you need to know me for who I am. A demon. And it's my destiny to have the Black Rose."

"Then we have a problem." Cassidy tightened her grip on the sword as the words caught in her throat. "I promised that I'd guard Celeste. If you try to hurt her, then that will make us enemies."

"No." He shook his head, his wild dark curls scattering across his forehead and his brown eyes sad. "Never enemies, Cass. Like I said, there is a ward on the Black Rose, so the only way I can get it is if a guardian gives it to me. Therefore, you have my word that Celeste won't be harmed at my hands."

"How do I know you're not lying?" Her heart pounded in her chest.

"Ask your mighty Thomas. I have many faults, but I do not lie. Not ever."

TWENTY-SIX

"Honey, if you don't mind my saying, you look as if you haven't slept in days," her dad said the following Saturday as he wiped the sweat from his brow

More like a week. Cassidy put down the resistance band she had been using to help him do his exercises and tried not to think about how horrible things had been lately. She was still training every morning with Thomas, who refused to tell her anything else about Travis than what she already knew, and the rest of the time she was following Celeste and trying to avoid Travis and his puppy-dog eyes. Not to mention doing schoolwork and spending time at home. Then she realized that her dad was still expecting an answer.

"I've just been busy with the play." She gave a vague wave of her hand.

"Sure it's nothing to do with the fight you had with Travis?" He studied her face, searching for answers.

"Travis who?" she asked in a light voice. "I'm just

happy I found out about him before he came here," she said truthfully, since the idea of a demon near her family made her throat tighten with anxiety. "And can we please change the subject?"

"Okay, fine. I know what we can discuss. Since I've graduated from crutches to a cane, I was thinking that we could do some grocery shopping. It's Thanksgiving next week, and there is no way I'm letting your mother handle it. She's so sensible that she would rather get a chicken than the largest turkey in the store."

"Dad, I know you're walking again, but facing the pre-Thanksgiving crowd is madness. Write me a list, and I'll do the shopping with Nash tomorrow after school. And don't even think of trying to sneak off to any Black Friday sales, either."

"Okay, but only because I know Nash has exceptional taste and won't let you get the bad cranberries. And speaking of Nash, I think I can hear his car. Where are you two going today?"

"Oh, we're just going to hang out." Cassidy smoothed her blue vintage dress and tied the laces of her Dr. Martens. She wasn't trying to lie to her dad, but as usual, she and Nash had no idea where Celeste would be heading. She grabbed her denim jacket, which she had tossed on the couch, and gave him a kiss before heading out the door. As usual, she had put her sports bag out the window so that her parents wouldn't question her about it.

They made the by-now-familiar drive to Celeste's house in record time and sat there for about fifteen minutes before the garage door opened up and her SUV backed out onto the street. As Nash followed her, Cassidy checked Celeste's Twitter and Facebook for an update, but there was nothing but a link to her favorite cosmetic company.

"We're just going to have to follow her old-school style," Cassidy said as Nash swung right at the lights. "Do you even know where this street goes?"

"Actually, I do," Nash said in surprise. "It heads toward the public library."

"Yes, but—" Cassidy began, assuming that Celeste's SUV would go whizzing past the imposing Georgian building, but instead, she pulled around the back into the parking lot and got out. "Well, I did not see that one coming."

"That makes two of us." Nash parked his car and looked confused. "First we find out Celeste's a virgin and now she's going to the library on a Saturday? In the fourteenth century those would've been considered signs of an impending apocalypse."

"And don't forget the nursing-home thing," Cassidy reminded him as they hurried in—Nash with his trusty leather satchel and Cassidy with her sports bag filled to the brim with weapons. There was no sign of Celeste, but since there were only two floors for studying, Cassidy knew she wouldn't be hard to find. However, before they reached the stairs, Nash came to a halt.

"Actually, while we're here, it would be wrong of me not to go into the William Manning Reading Room. I'll be only a few minutes. I might be able to find something out about . . . well, stuff," he finished off lamely, though Cassidy knew what he was really trying to find out was why Travis didn't look like the other demons. Why he didn't act like the other demons. *Why he'd kissed her.*

"Of course. And thank you." She watched him leave, knowing that he would probably lose all track of time once he got there. Still, at least he would be doing something useful. She climbed the stairs and scanned the first floor until she caught sight of the luminous tendrils of the Black Rose.

Cassidy took a seat three rows over so that she could still have a clear view, then randomly pulled out of her bag some books and her MP3 player, along with the grimoire and a small knife, which she put in her lap.

However, after two hours there was no sign of any demons, and the music that she'd been listening to hadn't managed to take her mind off anything at all. Celeste was still sitting at a desk working, and Cassidy idly picked up her cell phone to make sure her dad hadn't done anything stupid like go to the supermarket. But before she could scroll through her Twitter feed, Celeste stood up and headed over. Crap. Cassidy quickly leaned forward to look like she was studying, but it didn't work. A moment later, Celeste was leaning over the top of the cubicle, her long dark hair cascading down her shoulders in a shiny tumble in a way that Cassidy's never achieved.

"What a surprise to see you here. You really have turned into my shadow, haven't you?"

"Um, no." Cassidy shook her head and shrugged her shoulders. "I'm just studying." *While I have a knife in my lap and a mystical book by my side*. She groaned as she realized that this could all end very badly, but Celeste hardly seemed to notice as she held up a copy of *Romeo and Juliet*.

"Well, since you're here, you might as well make yourself useful. Do you want to read some lines with me?"

For a moment Cassidy just stared at her. "Are you joking?"

"Why would I joke? You are my understudy," Celeste reminded her before she narrowed her eyes. "Unless of course you're too busy with your new *boyfriend*. You know, that guy who screwed up the play."

"He's not my boyfriend." Cassidy flinched at the mention of Travis, causing Celeste to raise a curious eyebrow. She quickly added, "And I don't want to talk about it . . . but I would like to learn lines with you."

"Thank you." Celeste nodded. "There are some discussion rooms upstairs. We can go there. And by the way, thanks for distracting Rachel the other day. I've got a lot of stuff going on right now, and the last thing I needed was her trying to dig for dirt."

Cassidy wasn't really sure why it was so terrible that Celeste could fold a hospital corner, but then again she didn't understand anything about Celeste and her Queen Bee world, so she just shrugged.

"It was no big deal. I've kind of spent my life avoiding

people like her, so I guess it's just second nature to throw her off track."

"And you're not even going to ask me why?" Celeste asked, but Cassidy shook her head.

"Not unless you want me to. I know all about having things you don't want to talk about. Anyway, I'll just pack up my stuff and meet you upstairs," she said, and then waited until Celeste was gone before she put the knife and grimoire into her sports bag and sent Nash a quick text about what was happening. *And she'd thought that last week was weird.*

✤   ✤   ✤   ✤   ✤

By the time they left the library, Cassidy's lack of sleep was catching up with her, and she waited in the front seat of Nash's car while he walked with Celeste to her SUV, pointing out a particular section in the Renaissance art book she'd checked out. Nash had joined them in the discussion room after lunch to help them learn their lines, and because he was Nash, he'd been unable to stop himself from filling in the historical details of the play.

Personally, Cassidy didn't really care, but Celeste seemed genuinely interested, which was what had prompted him to go find the book for her. Cassidy yawned and was just deciding what she should eat when she got home when the foul smell of tainted blood caught in her nose. Her pulse thumped through her veins and rang in her ears. A demon.

With a start she pushed open the car door and raced

across to where Nash and Celeste were standing.

"Is everything okay?" Nash demanded, his sharp eyes immediately taking in her white knuckles, which were gripping the sports bag.

"Not so much," Cassidy said as she widened her eyes and nodded to Celeste, who was once again looking at Cassidy like she was crazy. Cassidy ignored it, her nerves jangling with anticipation as she continued to scan the parking lot.

Then she saw it.

It was over at the far end of the library building, its amber eyes flashing in anger and confusion. It could obviously tell the Black Rose was somewhere nearby, but thanks to Nash's amulet, it couldn't find exactly where.

"Hey." Celeste suddenly caught sight of it and moved closer to Nash. "That looks like the weirdo from Cade Taylor's party. Rachel keeps seeing him everywhere, too."

"What do you mean, Rachel keeps seeing him everywhere?" Nash demanded, obviously too curious even to notice that Celeste had grabbed his arm. But Cassidy ignored it as she turned to Nash and shot him a telling look.

"Okay, I'm going over," she said, fear and nerves raging through her body.

"What?" Celeste squealed. "Why would you go over there? That guy is crazy. He totally pushed me over at the party."

"Cass, no." Nash shook his head, his blue eyes filled with worry. "You can't."

"I have to." She tightened her grip on the sports bag. "You just make sure that nothing happens here."

"Only if you promise me that you won't do anything stupid. And that you'll call Thomas." Nash's voice was hoarse as he squeezed her hand, and Cassidy reluctantly nodded. Behind her she could hear Celeste demanding, "Who the hell is Thomas, and why is Cassidy Carter-Lewis so freaking weird?" At this point in time, Cassidy didn't feel equipped to answer that question. Instead, she hurried across the parking lot toward the demon.

"Thomas," she hissed as the gravel crunched under her shoes. The creature had noticed her now, and its swirling amber eyes ignited with fury as it charged toward her. *"Thomas, hello, come in. I need your help."*

But there was no sign of the owl, and so instead of racing directly toward the demon, Cassidy darted down an alley behind a deserted building. Her plan was to lure it away from the public, and from Celeste, but as the demon increased its pace, Cassidy began to regret her decision. She didn't want to fight it in a corner. Then she noticed that one of the doors to the deserted warehouse was kicked in. Without pausing she raced into the building, the demon just behind her.

The stench of blood and darkness clogged her nose while fear swirled in her belly as she pulled her sword and shield out of her sports bag.

"Thomas," she cried out again, as she realized just how

much harder it was when she was on her own. But before she could even think, the demon lunged at her, and she only just avoided having her neck hacked open by dropping to her knees. Her body instinctively remembered the drill Thomas had taught her, and she held up her shield just in time to block the next attack. But the force of it sent her falling back, and again she had to roll away before the demon knight could lunge at her.

She scrambled to her feet and cleared her mind.

Stance. Thomas's training came back to her. She braced her knees and held the sword high in the air, her other arm putting the shield up. The demon lunged at her again. *Block*. She lifted her shield up with more speed than she would've thought possible and felt the might of the creature's sword vibrate through her entire body as she stopped it from slashing through her like an onion. *Attack*. She stepped forward and lunged. Her first parry was blocked by the demon, but it lifted its shield too high and Cassidy, spotting an opening, didn't waste a second.

She thrust forward, sending the sword plunging into the creature's chest. The runes along the blade of the sword blazed with power as they sliced through flesh and bone until the demon's amber eyes widened and its sword clattered to the ground. She pulled her own sword out just before the creature fell forward.

Her heart was pounding so loudly now that she was surprised it was still in her body. She paused only long enough to pull her leather gauntlet off and fumbled for the lighter in her pocket and set fire to the hideous creature. It didn't take long for the flame to catch, and Cassidy then used the fire to cleanse her own sword.

Every part of her ached, and she had been just about to collect the sports bag and make her way out to see if Celeste and Nash were okay when she heard a rustling noise from over in the corner. She slowly turned around to see a group of demons standing there. It looked as if they'd been asleep, but as their swirling amber eyes settled on the spot where their fallen comrade had just been burned, it was obvious that they were now very much awake.

For a moment Cassidy just stood there, frozen.

Were they living here? But how? It didn't make any sense. Why were there demon knights in an old warehouse on the corner of Madison and Exeter—

Her conversation with Reuben came crashing back into her mind. He'd told her he'd seen a demon knight on Exeter Street near the deserted warehouses, but at the time she hadn't thought any more about it. And of course Thomas had instructed her not to worry about them unless they attacked Celeste.

"Thomas, *please.*" She fumbled for the leather gauntlet and tried to tell her aching body that it couldn't rest yet. Still, there was no sign of the owl, and three demons all raced toward her, fanning out to block her in.

Cassidy's breath caught in her throat as she took her stance.

These demons had been fighting their entire lives. She'd been fighting for about two seconds. The first one lunged at her, and she used her shield to block it, scrambling out of the way as the second demon came lumbering toward her. But she was already panting. There was no way she could—

"You know," a voice suddenly said from close by, "I'm pretty sure that Thomas would never have taught you that trick. He's not nearly radical enough."

"Travis?" Cassidy spun around just in time to see him thrusting a sword through one of the demons before pulling it out with a flourish. Gone were the jeans and casual T-shirt—today he was in full armor, which Cassidy was sure weighed more than she did. His dark curls were pushed back from his face, and there was a half smile pressed onto his mouth. Cassidy felt ill. It was one thing for Travis to be a demon. It was another thing entirely for her to have to fight him.

Travis raised his sword high above his head, no shield, just two hands so tight around the handle that she could see his knuckles through the thick gloves he was wearing. His dark eyes caught hers as slowly, almost carefully, he lowered the sword toward her. Then he coughed.

"Er, Cass, you might want to duck."

Then, before she knew what was happening, he marched toward her, using his shoulder to nudge her out of the way just before another demon came charging over. In one fluid motion, he brought his sword crashing down on the creature's chest, the force knocking it to the ground before Travis killed it with a direct cut through the heart.

Slowly, Cassidy realized the truth. Travis wasn't *fighting* her; he was *helping* her.

Another demon came crashing toward her, and Cassidy scrambled to her feet, her fear now replaced by adrenaline as she lunged forward, catching the demon in wide-eyed surprise, killing him with one deft stroke. A moment later Travis had killed yet another with his dagger.

Without a word he dropped to his knees, a look of intense concentration on his beautiful face as he pulled out a lighter and set the bodies on fire. They both watched in silence as flames jumped and licked their way into the air before a backdraft sucked it all back in and they were left alone in the warehouse.

Cassidy didn't want to look at Travis, but she couldn't help herself. His face was smudged and glistening with sweat. Dressed like a knight, he suddenly seemed alien, but at the same time familiar. He'd also helped her.

"What are you doing here? They were demons. You're a demon. Why would you do that?"

"Oh, come on, Cass, you don't need to look *quite* so surprised," Travis said in a wounded voice as he lifted his sword high in the air and let the flame from the lighter run the length of it, cleansing the dark, fetid demon blood that was coating it. Cassidy felt herself hypnotized by the flames, but once they flicked away, leaving the sword gleaming, she realized for the first time that Travis's blade, like her own, was covered in runes.

"Hey." She held up Thomas's sword in surprise and studied the two blades. "These are the same."

"Not exactly the same." Travis lowered his so Cassidy could see a tiny inscription underneath the quillon. *So below.* A chill went racing through her as she forced herself to stare at the words on Thomas's sword, engraved in the same hand. *As above.*

"*As above. So below.* My father had quite a sense of humor, didn't he?" Travis asked in a soft voice. "He still does."

"Wh-what do you mean? I-I thought your father was dead." Cassidy's mind was now in turmoil, her eyes never leaving the identical swords.

"*Non.*" Travis shook his head. "Baphomet, my true father, lives, but the man who raised me, he's the one who is dead. Killed by my brother's hand."

"Brother? You have a brother?" *A brother who killed his father?* Cassidy felt as if the oxygen was being squeezed out of her lungs as her body began to shake. And he had said *non* instead of no. She stared at his sword as she willed the room to stop spinning. "It's not possible. *You and Thomas?* Travis, please. Tell me it's not true."

"Sorry, Cass, I told you once before that I don't lie. Not even for you," Travis said, his soulful eyes never leaving her face. "Thomas and I are blood twins. He's older than me by several minutes, though I think we can agree that, of the pair of us, I got the looks and the charm."

Cassidy's breath came out in a shallow gasp. "But how? It makes no sense. You're a demon."

"*Oui.*" Travis gave a slow nod of his beautiful head. "And what runs through my veins runs through his. *As above. So below.* I'm guessing by the shocked look on your face, my brother dear has done more than forgotten to show up for today's fight. He's forgotten to mention that he's the demon knight who killed his own father."

TWENTY - SEVEN

*B*roken *bodies everywhere. Lying in the streets, hanging out of windows. Fire and smoke in the air. And blood. So much blood. Dripping from Cassidy's hands as if it would never stop. She screamed and tried to wipe it off, but the more she scrubbed, the more blood there seemed to be. Then she looked up to see swirling amber eyes staring at her through the dark. They were angry. They were condemning. They were begging, like she knew they would. In the distance was a voice. Pick me. Me, me, me—*

Cassidy gasped as she woke with a start, half expecting to see herself surrounded by carnage and demons, but instead, the faint morning sun was pushing in through her curtains and bouncing off the floorboards, turning them a luscious honey color, while the apricot and green trim of her room radiated tranquillity and calm. Over on her desk the grimoire sat, still open to the page Nash had been reading last night, looking for information on Baphomet. However, there was no glow coming from it, and Cassidy realized that it had all been a dream. A really, really bad dream.

Though not nearly as bad as yesterday had been.

After telling her about Thomas, Travis had obviously decided that, as with good comedy, timing was everything, and he'd made a hasty retreat, leaving her to think about his revelations. And she would probably still be there now if Nash hadn't found her and taken her home, where she had spent the night letting it play out in her mind.

Thomas was a demon knight. Thomas had killed his father. If Travis truly never lied, then what he'd said was true, and—

"Good, you're awake." Nash appeared in the doorway. Today he was wearing a pair of dark blue Levi's and a neat, buttoned-up black shirt. And he seemed unusually jumpy as he sat down on the floor and began to pull book after book out of his army satchel. "So? Have you spoken to him yet?"

"Of course I haven't." Cassidy joined him and hugged her knees. "I'm never speaking to him again."

"Why not?" Nash frowned. "You spoke to Travis again, and he's a demon knight. We know that not all demons are bad—"

"Yes, and we also know that not all demons are good," Cassidy reminded him. She appreciated that what Nash said was true, but it didn't change her mind. Thomas should have told her what he was. *And what he'd done.* "You can stop looking at me like that. I'll still protect Celeste as best I can, but that doesn't mean I have to talk to him."

"Actually"—Nash began to fiddle with the books he'd brought with him—"it sort of does. You see, I've been doing some research on Baphomet. Travis was right when he said that not all demons were bad. Turns out his father was sworn to protect the Black Rose from the other Demon Lords. And there're some things you should know."

Cassidy found herself leaning forward, not sure she wanted to know but unable to resist. "Like what?"

"A lot of it is just conjecture. He's a demon idol that Philip the Fair accused the Templar Knights of worshipping, though most historians seem to think that Phillip was just trying to get his mitts on their extensive fortune, since his own wealth was—"

"Nash," Cassidy said, to remind him to keep on point.

"Sorry. So what I did find out was that after the Black Rose was brought back from the Crusades, there was an incident that nearly burned Paris to the ground. I think you saw some of that through your connection with Thomas."

"Yes." Cassidy closed her eyes as the memory of the charcoaled bodies and screams crashed into her mind.

"After that, the Brotherhood of the Black Rose was formed. Knights whose sole duty it was to protect the Black Rose from alchemists, adventurers . . . and demons. However, as you've discovered, fighting demons is tough work, especially when you don't have a specially made rune sword or a grimoire, so Baphomet sent his twin sons to join the Brotherhood, knowing that their strength and power would help protect the Black Rose."

"How old were they?" Cassidy whispered as Travis's words came back to her, about how she'd always a choice but he never had.

"Six," Nash said in a soft voice. "No one but their foster father, Hugh de la Croix, knew the truth about them."

"And their mother?" There was a lump in Cassidy's throat.

"From what I can tell, she was human, but she died giving birth to them. Here, I found a sketch of her," Nash said as he opened up one of the old books that he'd brought with him and carefully passed it to her. Cassidy gulped as she studied the page. It was a pen-and-ink sketch of a woman's face.

She had Travis's gloriously warm, open smile, but the artist had shaded the eyes differently: one dark, one light. Then she glanced at her neck, where a familiar-looking crystal was hanging.

"Travis gave me his mother's necklace," Cassidy gasped.

"No wonder Thomas freaked out when he saw it," he said as Cassidy pushed the book away.

"Sorry, Nash, I know you like history, but trying to make me feel sorry for two demon knights isn't going to work. Yes, it sucks what happened to them, but it's not my problem. Like I said, I will protect Celeste as best I can, but don't think I'm going to talk to either of them again."

"Cass, that's not all I found. Do you remember that dream you had? About the feather that was split in two?"

"Yes." She looked at him surprise. "Why? Do you know what it means?"

"I think so." Nash picked up the book that she had just pushed away and turned to another page. "This is what I actually came around to show you. It's a prophecy about the demon twins. I think you should read it."

> The twin sons of Baphomet shall both seek the Black Rose when it is lost in time. Both will find it, but only one will succeed. Their fate shall be decided on the shortest day when the sun is gone by she who chooses. If the right twin receives it, the earth shall prosper, and Baphomet shall smile. If the wrong twin receives it, Baphomet shall weep, and crimson blood shall forever stain the scorched earth.

Cassidy was silent as she shut the book and thought of the voice that had been echoing in her mind for the last few weeks. *Pick me. Pick me.* She could tell by the tight line of Nash's jaw that the girl in the prophecy was her. And if it was true, it meant that one of the twins was good and one was bad. The only problem was, she didn't have a clue which was which.

❖ ❖ ❖ ❖ ❖

An hour later Cassidy walked Nash to the front door and hugged him. "Are you sure that you don't mind?"

"Of course not." Nash gave a supportive shake of his head. They'd decided that in order to avoid having to follow Celeste all over town, Nash would go over and read lines with her to stop her from leaving the safety of her house. *In other words, he was taking a bullet.*

"Liar." She mustered a smile before squeezing his hand. "But thank you anyway. I don't think I could face any following or fighting today."

Nash's lips twitched. "Okay, so hanging out with Celeste for the day isn't top of my list, but then again, seeing you get pulled in all directions isn't much fun, either. Besides, I said I'd do anything I could to help, and I meant it. And in return you need to promise to try not to drive yourself crazy with this."

"I won't," she promised, even though they both knew she was lying. Because seriously, how could she ever figure out which brother was good and which was bad? The way she was feeling, both of them were bad.

Once Nash had gone, she wandered back down the hallway. She could hear her mom puttering in the kitchen and was just about to slip past when her dad's head appeared in the doorway.

"Ah, there you are. I was starting to think that you'd run away and joined the traveling circus," her dad quipped as Cassidy widened her eyes.

"Dad, what are you doing? I thought it was Mom in here."

"And if you can't tell the difference between the delicious smell of my waffles and the store-bought ones that your mom uses, then I'm deeply offended," he informed her as he leaned against the counter to stay steady. "Unless, of course, you don't want my waffles."

"Are you crazy? I love them. You used to make them

every time I was"—she let out a groan— "*upset*. Every time I was upset you would say that 'misery loves waffles,' which must mean that you're worried about me. Is this because of Travis?"

"Actually, your mom was worried. She said you tried to talk to her, and she wasn't much help. I guess she's feeling guilty that she doesn't know the right things to say."

"Yeah? So why isn't she here making me waffles then?" Cassidy wanted to know, and immediately regretted it when her dad's face darkened. "Sorry, I didn't mean that," she hastily added.

"Try to give her a break. I know you're still mad at her for going to Boston—"

"She left for *five years*, Dad, and now she comes back."

For a moment her dad paused. "Cass, there's something you should know. Your mom never wanted to go to Boston. But there were things going on that she felt she needed to help out with."

"What are you talking about?" Cassidy wrinkled her nose.

"Remember when your mom's pop died and there was all that talk about his mismanaging some funds?"

"Yes, but it was just a mistake; it blew over in a week."

He shook his head. "It blew over in the *media* in a week. And it wasn't shareholder funds, it was pension funds. The life savings of ordinary workers. Your mom's spent the last five years trying to get those people their money back, and the job still isn't done."

"What?" Cassidy stared at him for a moment, as if he'd just told her that polar bears were pink or that Elvis was still alive. "Why didn't I know about this?"

"There was no particular reason. It certainly wasn't a conspiracy. At first you were too young, and then you were too mad and your mom didn't want to use it as an excuse. She still doesn't. I'm just telling you because I think you should know. She's not as bad as you think she is." Then, without warning, he suddenly shrugged his shoulders. "Now, are you going to tell me what happened with Travis?"

For a moment she stared at him blankly as she tried to think of her mom as doing some cool, noble thing, but then, with the mention of Travis, her more immediate problems came crashing back into her mind.

"I wish I could." Cassidy used her fingertip to draw a circle on the bench she was sitting on. "He just wasn't who I thought he was." *Neither was his brother.* "And no matter how much I want it to be different, it's impossible. Does that make sense to you?"

"I'm afraid it does." Her dad nodded before limping over to give her a hug. Then when he finally broke away, he shot her a weak smile. "Now, about those waffles . . ."

TWENTY-EIGHT

After the waffles Cassidy and her dad spent a couple of hours chilling out before one of his friends came around to watch a tennis match on television. Her mom had gone to the office, and after Cassidy had roamed around the house far too many times, she finally put her sneakers on and decided to go for a jog. Not that she normally liked jogging, but right now she felt that if she didn't find some way to get rid of her excess energy, she would go crazy.

It was still light out, but the sun was partially hidden behind a cloud and the street was virtually deserted as her feet pounded along the pavement. She purposely turned left at Turner Road so that she wouldn't go near the woods, and after ten minutes the houses had given way to an open field. Still energy poured through her veins, and she picked up the pace, so busy concentrating on the rhythm of her feet that it wasn't until the owl was flying next to her that she even realized it was there.

"Go away, Thomas," she yelled, keeping her gaze firmly in front of her. The owl ignored her as it continued to fly beside her. Cassidy increased her pace, going so fast that she doubted her PE teacher would even recognize her. However, the owl matched her easily, its dark brown feathers making a swooshing noise as it flew. Finally, Cassidy realized that even with the superstrength of the grimoire, she was never going to outrun the bird, and so she reluctantly came to a halt by the side of a field.

The owl landed several feet from where she was standing, its large amber eyes solemnly staring at her. Demon eyes. Why hadn't she made the connection sooner? She stamped the damp grass in annoyance. Then the owl was gone, and Thomas was in its place. Or, should she say, the apparition of Thomas.

"I don't want to speak to you. I'm so mad." Her voice shook, and she refused to look at him.

"I take it you know."

"No thanks to you." Her throat tightened as she studied the ground. The words choked out. "How could you lie to me like this?"

"I didn't lie," he protested before letting out a sigh. "I just didn't tell you everything."

"You told me *nothing*." Cassidy folded her arms and walked away from him, her frustation mounting. "If it wasn't for Travis, I would never have even known."

"Don't be so fast to trust my brother, Cassidy. He is not as he seems."

"So are you saying that *he* lied to me?" She swung around and raised her eyebrows, finally looking at him.

"*Non,*" Thomas said, though it seemed like it cost him some effort, and she watched as he clenched his hands until his knuckles were white. "He doesn't lie, but he can distort things to suit his own desires."

"Sounds like someone else I know," Cassidy retorted. "And in case I'm being too cryptic for you, I'm talking about you, Thomas. Did you think that you'd have a better chance of convincing me to do this for you if you didn't tell me the truth? That if I thought you were the nice guy, I would choose you?"

Thomas flinched for the merest second as he let out a small gasp. "You know about the prophecy?"

"*Oui,*" Cassidy mocked. "I guess that was another thing you forgot to tell me about. Was anything true?"

For a moment Thomas didn't answer. Instead, he bowed his head and ran his scarred hands through his hair before finally looking up, his face leached of color. "It's all true. Everything. The Black Rose *needs* to be protected. Please, I know that the hatred you feel for me burns through you like fire. I know that you don't ever want to see me again, but everything is as I told you. If the Black Rose is used, the world will be destroyed. *You saw Paris.*"

"The Crusader who inhaled the essence was human." Cassidy found herself repeating Travis's words.

"My brother has no proof that demons can control the Black Rose any better than the Crusader could."

"He told me something else as well," Cassidy said, emotions spinning through her body. "About your father. He said you—"

"He's right," Thomas cut her off quickly and was then silent. Cassidy stared at him in sickening horror. "My foster father, Hugh de la Croix, died by my hand."

"That's it?" Cassidy felt as if she was being kicked in the stomach as she studied his impassive, unyielding face. "You're not even going to give me an explanation? You once told me that you had no time for sentiment, but to be so cold about killing your own foster father. W-was he that evil?"

"*Non*. He was the best of men." Thomas looked away. "I'm sorry. I know you want more, but this is not something I can talk about. I-if you want answers, then you must trust my sword."

"What?" Cassidy started to protest, but before she could even finish, there was a rustle of feathers and Thomas was gone, leaving her alone in a field and more confused than ever.

He admitted to being a demon knight and to killing his father, the same way he might've admitted to spilling ketchup on the carpet. Cassidy felt sick and betrayed. She wasn't sure how long she stood there before slowly jogging home, her excessive energy completely gone, leaving her weak and drained.

By the time she reached the house she was exhausted, but her mind kept swirling around with images of Travis and Thomas. Two brothers who both seemed to be telling her the truth, despite the fact that only one of them could be right. And the voices in her head begging her to *"pick me."*

There was a text message from Nash to say that he'd managed to keep Celeste inside the entire day, which was one less thing to worry about. Then she caught sight of the corner of her sports bag, which was poking out from under the bed. Thomas had told her that if she wanted answers, then she must trust his sword.

What did that even mean?

She dropped to her knees and retrieved it. His father's sword.

The late-afternoon sun bounced off the metal blade, lighting up the runes one by one until they all glowed with a piercing white light, so strong she had to shield her eyes. Instinctively, Cassidy lay flat on her bed and let the sword rest on top of her, her hands firmly clutched around the handle. The bedroom ceiling began to swim and undulate above her, and then everything went blank, apart from the sensation that she was falling. . . .

TWENTY-NINE

The cold made her skin prickle, and Cassidy knew instantly that this was no vision. Darkness surrounded her, and the smell of damp soil and stale air invaded her nostrils. The light didn't improve so she crawled on her knees, dirt and stone scratching her skin. She groped to find a wall and was greeted by more earth. She reached higher, and the dirt made way for rough wooden beams.

Was she underground?

Cassidy thrust her hands into her pocket, grateful for Nash's Zippo. The small flame gave her enough light to confirm that she was definitely in a tunnel. Panic pounded in her chest, but before she could give in to her emotions, she heard a noise coming from farther down the cavernous tunnel. She looked up to see a flickering flame moving toward her and two voices, both achingly familiar.

Thomas and Travis.

They were arguing. and Cassidy pressed herself against

the wall, willing herself to be small and invisible. As they marched past, she realized that while this wasn't a vision, it wasn't quite real, either.

The brothers couldn't see her. She let out her breath and followed them.

"I tell you, it's true," Travis hissed in a low voice as they approached a thick wooden door. "Our foster father plans to betray us."

"You are mistaken." Thomas thrust his torch into a wall bracket with an economy of motion that Cassidy knew so well. Then he stepped into the light, and Cassidy cried out loud at the sight of him.

He was younger. Perhaps fourteen, and if it wasn't for the mismatched eyes, she wasn't sure she would've recognized him. Despite his youth, he was wearing full armor and a long white tunic with an inky black rose embroidered across the chest. On his hip was the leather sheath and the sword she was now so familiar with. His hair was darker and longer, and his normally pale face was tanned. *But most of all, there was no sign of the angry red scar that was now his constant companion.*

Her heart pounded as she turned her attention to Travis, though the change in him wasn't so great. His beauty and warmth were still there, though there was a hint of harshness around his mouth that she'd never noticed before.

"How can you be so sure? Now is the perfect time for our father to take the Black Rose. With everything that's happened in Paris, it's only a matter of time before Philip turns his eyes to the treasure here at Landévennec. I tell you, our father means to use the confusion to take it for himself."

"Our father is no traitor, Travis. Your words are unfounded, and you do him no justice," Thomas snapped in his blunt manner. Travis flinched as if Thomas's words had actually hit him. But instead of showing his anger, he merely shrugged.

"Well, shall we go to see which brother is right and which brother is wrong?"

Without waiting for an answer he pushed the wooden door open, and the two brothers marched through, their heavy armor announcing their presence. Cassidy followed them. Unlike the dark passage, the chamber was well lit, though she soon discovered that most of the glow didn't come from flickering flames, but rather from the treasures that were casually lying everywhere: gold coins, plates, goblets, and semiprecious stones and jewelry. Then her gaze fell on the man who was sitting in the far corner of the room in the middle of a crudely drawn circle.

He looked to be about forty, with a weathered face and long blond hair that was streaked with gray. To one side of him was a plain urn, and in front of him was . . . the grimoire! Cassidy's eyes widened with recognition. Unlike the twins, he wasn't wearing armor, but rather a coarse brown shirt that fell down around his hips. He didn't look up when they entered; instead, he appeared to be in a trance. Cassidy guessed he was their foster father, Hugh de la Croix.

The tattoo on Cassidy's arm burned, and the voice in her mind screamed, *"Pick me. Pick me."*

"It's too late." Travis's face paled as he hurried toward him, but before he could step across the line of the circle, he was hauled back by Thomas, the strain of his steely muscles showing on his face.

"Step down," Thomas growled.

"What are you doing? We must stop him." Travis spun around, his amber eyes swirling with urgency. "We can't let him get the Black Rose."

"It is not our foster father who seeks the Black Rose, *brother*." Thomas's voice was low and dangerous, and for the first time his mismatched eyes were gone and were replaced by two swirling pits of amber. Demon eyes. Cassidy gasped as her emotions threatened to choke her. "We know what you were planning. Our foster father is putting a new ward on the Black Rose. To protect it from *your* betrayal. It means that never again will you be able to touch it. It will now be lost to you forever. You have failed."

"You and your noble beliefs. Thomas, you know nothing. You understand *nothing*," Travis suddenly spat as he once again tried to reach his foster father, but Thomas was there, formidable and deadly, as he took his stance with his sword. "The Black Rose is not what you think it is. It can be used for good. It can be used to heal. But not if a human like our foster father uses it. It needs to be a demon. Let me prove it to you, Thomas. Help me and we can both be free."

"Enough. You cannot sway me from my duty," Thomas snapped as Travis raised his own sword.

Cassidy screamed, despite the fact that they couldn't hear her, and was forced to watch them face each other, the runes of their swords blazing. It was a terrifying sight. Thomas, his movements so concise and minimal, while Travis kept pressing and countering with a flourish that Cassidy had seen when he'd helped her fight the other demons.

Back and forth they went.

Two brothers who had obviously sparred together for years. They matched each other stroke for stroke, strength for strength. Neither of them spoke as the sweat beaded on their foreheads, their amber eyes both blazing with determination. However, for all his flourish, Travis couldn't reach the circle, and the frustration started to show in some of his movements. Inch by inch, Thomas pressed him back, and Cassidy marveled at his sheer strength.

Travis ducked, and with his foot he stretched out and kicked one of the heavy candelabras that were sitting on the floor. Cassidy watched in horror as the thick waxy candles went crashing into a bolt of silk. Soon small plumes of smoke began to rise up from it. For the briefest of seconds, Thomas blinked, and in that moment Travis's sword sliced down the side of his face. Cassidy flinched as if her own skin had been cut.

"Please, stop. Both of you. You need to put out the fire," she cried, but her words were unheard just as her presence was unseen. Then from behind her, there was a flash, and the trance that their foster father had been in was suddenly broken.

Cassidy had no idea what ritual he'd been doing, but it was obviously complete, and she watched as he rose to his feet, his quick eyes taking everything in: The battling twins. The betrayal. The small fire that was quickly gathering purchase, fueled by the wooden chests that were placed about the room.

Travis saw the movement, too, but Thomas, his back turned, didn't seem to have noticed. Suddenly, Travis darted to the side just as their foster father went racing toward the flame. Thomas, his aim true, pulled out the small knife tucked in his belt and threw it directly at his brother, but at the last moment Travis dropped to the ground and the knife went slicing through Hugh de la Croix's coarse brown shirt, and he fell to the floor in a heap.

The room was silent, with only the sound of the crackling fire as it searched for fuel. Thomas dropped to his knees and desperately tried to stop the dark crimson blood that was flowing freely from his foster father's wound before pooling on the earth below, mixing with the blood from his own injured face.

Cassidy's hands flew to her mouth, and the tears stung in her eyes. Thomas's face paled, and for the smallest moment Travis stared at the dying man and his brother before turning his back and stalking toward the plain urn.

His whole face radiated with joy as he held the urn up to his mouth. But his happiness was quickly replaced by anger as whatever he had been hoping for didn't happen.

"*Noooo.*" The howl echoed around the chamber. Then he narrowed his eyes and hurried back to Thomas, joining him down on his knees. "You need to remove the ward. Brother, you need to help me. Remove the ward and we can all be free. We can save our father. We can both live a real life. Join me, Thomas. My twin. Please, I'm begging you, remove the ward and trust me. I know I can save him."

"*Non.*"

For a moment Travis just stared at him, his beautiful face ravished with pain and anger. Then he snarled. "Fine. Let our father die just so you can be right. But remember, you are not the only guardian. There are sixty knights who can help me. One of them will remove the ward, and then you may very well regret this day's work, brother."

From the ground the dying man began to groan, and Thomas leaned over him and whispered something in a soft voice that Cassidy couldn't hear and didn't want to know even if she could.

Then he turned to his brother and Cassidy braced herself, waiting for the scathing reply that she knew was coming. But instead, he had tears in his eyes as leaned forward to embrace Travis. It was such a startling action that Travis was caught unaware. Before he knew what had happened, Thomas's arms were around his chest, squeezing the air from his lungs, and Travis fell into a heap next to his dying foster father.

He wasn't dead.

She knew he wasn't dead, but still Cassidy couldn't help herself from screaming as she watched Thomas rise to his feet and hastily retrieve the urn and the grimoire before racing from the room. The fire was growing worse, and Cassidy longed to do something, but she was helpless. She watched as Travis slowly rose to his feet and let out a tormented scream. He looked down at his foster father and pushed back a strand of hair.

"I'm sorry that I failed you," Travis whispered before racing out of the chamber in search of Thomas, whom Cassidy could only guess was by now long gone.

The fire was everywhere, and Cassidy suddenly wondered how she was supposed to get back to her body seven centuries away. Did she just close her eyes and will it to be so? Panic welled in her chest, but before she could decide what to do, there was a sudden coughing noise, and she turned to see Hugh de la Croix, his dying eyes staring straight at her.

"It's you. You're the one. She who chooses," he croaked, his breath short and his face waxen. "Please be gentle; this is not their fault. Both my sons are good at heart, but they are broken. Just remember that whoever you choose will be made whole again." For a moment he smiled through his pain before his face once again crumpled under the weight of his wound. "But the other one will be lost to us forever. I fear for them, and for you, with this burden you carry."

Pick me, a voice cried from somewhere, and Cassidy opened her mouth to speak; instead, she fell to the ground and everything went blank.

THIRTY

"Stand still," Celeste Gilbert's mom said around a mouthful of pins as she glanced up from where she was pinning the hem of a blue dress. Cassidy was pretty sure that understudies didn't normally get their own costumes, but she'd underestimated Celeste's quest for the perfect play—not only had Celeste roped her mom into doing all the costumes, but she had insisted that Cassidy have her own wardrobe. *Something that had sounded a lot better in theory.* She let out a sigh, causing Mrs. Gilbert to growl, "Cassidy, you have a choice. Either you stand still or you get jabbed in the leg with a pin."

"Oh, however will you make such a tough decision?" Travis sauntered across the room, looking more gorgeous than ever in pantaloons and a loose white shirt that brought out the creamy richness of his skin and his dark curls. He raised a quizzical eyebrow at her. "And speaking of decisions, there is that other matter you still need to make up your mind about. Not wanting to pressure you, but there are only three days until the solstice, so if you're going to choose me, then I need to start planning."

"Travis." Cassidy glared at him, but Mrs. Gilbert didn't seem to notice as she got to her feet.

"We'll do the other one tomorrow, because I don't think I can face any more wriggling." Then without another word she headed to the other side of the room and began to gather up an armful of dresses. It was obvious from whom Celeste got her attitude. Once Mrs. Gilbert was out of hearing distance, Cassidy turned to Travis and narrowed her eyes.

"I told you that when I decide you'll be the first to know. Though right now I'm tempted to send the Black Rose to China." Cassidy jumped down off the box she'd been standing on and tried to tug the dress over her head. Mrs. Gilbert had tried to get her to take her retro bowling shirt and jeans off for the fitting, but Cassidy had refused. Something she was now regretting as the dress felt too tight to pull over her head.

"Need a hand, Ms. Snappy?" Travis asked in a wolfish voice as she felt the dress gently lifted over her head until she was staring into Travis's handsome face. "I take it from your foul mood that you still haven't spoken to my brother. I'm not actually sure whether to be flattered or offended that you're speaking to me and not him."

"Travis, please." Cassidy spun away, annoyed that he

could read her so well. It had been a little over four weeks since she'd witnessed the battle between the two brothers and the death of their foster father. Since then Thanksgiving had passed, and while it wasn't strictly true that she hadn't spoken to Thomas, she'd made sure that conversation had been kept to a bare minimum, and she had made it clear that if it didn't involve her training, then she wasn't interested. To his credit, Thomas had never asked if she'd followed his advice and used the sword to see the terrible tragedy that had taken place, and so they'd managed to survive in an uneasy stalemate.

Travis had been harder to avoid.

Not only because of his physical presence but because he didn't seem to think there was anything wrong with discussing how his father had died. Nor did he seem to mind that she had seen his blatant desire for the Black Rose. All he would say was that he wasn't embarrassed by who he was. None of which made her choice any easier. Well, calling it a choice wasn't really fair, since as far as she could see, there was just no way she could decide, and so she'd ended up putting it into the too-hard basket and spent her time hanging out with her dad, who was planning to go back to work in two more weeks, plus learning her lines for the play and doing as much training as possible.

The only problem was that the solstice was going to be there in three days, whether she had decided or not.

"Well, just remember that I'm the one who is nice to you.

And who brings you Diet Coke whenever you want it." He waved a bottle in her face before putting it down next to her.

"Yes, getting free Diet Coke is a very good reason to hand over the most dangerous treasure ever invented."

"It's not dangerous," Travis reminded her, with a slight edge to his voice. "It's the user who determines what happens with it. Of course, if you give it to Thomas and he disappears back to the lack of hygiene that is my century, you know that, despite his impressive fighting skills, the Demon Lords will eventually get it, and when they do, it will be an even bigger mess than Paris. Because unlike my own sweet self, Demon Lords will not use it for good."

"Travis, stop." Cassidy wished that the pounding in her head would disappear. "It's not helping me. And you keep saying that Thomas is the bad one, but at least he didn't pretend to like me just so I would pick him."

Which was why she was also convinced that it wasn't Thomas's voice in her mind saying, *"Pick me."*

Travis's face darkened as he stalked around the room several times before making his way back to her, his eyes not quite amber, but not quite brown, either. "Cass, there has never been any pretense. You are like no one else. Perhaps if I liked you less, I could've compelled you more." Then without saying another word, he leaned forward and dropped the lightest kiss on her cheek. "Choose wisely, sweet girl, because if you get it wrong, it might not be the end of the world, but it will sure as hell be close to it."

Then he was gone, and Cassidy sat down on the box she'd

just been standing on, her hand fluttering up to her cheek. She longed to put her hands over her head and pretend that it wasn't happening but was stopped by the sound of the stage crew hurrying past her. Rehearsals must be finished, which meant she had to go to meet Celeste.

She wouldn't go as far as to say that they were friends, but thanks to Nash's almost constant presence, Celeste hadn't seemed to have minded how much time they were spending with her—and had even offered Cassidy a lift home when she'd discovered Nash wasn't going to be there.

Celeste was waiting for her by the stage door, and so Cassidy hurried over, her sports bag close in hand. In the last four weeks she'd fought and killed fifteen more demons, each time with either a grim Thomas by her side directing her or with Travis and his more flamboyant sword tricks, though never with both of them at once.

"So," Celeste said as they hurried toward her SUV, the December wind pecking at their skin. "Since Nash isn't here, there's something that I've been meaning to ask. Do you think that—"

"No," Cassidy cut her off because she had a pretty good idea where this was heading, and it wouldn't have been the first time she'd been forced to give a love-struck Nash fan the It's Really, Really, *Really* Not You, It's Him speech. However, she didn't want to give it to Celeste, especially with so little time left before the winter solstice. If Celeste was pissed with Nash, then it would be harder to protect her.

"No?" Celeste wrinkled her pert nose and flicked back

her glossy hair. "How do you know what I was even going to ask you?"

Crap. Cassidy winced. "Sorry, I just thought you were going to ask me about Nash's dating preferences."

"I was going to ask about Nash's Christmas present," Celeste corrected before flushing. "I just saw this really nice old book on the history of telescopes when he took me into the antiquarian bookstore. It was by someone called Patrick Rivers. I was wondering if he already had a copy."

"Oh." Cassidy's mouth opened and then shut again. Then she paused for a moment and decided that she needed to start from the beginning. "So *when* did Nash take you to the bookstore?"

"The other day," Celeste said in a breezy voice. "After you ran off mumbling something about being late for a dentist appointment."

"Oh," Cassidy said again and nodded, since these days being late for any kind of appointment was actually code for "There's a demon running down Gibson Terrace." Nash had obviously decided to take Celeste into the bookstore to distract her.

"So?" Celeste shot her a you-are-still-sooooo-weird look. "Do you know if he has the book?"

"Sorry. I wouldn't have a clue, but I'm sure I can find out if you like."

"Really? That would be great." Celeste seemed extraordinarily happy as she drove the rest of the trip to Cassidy's house, humming a David Bowie song. Cassidy groaned since, while most kids their age didn't listen to much Bowie, he was one of Nash's idols. But it was quickly forgotten as her house came into view, and Cassidy realized there was an ambulance parked outside it.

"What house do you think that's for?" Celeste asked, but Cassidy hardly heard, and as soon as the SUV came to a stop she jumped out and raced over as the two paramedics came out, with her dad strapped onto a stretcher. Cassidy's knees began to buckle, but she forced herself to ignore it, heading straight toward her mom. Her mom's face was pale, and her hands were shaking.

"What happened?" Cassidy's voice was a little above a whisper.

"He was complaining of a headache, and we were just about to take him to the doctor when he collapsed." Her mom took a deep breath. "Cass, they think he's had a stroke."

THIRTY-ONE

No. It couldn't be happening. Cassidy sat in the corner of the hospital room. Out in the corridor her mom was having an intense conversation with the doctors, while there in the middle on a metal bed with IV tubes and monitors attached to him was her father, the person she loved most in the world. Yet she couldn't tell him that she loved him most in the world because he had slipped into a coma.

It had been two days since her dad had been rushed here, and they had taken him straight through to have an MRI, only to confirm that his stroke had been caused by a massive blood clot in his head. It was too big and too dangerous to operate on, and by earlier this morning they had been warned to prepare for the worst. He hadn't moved once.

Cassidy turned away. She couldn't look at him lying there. He had told her he was fine. He had promised it. Had even laughed at her for worrying when she had first bought the tattoos almost two months ago. Her throat tightened, but she forced the tears back down. If she cried, it was real, and if it was real, then—

No. She paced over to the door. She had to get out of there. Just for a few minutes. Just so that she could convince herself that it wasn't really happening. Her coat was lying on one of the chairs, and she grabbed it as she hurried out.

"I'm just going to get some air," she told her mom as she passed, careful not to make eye contact as she rushed by. The December weather had turned bitter and icy, and the frost-tipped grass crunched as she made her way to a bench seat. Her skin tingled and her breath was heavy in the cool air, but Cassidy didn't care. All she cared about was not thinking.

In her pocket her cell phone beeped but when she checked the screen it was only Nash. He had been with her most of the time but had left this morning to go follow Celeste. Cassidy hadn't minded, since she knew he was feeling pretty helpless to do anything. She texted him back to tell him there was no news and then settled back down, staring into space. She wasn't sure how long she had been there when she heard footsteps, and she looked up to see her mom walking toward her, two coffee cups in her hands.

"I thought this might warm you up." Her mom passed her a cup and sat down next to her so that they were both looking straight ahead at a large willow tree. Finally, her mom spoke. "He wouldn't want you to be upset, you know."

"Well, he shouldn't have gotten sick then," Cassidy retorted as tears stung at her eyes and anger pricked at her chest.

"Honey, that's not fair." Her mom tightened her grip on the cup so that her knuckles were white and strained.

"Jeez, Mom, he's forty-five years old and in a coma. What's fair got to do with anything?" Cassidy could feel her lower lip tremble in annoyance.

For a moment her mom was silent, and Cassidy braced herself for the lecture that was about to come, but instead her mom just leaned back on the bench and sighed. Her face was almost gray, and the bags under her eyes made Cassidy wonder if she'd gotten any sleep at all when Nash had driven her home for a quick nap and a shower.

Then she noticed how stiff her mom's shoulders were, and anger was suddenly replaced by guilt. Her mom had done many things over the years to piss her off, but this wasn't one of them.

"I'm sorry. I shouldn't have said that." Cassidy's throat contracted. "That was out of line."

"No, actually, it wasn't." Her mom was still looking straight ahead as she closed her red-rimmed eyes. "But don't you see, Cass? That's the whole damn problem. If your father was here, he would never have said the wrong thing in the first place, and you wouldn't need to apologize."

"You didn't say the wrong thing," Cassidy forced herself to admit. "Because, let's face it, there is nothing you can say to make this okay."

"You're like him, you know," her mom suddenly said. "Strong. Kind. Caring. Like two peas in a pod. I often wished

I could be more like the pair of you. Less uptight." Then she let out another sigh and finally turned to Cassidy. "I know I haven't always been the easiest person to be around, but Cass, you can talk to me, you know."

"I know," Cassidy said, and her mom flinched, as if she thought Cassidy was joking. It was probably no less than she deserved. "Dad told me the truth about Boston. I guess he didn't want me to keep giving you a hard time for the next hundred years."

"A hundred years? Is that the going rate for parental punishment right now?" Her mom shuddered before wincing. "I'm sorry. I probably should've told you myself. I just hate justifying my actions, and if I'm honest, I didn't want you to feel manipulated into feeling like you should be happy when you were obviously mad at me. Of course, I hadn't expected you to stay mad for quite so long."

"I guess I get the stubborn gene from you," Cassidy said, giving her mom a weak smile, then studying her face. "Do you regret going? I mean, with everything that's happening?"

"Of course. Every single day I have regrets, and please don't think that my decision was an easy one. I do believe it was the right one, and the fact that we managed to rebuild all the pension funds definitely made it worth it, but I think you know as well as I do what the consequences were. You and your father. Vacations. Dance recitals—"

"Just one dance recital, and if Dad told you it was good, then he was lying. I was lousy."

Her mom gave a watery laugh. "Doesn't change the fact that I still missed it," she said as a flash of pain crossed her face. Cassidy gave her a curious look.

"But you still went even though you knew the consequences?"

"Like I said, I didn't think things would end up quite so bad between us," her mom said in a soft voice before regretfully nodded her head. "But yes, I still went. Knowing what I knew, I just didn't think I could live with myself if I didn't try to help all those people from whom my father's company had stolen. I would've had their blood on my hands. Most days I'm still not sure that I got it right."

"You got it right," Cassidy said in a soft voice as her mom's cell phone buzzed. Her mom studied the screen and got to her feet.

"No news, I'm afraid. Just more paperwork. Don't stay out here too long, okay?"

Cassidy waited until her mom was gone before taking a sip of her coffee. It had way more sugar and milk than she usually liked, but she found it strangely comforting. As she drank, she wondered if she could just stay there forever. Would that stop the world from moving and anything bad from happening?

She finished her drink and thrust her cold hands deep into the pockets of her coat. Normally, there were a few old tissues and ticket stubs in there, but tonight her fingers found something else. It wasn't until she pulled it out that she realized it was an owl feather. She must have slipped it in there, back before she knew who the owl really was. She unconsciously ran the soft down along her cheek. How could this be happening? How could she live in a world where demons were real? Where Celeste Gilbert could be a mystical vessel? But where her dad was . . . *dying*.

She'd finally said it. He was dying. More tears came, and deep gasping sobs racked her body. Cassidy lay down on the small seat and curled herself into a ball. She wasn't sure how long she lay like that, but when she finally stopped, she looked down to see the once-beautiful feather was sodden and ruined. Poor feather. Poor broken feather. For one idle moment she wondered if Thomas would hate her for ruining something so perfect. Then she decided that he wouldn't care. He didn't care about sentiment. He cared only about duty. Everything he did was out of duty—

She froze. Thomas had used magic to heal Nash out of duty.

She had touched Nash's arm, and then Thomas had sent his magic through the grimoire so that it came out her fingers in a dazzling surge of energy. Her tattoo had blazed, and then Nash had been better.

Thomas had made Nash better.

Understanding slammed into her chest as she fumbled for her cell phone. She sent her mom a quick text to say that she was going for a walk to clear her head, and then she raced over to one of the taxis that was parked by the front of the hospital. She directed it to the clearing in the woods, the one place where she knew Thomas would find her. At the back of her mind she wondered if she should've told Nash where she was going, but it was overridden by one pressing thought. *Thomas could save her dad.*

THIRTY-TWO

By the time she reached the clearing, the clouds had shifted and dull threads of sun pushed through into the small space, giving it an almost ethereal feeling. And in the middle was Thomas, waiting for her, as still as a statue. But for once Cassidy didn't care. All that mattered was that he was here. He was here.

"I need your help." She came to a halt, her breath still coming thick and fast. His face immediately darkened.

"What has happened? Is it Tr . . . Is it my brother?" he corrected, as if saying Travis's name was too painful. "Has he done something to you? Threatened you?"

"No." She gave an impatient shake of her head. "It's not Travis. Something's"—she broke off for a moment and took a deep breath, schooling her thoughts so that the tears that were threatening to choke her could be held at bay—"something's wrong with my dad. He's sick, Thomas. I need you to heal him."

For a moment he lowered his eyes before finally looking up, his face full of pain. "I'm sorry, Cassidy. I cannot do anything."

"Yes, you can," she insisted as she stamped her foot on the ground. "You *have* to. This is important. You saved Nash. I saw you. We've got the grimoire; we can go there now. I'll take you to the hospital and put my hand on his chest and touch the grimoire. Thomas, please. You begged me once for help, and now I'm begging you," she said in an urgent voice. "It's my dad. We've got to help."

"This is different. I healed Nash because—"

"Do not say duty." Cassidy could feel her eyes begin to blaze with fury. "Don't you dare say duty to me, Thomas de la Croix."

"I healed Nash because he wasn't dying," Thomas explained in a soft voice. "I'm sorry, Cassidy. I truly am. Now we still need to discuss the solstice tomorrow night."

"The solstice?" Disbelief stung her words. "I don't care about the solstice *or* the Black Rose. Why can't you see that? I care only about my dad." Cassidy dropped to her knees, her hands clutched together. "You're better than this. I know you. *I know you had your reasons to leave your own father.* But you can help me. You have to help me."

For a moment something flickered across his face, but then it was gone. and he was still again. "My power isn't strong enough to bring someone back from the Great Wheel. There is nothing I can do."

"Now, now, brother, that isn't entirely true," Travis's

voice suddenly said, and Cassidy spun around to see him wandering into the clearing, staring directly at the vision of Thomas.

"Travis, you know the powers of earth magic as well I do. I cannot hold back a life force if it has already started its journey on the Great Wheel."

"You can't," Travis agreed as he made his way over to where Cassidy was still kneeling in the dirt, and he gently helped her up. "But brother dear, I'm not talking about the earth magic. I'm talking about the Black Rose." Travis reached up and softly ran his finger across her face. "I'm sorry to hear about your dad, Cass. It's not something I would wish on anyone, least of all you."

"Enough, Travis," Thomas roared, his face clenched in a pale mask of fury. "Do not do this."

"Do what?" Travis took his hand away from her face and turned on his brother. "Tell Cassidy what the Black Rose can really do? Tell her that it could save her father? *That it could save many fathers?*"

"The Black Rose?" Cassidy felt like she was in the school play and the curtain had suddenly been drawn back to reveal the lights and the audience as she slowly turned to Travis and let a wave of understanding race over her. "It can save him?"

Travis nodded before he caught sight of his brother's outraged expression. "What? You would deny her this?"

Thomas's whole body shook with rage. "I would deny her *nothing*. But this is not the truth that you're offering her.

It's not real. The Black Rose cannot help her; it can only hurt everyone." He turned to Cassidy, his mismatched eyes desperate and full of pain. "I'm a plain speaker. I don't have a smooth tongue to woo you with fancy words. But please, remember Paris. You saw what I saw. *You felt what I felt.* Can you risk that again? Even for your father?"

"Just because you could walk away doesn't mean that she has to," Travis retorted, and Thomas looked as if he'd been hit. Cassidy tried desperately not to think of Thomas's knife going into his father's chest and how he then walked away with the grimoire and the Black Rose, without looking back. "I've watched one father die. I don't want to watch another one."

Cassidy's cheeks felt so hot it was like a fever burned inside her. "What if there was another way? What if I could use the Black Rose just for a moment and then send it back to you?"

"It wouldn't work," Travis cut in. "Once the Black Rose is released, if you do not send it directly to its next home, it will return to the vessel and the chance will be wasted. So you can either send it to Thomas so he can continue to conceal it from the world, or you can send it to me so that I can heal the world. Or it can go back to Celeste and wait until a demon knight rips it from her beating body."

"Stop it," Thomas hissed, his restraint completely stripped away so that his face was bare and racked with emotions. "This fantasy of yours is not real. It is our duty to keep the world safe from the Black Rose."

Suddenly, Travis stiffened and his dark eyes were lost in swirling amber. "Keep the world safe?" He stalked toward his brother, so close that if Thomas had been really there, their noses would've been touching. "There is *nothing* safe about this world. It is not a good place. Not a kind place. It is polluted. *Unjust*."

"Brother, your desire for the Black Rose has corrupted you," Thomas said, his words dripping with venom. Travis flinched, much as he'd done when they were fighting in the darkened hallway by the chamber where their father was killed. Then he took a step back, his demon eyes blazing.

"Tell me, *twin*. Before you made my father put the ward onto the one thing that I needed most, did you ever stop to ask yourself *why* I desired it?" he asked in a soft voice, and suddenly the clearing was quiet. Cassidy held her breath as she watched two brothers staring at each other through time and space. However, when Thomas didn't answer, Travis threw his head back and laughed. "No, I thought not. Well, let me show you, shall I?"

Without another word Travis took off his coat and lifted the T-shirt he was wearing. But instead of seeing a golden torso, his entire chest was wrapped in a bandage, which he painstakingly unwrapped to reveal his blackened and torn flesh, like a bloodstained battlefield. Cassidy screamed at the sight, and Travis lowered the T-shirt before he turned to her.

"I think I told you that all demons suffer. Our souls are not meant to be in this flesh. Most demons can survive for thirty or forty years, which, where I come from, are good odds. But my suffering has come earlier than most. I am dying. I need the Black Rose to live. To stop the pain," he said before slowly wrapping the bandages around his torso again.

Cassidy turned to Thomas, her voice hoarse. "Did you know about this?" But his shocked face told her everything. He lowered his head, as if composing himself.

"Cassidy, I'm sorry for your father. And for my brother. I—" He paused for a moment. "I share his pain in my flesh, but not like that. I can't imagine the torment."

"And yet you still deny me relief from it?" Travis demanded.

"In any other way I would help you. We are flesh and blood. But my duty is to the Black Rose." The words seemed to be choking him, but he turned to Cassidy. "On the solstice, you must send it back to me so I can protect it."

"You mean so that you can disappear with it." Travis smoothed down the T-shirt that hid his ravaged body from the world. "I know I played a part in my foster father's death, and I accept that. But seeing him die like that when I knew the cure was so close at hand was not what I wanted. It was never what I wanted and Cass, more than anything, I don't want that for you."

Cassidy thought of her strange conversation with Hugh de la Croix. He said that both his sons were broken. Her choice would help make one whole, but what would it do to the other one? If Travis got the Black Rose, Thomas would've failed his duty, and Cassidy knew that he would retreat so deep into his harsh persona that he would probably never emerge again. However, if Thomas got the Black Rose, Travis's body would end up betraying him.

Then there was her dad. Her father. The most important person in the world to her. The tattoo on her arm burned, like it was moving, and the voice in her mind echoed, *"Pick me, me, me."*

She turned to Thomas and tried not to cry.

"Don't," he said in a soft voice, obviously realizing her decision before she even told him.

"I'm sorry," she whispered as she pressed her finger to where his mouth would've been if he were flesh and blood instead of just an apparition of a guy stuck back in the fourteenth century. "But what if he's right? We've only seen what happens when a human inhales the essence. What if it's different for demons? What if the Black Rose *can* heal? It could help so many people—my father, Thomas. Don't look like that. It's not a crime for your brother to want to live. For me to want my father to live. I'm sorry."

"Cass." Travis's voice cut though her pain. "Let me take you home. You look exhausted." Then once Cassidy nodded, he turned to Thomas, his dark eyes full of compassion and infinite sadness. "I know you won't believe me, but this is never what I wanted. Tomorrow night at the solstice perhaps you will finally see that."

"Cassidy," Thomas called out to her in a tight voice. "Please, don't make this choice—"

"Thomas, it's my dad," she said, but it was too late, and he was gone.

She felt as if she'd been hit in the chest, and even the feel of Travis's arm around her shoulder, leading her out of the woods, was no comfort. Cassidy thought she could hear the rustle of feathers flying along somewhere above them, but when she looked up, the owl was nowhere to be seen.

She'd just made the hardest decision of her life. Hugh de la Croix was right. Both of his sons were good at heart, and tomorrow, as long as her dad could hold on, she was going to do something that would destroy one of them forever. She felt certain she was doing the right thing, so why did it hurt so much?

THIRTY-THREE

Cassidy sat in the hospital room the following evening and stared at the machine. It was too painful to look at her dad's unmoving face, so she had taken to looking at the heart monitor instead. Besides, it was the thing that told her that he was still holding on.

Fear and nerves jangled in her stomach as she looked at her watch. Nash would be there soon, and then they would collect Celeste to go to the woods to wait for the solstice. She toyed with the carnelian necklace that Travis had given her. Suddenly, she was pleased that the twins' mom wasn't there to see what Cassidy was about to do to one of her sons.

"I don't have a choice," she whispered as she tightened her grip on the carnelian. "Please, you've got to understand."

However, Thomas's and Travis's long-dead mother didn't answer, and Cassidy thrust the necklace back into her pocket with the owl feather. She knew she was making the right decision, but it still weighed heavily on her mind.

And her greatest fear was that it would be too little, too late.

Finally, she forced herself to look at her dad. His hair was looking grayer and the tan on his face had faded, but the softness around his mouth was still there. Cassidy felt the tears threaten to choke her again.

"Just a bit longer, Dad," she told him in a stern voice as she wiped away her tears. It was pointless to cry when she was going to fix everything. When she was going to make him okay again.

"Did you say something?" Her mom walked into the room, looking even more pale and wan than she had yesterday.

"I was just telling him to hang on." Cassidy looked up, not sure if her mom would think that she was being silly. "The nurse said it was okay to talk to him."

"Of course it is." Her mom wrapped her arms around her chest and then nodded at Cassidy's arm as her eyes watered up. "And I'm sorry I wasn't very supportive of the tattoos when you first got them. I'm pleased that you went back and got another one. I'm starting to understand how important hope is. It's there for us even if we don't know it."

Cassidy rolled her sleeve back, and the black rose on her arm tingled in recognition. Her mom had no idea just how much hope the tattoo was going to give them. Her dad just needed to hold on for long enough.

"Look, here's Nash." Her mom wiped her eyes. "It's good that he's convinced you to take a break from this place. Pity there isn't much day left. I think it's the shortest day of the year. The—"

"Solstice," Cassidy finished off as she got to her feet. Suddenly, her mom looked tiny, hunched over in the chair, her dark auburn hair pulled back into a messy knot. Without thinking, Cassidy leaned over and gave her a hug. She was strangely touched that her mom's stiff shoulders softened and relaxed. "Keep your hope alive, Mom. Promise me that you won't give up hope while I'm gone."

"I promise." Her mom's voice was full of tears, but as Cassidy pulled away she could see the determination that had set in around her mom's mouth. And for the first time in days Cassidy felt a small smile tug at her lips. Her mom might have missed a lot of birthdays and other milestones over the years, but being stubborn was something that she had never failed at. Suddenly, she was grateful for that.

Then Cassidy gave her dad one final look before she hurried out to where Nash was waiting. Without speaking, he enveloped her in his arms like the true friend he had always been to her, and Cassidy felt the tears slide out. Then she realized he was wearing his Smiths T-shirt, and she wriggled away.

"It's your favorite," she explained. "I don't want to get it all snotty."

"If you think that I care about snot on my shirt, then you're an idiot," Nash retorted. "Fortunately, idiots are my favorite kinds of people. You look tired."

"I think what you mean to say is that I look like shit," Cassidy corrected as they walked through the never-ending hospital corridors until they reached the elevator. As they went down her decision continued to play out in her mind.

Save one brother and destroy another. *Pick me. Pick me.*
And if she chose the wrong brother, then, while her dad
might recover, the world might not be so lucky. It could be
Paris all over again.

"Are you thinking about it again?" Nash asked in a
soft voice, and she silently nodded. They'd spent most of
the night talking about it, but even Nash and his brilliant
philosophical mind was stumped. Of course, the alternative
was to do nothing, but then she'd have to keep protecting
Celeste from demons until the next winter solstice. And who
was even to say that she would be successful? Not exactly an
easy option.

Besides, no matter how difficult the decision was, she'd
made it now, and Nash had spent the rest of the time
showing her the ritual in the grimoire so that Cassidy could
be prepared to release the Black Rose.

Celeste would be unaware of what was happening.
Cassidy would draw a circle and chant a long, tedious
poem. The essence of the Black Rose would then rise out
of Celeste's body. Cassidy then had only seconds to direct it
toward Travis, and he would inhale the essence, making him
strong, whole, and capable of saving her father.

"Cass, there's no right or wrong. You're just doing the
best you can, considering the circumstances."

"Are you sure that she won't feel the ritual at all?"
Suddenly, Cassidy felt bad that she kept forgetting about

Celeste. She was the person who didn't really have a choice. She was still clueless about what was happening around her, or just how many people wanted to get the thing out from inside her.

Of course she had far too much school spirit for Cassidy's liking, and a love of shopping that made Nash shudder, but they were both in agreement that they didn't want to see her get hurt. Plus, while Cassidy was at a dress fitting, Mrs. Gilbert had taken a call, and from the sound of it, her husband had walked out on them a few months ago and money was tight. It suddenly explained why Celeste had been working in the nursing home.

Nash shook his head. "The spell in the grimoire will put her into a dreamlike trance. She won't feel anything but happiness and bliss. According to Thomas, in the past, when the Black Rose was housed in human vessels, it was considered a desirable job, not because of all the people and demons trying to rip your flesh apart, but because of the euphoria that it allowed."

"Y-you have spoken to Thomas?" Cassidy asked in surprise.

Nash dipped his head before shooting her an apologetic look. "I just wanted to make sure that I got the spell right. Celeste is a pain in the butt, but I didn't want to turn her into a toad or anything."

"D-did he say anything about me? Did he try and get you to help change my mind?"

"No, definitely not. He was even more reticent than ever until he told me about the human vessels and how it was an honored role in the past."

"Oh." Cassidy bit back her disappointment. Not that she really wanted any extra pressure, but for some reason it still bugged her that Thomas hadn't made more of an effort to change her mind. Then the elevator opened up and they hurried out to the parking lot. *It was time*.

THIRTY-FOUR

"Wow, this is so beautiful." Celeste let out a happy sigh as Cassidy and Nash exchanged bemused glances. They were tramping through the woods in the dying light of the day, and so far Celeste had caught her dress three times on the low-lying scrub, but she didn't even seem to notice. Nash obviously hadn't been exaggerating the effects of the spell on her. Still, Cassidy was almost jealous as her own stomach churned with anxiety. She could tell by the way Nash.was studiously avoiding the question that he was worried, too.

None of it was helped by a certain eeriness that clung all around them as the sun, after not showing up all day, now tried to push bright, almost overpowering, fingers of pale pink light through the trees. Cassidy tried not to look at it as they hurried toward the clearing, stopping only when Celeste wanted to admire a mushroom and a broken twig.

Finally, they arrived and Nash opened up the grimoire

before spreading out the numerous things that he'd brought with him in his satchel.

"Pretty." Celeste let out a gasp of joy. "Look at my arm. It's shining like the sun. So gorgeous."

"Are you sure that spell you did on her is okay?" Cassidy looked at Nash in alarm, but he quickly nodded his head.

"Yes, but I don't think she's hallucinating, I think she's actually seeing the Black Rose the way you do. My guess is that it's happening because it's so close to the solstice," he explained, but before Cassidy could answer, the owl appeared, and a second later Travis wandered in, looking more gorgeous than ever in pair of dark jeans and a soft knitted sweater that covered his scarred, broken torso.

"Hey, Cass. Nash." He nodded to them both before turning to the owl. "And Thomas. I'm guessing that you're here to change her mind. Can't you accept that this is Cassidy's choice?"

"This isn't about choice: it's about doing what's right," Thomas said as the owl disappeared and suddenly he was standing there, once again in the dark brown, coarse woolen shirt, his face the color of fresh snow. "And I am here to see it through to the end. Whatever the outcome."

"Oh, he's cute." Celeste looked up from studying her glowing arm to where the apparition of Thomas was standing. "Not as cute as Nash, of course, but he has a Sam Worthington thing going on." Then she wrinkled her nose. "By the way, who is he?"

"That's Thomas. He's Travis's brother," Nash said as he

glanced at his watch and then shot Cassidy a concerned look. "Ten minutes until the solstice."

"Really?" Celeste asked in surprise. "So why can't I understand a word he's saying? It's like he's speaking French or something—but weird French. And look what he's wearing. Was he an extra in the play?"

"It's complicated," Nash said in a patient voice, obviously not wanting to go into the whole grimoire thing that allowed both her and Nash to understand what Thomas was saying. Then Cassidy frowned for a moment as she turned to Travis.

"Actually, Celeste is right. I can understand Thomas because of the grimoire, but there's still no hiding that he's from the fourteenth century. But why don't you sound like that? I mean, you talk like more of a modern teenager than Nash does."

"Hey, I resent that," Nash protested. "But Cassidy does have a point."

"My magic is strong. Stronger than that which my brother uses. That is how I could come forward in time. It's also why I know how to speak and dress correctly. And text . . ." He turned to Thomas and held up his cell phone, his face intrigued. "Twin, if you were here, you would love these things. They're like nothing we've ever seen before."

But when Thomas didn't answer, Travis just shrugged and put his cell phone back into his pocket.

"Sorry, Cass." Nash tapped his watch. "We've only got five minutes to go. Do you remember everything you need to do?"

She nodded as she gently touched Celeste's arm. "Hey, Celeste, do you want to lie down now? I think you're getting sleepy."

"Okay." Celeste nodded happily, not even looking at the soft dirt and leaves below her. Once Celeste was settled, Cassidy took a deep breath and looked around her. Next to her was Nash, his generous, clever face focused solely on her. She smiled. Then she turned to Travis. Beautiful Travis, who lived in pain and wore his scars under his shirt. When he realized she was looking at him, he grinned at her, his smile full of warmth and sunshine despite the weather. And finally, she turned to Thomas.

Silence greeted her.

The strange sinking sun pushed pinky blue rays straight through his there-but-not-there body, but despite the odd illusion, she still felt that if she were to step outside the circle he would be flesh under her fingers. Would this have been different if he had been really here? If she could've touched him. *If he could've touched her?*

Cassidy shook the question from her mind as she thought of her conversation with her mom, who'd been forced to make a painful decision, sacrificing her family so that she didn't feel like she had blood on her hands. Cassidy was doing the same. She was sacrificing Thomas for—

She froze.

Blood.

She stared at her hands as she felt the breath catching in

her lungs. Blood. Suddenly, she turned to Travis and tried to ignore her pounding heart.

"You promised me that you don't lie, so I need you to answer a question for me. Where did you get the blood from?"

Suddenly, Travis was deathly still, and even Nash gasped. Thomas just stood there, unflinching and silent. Cassidy persisted. "When I first met Thomas, he told me that he couldn't come forward in time because it took blood magic. His entire life is all about duty to the Black Rose. I saw him walk away from his dying foster father, whom I know he loved, just to protect it, but despite everything, he refused to use blood magic. So I'm asking you, Travis, where did you get the blood from? D-did you kill someone?"

For a moment Travis clenched his jaw, making him look, ironically enough, like his brother for the first time. Then he slowly nodded his head. "*Oui*, I have killed men before. But Cass, you don't understand how much it hurts. The pain. I-I need to fix it."

Cassidy dropped to her knees, horror pounding in her ears, blocking everything out. "How many?"

"I . . . I don't know how many. But this doesn't change anything. I am still me. I've never lied to you, and I'm not lying now. The Black Rose can help people. You must believe me. Its essence can save. It can heal. It can transform."

"The worst thing is that I do believe you," she said in a soft voice. "But I also know that you did lie to me once."

"Never."

"Yes, you told me that you didn't have a choice. That you were born a demon. But you did have a choice, Travis. You and Thomas both had a choice. And yours was to take a path where he couldn't follow."

"What?" Travis's voice was hollow.

"I know all about making choices. I can spend more time trying to pick a pair of shoes than most people take to buy a house or plan a vacation. But I also know that you need to live by your choices."

"Are you saying that you're not going to give it to me?" Travis asked, color leaching from his face. Cassidy felt a sickness in the hollow of her stomach. If she turned her back on Travis, she was turning her back on her father. But was her father's life worth someone else's blood? Would her hands ever be clean if she did this? Tears poured down her face.

Pick me, me, me, the voice continued to whisper as the tattoo on her arm hummed with energy. She didn't need Nash to tell her that solstice was almost here.

"I'm saying that it shouldn't have to be this hard," she sobbed.

"No." Travis raced forward, but this time it wasn't Thomas who hauled him back, it was some kind of invisible force, and he fell into a heap on the ground.

"Hey." Nash widened his eyes. "It worked. I was experimenting with a ritual to make sure that Cassidy was safe while she was performing it."

"Cassidy, no." Travis jumped to his feet, and this time he raced toward Nash. "I don't want to hurt him, but I will if you don't give me the Black Rose. Can't you understand how much I need it?"

"Nash!" Cassidy screamed. She scrambled to her feet to race out of the circle, but before she could, the owl launched itself at Travis with such ferocity that he fell backward. He let out a shout of pain as some kind of invisible rope seemed to be holding him back. An instant later Thomas reappeared, his fierce, unwavering face pale but determined.

"The Brotherhood is using their magic to hold him. Not blood magic, earth magic. You can continue with the ritual—" Then he paused and bowed his head before her. "And you can choose as you will."

Hysteria rose up in her chest, while Celeste, who was still lying down, eyes closed and a smile on her face, was oblivious to all the drama. The irony was that she probably would've loved it. The pink rays of the sun spread out across the clearing as Cassidy repeated the ritual Nash had taught her, prompted by the grimoire, which was glowing like a beacon thanks to Travis's presence.

Then she watched as a sliver of pure white energy rose up from Celeste's body and formed a perfectly shaped rose. Cassidy's hysteria was replaced by euphoria as the essence enveloped her in its majesty. Everyone gasped, even Travis, who was still tethered to the ground by unseen binding.

The tattoo on her arm tingled in recognition, reminding her of her father. Not dying in a coma, but as he normally was. Happy, hopeful, strong. Then Nash tapped his watch to let her know it was almost time for her to decide. She stared at the shimmering essence that was blossoming up around Celeste's body.

How could it look so pure when it had caused so much pain? It had killed people. Divided brothers. Then she froze. If Cassidy released it to either brother, it would start all over again. And even if she wasn't the one fighting demons, someone else would be. Perhaps someone else would become a vessel and his or her life would be in danger. It was too much. She didn't want Travis to be in constant pain. Or Thomas to be bound by his duty. But most of all, she didn't want her father to die.

And yet if she chose any of them, someone else would suffer. She just wanted it to stop.

Me. The familiar voice called out to her. *Pick me, me, me.*

Her tattoo pulsed on her arm, but this time, instead of blocking it out, she let the voice wash over her again and again until she finally heard it. Of course! It didn't belong to Travis *or* Thomas. It belonged to someone else. Actually, it belonged to *something* else.

It belonged to the Black Rose itself. Her tattoo resonated in agreement, and suddenly her choice was clear. Regardless of what happened, she had to choose the Black Rose. It could decide its own fate.

So as the last of the pale rays of light sank down, marking the solstice, Cassidy lifted her hand up and gently touched the pulsing essence in front of her. Suddenly, all the joy she had been feeling was amplified as the Black Rose exploded into a thousand tiny shards, flying out in all directions like a firework. In the distance she could hear Travis, Thomas, and Nash all screaming at her, begging her to stop. But she ignored them as she continued to release the essence, which had been trapped for so long. And just before she passed out into the welcoming darkness, she heard the voice one more time.

I'm free. Thank you.

THIRTY-FIVE

"Cass, you've got to wake up," Nash's voice said from somewhere in the distance, but she tried to ignore it as she floated on a soft breeze of nothingness. "Cass," he said again. This time he was louder, closer. His hand was shaking her arm, forcing her to leave behind the nothingness and reluctantly open her eyes, her mind still full of fog. "How do you feel?"

"I-I don't know." She gingerly wriggled into a sitting position and looked around her. That's right. She was in the woods. The clearing was dark now, lit only by the flashlight Nash had thought to bring. Somewhere behind her she could hear Celeste squealing in excitement at what sounded like a toad, but there was no sign of Travis or Thomas. "Wh-what happened?"

"Don't you remember?" Nash asked, his voice gentle as his arms wrapped around her in a soft hug.

"No." She tried to shake her head but was met by a

wall of pain, and so she sat perfectly still until the fog and pain receded and the memories trickled through. "Yes, I was doing the ritual, and the Black Rose appeared. It was beautiful. *Alive.* Amazing. It asked me to free it, and so I touched it. I made my choice and released—"

Her dad.

The euphoria she had been feeling was gone, replaced by horror as the reality of her decision pressed against her chest. She had thought she was doing the right thing, but now as the freezing December air clawed at her skin, she realized the price she had paid. She had set the Black Rose free at the expense of her father.

A low moan escaped her lips. What had she done? She struggled to her feet, ignoring the nausea that was threatening to overtake her, but Nash pulled her back down.

"Hey, whoa. No fast movements. Cass, just sit still."

"I can't." She wriggled to break his hold on her but whatever strength she had from the grimoire was gone now, proof that the Black Rose really was gone. "Please, you don't understand."

"Yes I do," he insisted. "You need to sit still so that you can contact your mom. She just called from the hospital, and trust me, you're going to want to speak to her."

Cassidy stopped fighting him and realized that his beautiful porcelain face wasn't filled with pain or sadness. He was smiling. A wave of confusion swept through her.

"Nash, what's going on? I let the Black Rose go free. The doctors said that there was nothing they could do for my dad, and since I didn't do anything for him—"

"I wouldn't be too sure about that." He pressed a cell phone into her hand. "Call her. She has something really exciting that she wants to tell you."

✦ ✦ ✦ ✦ ✦

"He's alive," Cassidy said for the hundredth time as she sat on the log in the clearing. Whatever trip Celeste had been on was now over and she was curled up in Nash's coat, sleeping on a blanket at their feet. Cassidy's call to her mom had lasted for over half an hour, and despite how many times she had asked her, the news had been the same each time. Her dad had come out of his coma, and there was no sign of the clot, which had been so close to ending his life. They were going to run some more tests tomorrow, but the doctors seemed as baffled as everyone about it. She turned to Nash, her happiness competing with confusion. "Do you really think it was the Black Rose?"

"Not that I'm doubting the wonders of modern medicine, but I really do," Nash said as he turned the pages of the grimoire. "There is nothing in here to suggest it, but then a bunch of medieval knights who are trained to fight demons probably aren't going to consider if an immortal essence deserved free will or not. Perhaps they all experienced the same voices you did and they just ignored them? It is truly most extraordinary."

"Yes, but that still doesn't explain why it would heal my dad."

"Perhaps Travis was right?" Nash flicked his Zippo, as was his habit when he was thinking. "He believed that the Black Rose was capable of great healing, and when you touched it, it could probably see what your greatest hopes were."

"You think it read my mind and knew I wanted my dad to be better?" Cassidy widened her eyes.

"It makes sense. You were the first person in centuries to listen to it and find out what it actually wanted, so why shouldn't it repay you? I guess the thing we need to figure out is what else you were thinking about when you released the Black Rose and—"

"That's a question I would like to ask, too," a deep voice said as a young guy stalked into the clearing, the flashlight that was propped up on the ground creating eerie shadows on his familiar scar-crossed face. "Starting with the fact that one moment I was in a stable in Saint-Malo and now I'm, well, I don't know where I am."

"Thomas?" Cassidy let out a strangled cry and was up on her feet, running toward him, disregarding the darkness and any obstacles between then. Her heart hammered in her chest as she finally reached him. Then she caught her breath in awe. She had been wrong to think that the apparition of Thomas had been real, because now, as he stood before her, she understood that what she'd seen before was merely a faint, undefined shadow of the real Thomas.

Up close he was taller, his muscles broader, and the skin around his badly scarred face so much softer than she ever expected it would be. She also felt infinitely drawn to him in a way that she would never be able to explain.

"Cassidy, I'm waiting," he growled, his mismatched eyes flashing with anger. "What did you do? Where the hell am I?"

But instead of flinching, Cassidy just grinned as she lifted up onto her toes so that she could gently touch the outline of his scar. Then she leaned in and gave him the softest of kisses. "You're here, Thomas. With me."

THIRTY-SIX

"Are you kidding me with this?" Nash asked in a stern voice three days later as Cassidy chewed her lip and held up an apricot T-shirt and her favorite old lace blouse. "You made one of the most philosophically important decisions in the world, and now you can't decide which top you should wear?" Then he shot her a soft smile. "So has he forgiven you yet?"

"No. Of course not." Cassidy shook her head while suddenly wondering if a dress would be better. "He is pissed like you would not believe. All he keeps saying is that he doesn't belong here and that I should never have brought him forward in time. But the thing is that I didn't mean to bring him forward in time. I just hoped he would be happy, and then the Black Rose did the rest."

"He's probably just feeling testy because he's spent his life following his duty and protecting the Black Rose, and now that it has been released, he's lost," Nash suggested. "Just give him time. I'm sure he'll come around once he finds a new destiny."

"I hope you're right," Cassidy said as she picked up the first top again and studied it in the mirror before discarding it. Thomas wasn't the only one who was struggling to get used to what had happened. They had discovered that as well as healing, the Black Rose could also punish, and according to the Brotherhood, Travis was now back in the year 1310. They also said that his horrific wounds were healed, but Cassidy had the feeling that his anger wouldn't be nearly so easily cured. Nor would his sense of injustice. For a moment she longed to be able to see him and explain, but she knew it wasn't possible. The Black Rose had sent him back there for a reason, and she just had to accept it.

Also, as her mom had taught her, every decision had a consequence, and despite how much she cared for Travis and could see how broken he was, she knew that he had crossed a line—a blood line—and he couldn't be saved from it.

"Anyway." Nash unfolded his long legs, smoothed out his tuxedo trousers, and adjusted his long jacket. "It's Christmas Eve, and my parents have decided that my presence is required since they haven't seen much of me lately. Personally, I find their sentimental attachment to traditional holidays a bit smothering, but I'd better play nice. Will you be okay if I leave you with this monstrous decision?"

"Yes, Nash. I think I will manage." Cassidy walked him down the hallway. Once he was gone she wandered into the living room where her dad was sitting, his knee elevated and his navy eyes twinkling. The doctors still hadn't been able to discover why he had recovered the way he had and had suggested that he stay on medication for the rest of his life, but Cassidy secretly knew that he didn't need it.

"Why are you smiling so much?" her dad wanted to know as she sat down on the floor beside the couch and began to fiddle with the resistance band that he used for his knee exercises. "Do you think it will make me go easy on this fellow of yours?"

"You'd better," she warned. "Because meeting parents isn't his specialty, and this could scar him for life."

"How many other parents do you think he intends to meet?" her dad pondered before grinning. "And don't worry, I'll be nice. Actually, I even think your mom will, too. She's out in the kitchen attempting to make cookies to impress him."

"Mom's baking?" Cassidy lifted an eyebrow.

"Well, she's trying to. And thanks for going easy on her. I've never seen her so happy."

"I think that probably has something to do with the fact that you're no longer in a coma," Cassidy said before her lip began to wobble. "I am, too. It was pretty scary."

Her dad's grin faded, and he put a hand on her shoulder. "For all of us. And you know what was really strange? I don't remember much, but I do remember that tattoo you got me. For a moment it felt like it was still on my arm and I could feel it tingling. Actually, I've even been thinking that when I'm back up and moving, I might go and get a real one in the same design. To remind me always to have hope."

"I think that's a great idea," Cassidy said as she traced the space on her arm where her own tattoo had been. It had disappeared the night she had freed the Black Rose, and she was already missing it. "Maybe I'll get one, too."

"Not on my watch you won't," her dad growled, and Cassidy grinned. It had been worth a try, and she was just about to see if she could at least get a visit to the vintage shop out of the deal when she caught sight of an owl sitting on the branch outside. She jumped to her feet.

The owl was no longer possessed by the spirit of a medieval demon knight, but once again just a regular bird who had taken to following Thomas around wherever it could.

"He's here."

"Now you've become a psychic?" her dad queried just as the doorbell rang. He nodded his head. "Okay, so you *have* become a psychic. Well, I guess you'd better go and let him in."

Cassidy didn't need to be asked twice, and she raced down the hallway and opened the door to see Thomas awkwardly standing there.

He was wearing the jeans that Nash had helped him buy and pulling at the woolen sweater that was covering his broad, corded muscles and chest. His red scar looked sore and angry, but the rest of his face almost looked nervous. Then Cassidy grinned as she drank in the sight of him. Besides, he had every right to be nervous. It was Christmas Eve, and he was about to meet her parents.

"Hey," she said, but instead of answering her, he just reached out and entwined his fingers in hers before kissing her. Deeply, passionately, and enough to make her toes curl up in her Dr. Martens. Finally, he pulled away and shook his head.

"Cassidy, this is a bad idea. I cannot meet your parents. They will want to know what I can offer you, and I have nothing. The Brotherhood doesn't pay us. It's something we do for—"

"Duty?" Cassidy guessed as she wrapped her arms around his waist and shivered at the feel of his hard, coiled body. Then, after kissing him some more, she peered up at him. "Thomas, you once told me that you trusted me."

"I do." He nodded, and Cassidy felt her heart melt.

"Well, trust me when I tell you that as long as you don't mention swords, prophecies, demon knights, and magical essences that offer eternal life to any who inhale them, then I promise you'll be just fine. Do you think you can do that?"

For a moment he paused and kissed her again. Then he looked at her and grinned. *"Oui,"* he said. "I can do that."

Turn the page to read a sample of another great
book from Amanda Ashby,

one

$\mathcal{M}$ia Everett was doomed. It was a fact she had known ever since Rob Ziggerman walked into biology class half an hour earlier. Instead of sitting next to her, as had been his habit for the last month, he'd made a beeline for Samantha Griffin. All of which meant the rumors must be true.

"How can this be happening?" she demanded in a low voice as she turned to Candice, who was carefully inspecting the skin of her elbow by poking it with a pencil.

"I have no idea." Her friend shook her shoulder-length red hair in disgust as she offered up her arm for inspection. "I'm only seventeen. It hardly seems fair, but it's definitely leprosy. No doubt about it. See the way the skin is falling away like that? Textbook case."

"Candice, I'm not talking about you, I'm talking about how my life is about to be ruined." Mia sunk farther down into her seat as their teacher, Mr. Haves, continued to talk in an animated voice about something bug-related. Normally Mia liked biology, but then again, she normally had Rob Ziggerman in all his blond, beautiful glory sitting next to her, so what was there not to like? "It's important."

"And leprosy isn't?"

Mia gritted her teeth, once again wishing Candice wasn't such a hypochondriac. This week it was leprosy, the week before it was some weird tapeworm that you could only get from a certain part of the Amazonian rain forest. Which, considering Candice hadn't even left the state of California, was highly unlikely.

"*What?*" Candice raised an eyebrow. "Why are you looking at me like that? I'm serious. My arm could fall off by tomorrow."

"Yes, it could. *If in fact you had leprosy.* All you've got is a bad case of dry skin." Mia forced herself to keep her voice low. "Now, can we please start focusing on my crisis? Did you find out anything?"

"Fine." Candice let out an exaggerated sigh and reluctantly pulled her sleeve down. "So this is what I heard. When Samantha broke up with Trent three weeks ago, she assumed that the guys would be lining up to ask her out. Unfortunately, she forgot to take into account that while she might have a hot body from doing all that cheerleading, she still has a major personality flaw—aka, she's a total witch. Anyway, with the senior prom only four days away and still no invitation, she's decided to focus on Rob."

"She doesn't have a prom date and so now she wants

mine?" Mia wailed as she felt her stomach churn in a way it hadn't done since she had first heard that *Buffy* was going to be canceled.

"Looks like it," Candice agreed in a whisper as Mr. Haves turned off the lights and started to fiddle with his laptop until a picture of a cockroach flashed up on the whiteboard.

"But that's so unfair. Why would he take me out on six perfect dates"—*well, okay, five actually, because going to watch him practice football probably didn't count as a date in the technical sense of the word*—"and then ask me to the prom, if he was going to run off with Samantha Griffin the minute she looked his way and tossed her hair? I mean, he said I was cute and that he liked the fact I wasn't high-maintenance. He said it was refreshing."

"He also said that Indiana was the capital of India in geography the other day," Candice pointed out.

"Okay, so he's not exactly a brainiac," Mia conceded. "But unlike most of the other jocks around here, he doesn't think he's God's gift to the world, either. He's just a regular guy who is sweet and kind—"

"And has abs that would make David Beckham weep," Candice added, and Mia found herself nodding. Yup. There was no denying that Rob Ziggerman was gorgeous. With a capital GORGEOUS. None of which was helping with the problem at hand.

"So where does this leave me?" Mia stared unhappily at the back of Rob's head. His blond hair was styled in a sculptured mess that she longed to run her fingers through (not that she would, of course, because despite being sweet and kind, he did have a thing about his hair). Sitting as close as she could get, Samantha was leaning all over him, leaving no doubt about what her intentions were.

"With a spare prom dress?" Candice guessed before shooting her an apologetic grimace. "Look, you've lived across the street from Samantha for the last ten years, so you know as well as I do that what Samantha wants, Samantha gets. Just accept it and be happy you dated a football player for a few weeks."

"Well, she's not going to get her own way this time. No way." Mia gave a firm shake of her head. "We just need to think of a plan. Ooh, maybe if I start using makeup and do my nails, I can beat Samantha at her own game."

"That's your plan?" Candice peered at her from under her mascara-free eyelashes as if to remind Mia that their makeup kits didn't consist of much more than Clearasil and lip gloss. Then Mia glanced back to where Samantha was now laughing at something Rob had said, and she felt her resolve strengthen.

"It's not such a dumb idea," Mia defended. "I mean, it's a slight problem that I don't have a PhD in eyeliner application, but how hard can it be? Besides, I could always ask Grace to help."

"You hate your sister," Candice reminded her. "And more to the point, Grace hates you. Plus, she's friends with Samantha.

It's that whole cheerleading-club thing. She would never go along with it."

"True," Mia reluctantly agreed as she realized no good could come from telling her fifteen-year-old, pom-pom-wielding, vacuous-Barbie-doll sister about this. "But I've got to do something or I'll be the laughingstock of the school. I mean, how can I go to the prom if Rob dumps me?"

"Oh yes, how embarrassing to not have a prom date. We wouldn't want that," Candice bristled, and Mia found herself wincing in guilt. They'd made a pact to go to the senior prom together to prove they didn't need guys to have fun. Though in all fairness, they'd made this decision based purely on the fact that with Candice's ongoing medical obsession and Mia's encyclopedic knowledge of anything *Buffy*- and *Angel*-related, neither of them had any expectations of being asked in the first place. Let alone by a guy like Rob Ziggerman.

"Candice, I didn't mean that." Mia shot her friend an apologetic look. "It's just, if he hadn't asked me, then no one would've cared less if I did or didn't have a date. But now. . . "

"But now, instead of everyone just thinking you're that weird girl who once tried to get the school to have a Joss Whedon day, they'll think you're the girl Rob dumped," Candice finished, and Mia let out a groan.

"I've really screwed up, haven't I?"

"No, you haven't," Candice finally relented. "Your only sin was being so refreshingly adorable that Rob couldn't resist you."

"Thanks." Mia shot her friend an appreciative glance and sighed. "Now if only I could figure out how to make it happen all over again."

"Got it," Candice suddenly whispered. "Since Rob seems incapable of taking his eyes off Samantha's disgustingly low-cut top, we have to assume that boobs are his fatal flaw. So what about getting a push-up bra to help distract him? We could cut the next few classes and go to the mall."

"But the senior assembly is this afternoon." Mia looked at her friend in surprise. "That's when the football team will be getting their awards. Rob will be there."

"Yes, and if you don't act soon, you'll get to see Samantha and her thirty-six-Ds bouncing up to congratulate him afterward," Candice said in a matter-of-fact way.

"You're right." Mia glanced down at her own less-than-impressive chest. "A push-up bra it is, and maybe we could also—"

"Maybe you could both pay attention?" someone suggested in a mild voice, and Mia looked up to where Mr. Haves had suddenly appeared by her side. "So, Mia, would you like to tell us what happens next?"

Mia hoped no one had heard her push-up-bra plan as she looked up at his encouraging smile. Normally, when teachers did that it was because they were evil passive-aggressive maniacs who liked to see students squirm, but Mr. Haves just genuinely seemed to like helping kids learn. Which as a rule was a good thing, just not today. She peered over to the whiteboard, where there was an amplified photo of a cockroach. Gross.

"Well?" Mr. Haves continued. "What do you think is going to happen to our friend, *Periplaneta americana* next?"

"Um... it's going to fly away?" she guessed, and then wished she hadn't as the sound of Samantha Griffin's unmistakable snicker sounded out. Which was more than a little annoying since Samantha wasn't exactly an A-plus sort of student.

"Not quite. Can anyone else tell me?" Mr. Haves looked hopefully around the class, but when no one raised a hand, he glanced in the direction of his favorite student, Chase Miller—aka the new boy. Well, he'd been at Newbury High for about six months now, but for some reason Mia had never really talked to him. Apparently he was from Boston or somewhere like that. He was tall with short light brown hair and green eyes that were set above a pair of razor-sharp cheekbones. He also tended to keep to himself.

"The jewel wasp is going to put venom into the cockroach's brain so it can control its mind and body, making it a brainless minion."

Okay, and now she remembered why she never talked to him, because he was weird. After all, who in their right mind would know stuff like that?

"Excellent. Well done, Chase." Mr. Haves clapped as he walked back to the front of the room and brought up the next photograph. "The jewel wasp will lay its eggs on the cockroach. After the eggs hatch, the larvae will feed on the roach. Then the larvae use the roach's abdomen as the perfect living-dead incubator until the newly hatched wasps can feed on—"

Much to Mia's relief, the rest of his words were drowned out as the bell rang, quickly followed by the sound of scraping chairs that echoed around the room.

"Can you wait for me? I won't be long." Mia turned to where Candice was busy studying something on her cell phone.

"Sure." Her friend gave a vague wave of her hand without looking up and so Mia piled her books into her bag and took a moment to pat her shoulder-length brown hair into place before hurrying toward Rob. However, just before she got there, Mr. Haves appeared in front of her.

"Mia, could I have a quick word, please?"

"Oh." She gulped as she watched Rob stride out, engrossed in something Samantha was saying, the faint smell of his cologne catching in her nose as he went. Mia realized this probably wasn't the time or the place. "Uh, I guess so."

"Actually, I'll meet you outside." Candice waved her phone in the air. "I've got to make an important call. When it comes to leprosy, you've got to move quickly."

"Did she just say 'leprosy'?" Mr. Haves lifted a surprised eyebrow as he beckoned Mia to follow him to the front of the classroom.

Thanks, Candice.

"Yeah, Leprosy. They're, uh, this great band. She wants to

get concert tickets," Mia improvised as she reluctantly headed over.

"I'll have to listen out for them," Mr. Haves said as he reached into his desk and pulled out a piece of paper, which bore a striking resemblance to the test she'd taken a couple of weeks ago. That was the day after Rob had asked her to the senior prom. Then he waved a second piece of paper in the air. That one looked like Friday's test. The one she'd taken after hearing the rumors that Samantha was after Rob.

"So, about these," Mr. Haves said as Mia studied her shoes. As she recalled, she didn't exactly nail either of them. "I don't need to tell you you're one of my better students, which is why I'm concerned about these grades. Is there something going on?"

What? Like the fact that the guy she'd secretly had a crush on for four years suddenly asked her out on a date for no apparent reason? And then after five more dates, he had made her the happiest girl in the whole entire world by asking her to prom. *And now he had apparently decided to get with Samantha Griffin.*

"Everything's fine. I've just been a bit stressed. It's no biggie," she said.

"Are you sure?" Mr. Haves wrinkled his eyes together and looked concerned. "Because I noticed Rob is now lab partners with Samantha. Does that have something to do with it?"

What? Why? What had he heard?

"No, of course not," she said instead as the blood started to pound in her ears. If Mr. Haves knew about it, then there was a fair chance that the rest of the school did, as well. "And I'm sorry about the tests. I, er, had food poisoning last week."

"What sort?"

"Excuse me?"

"What sort of food poisoning?"

"The poison sort. Anyway, if that's everything, I'd better get going."

"Of course, but remember Mia, if you ever have any problems, you can talk to me. You're a bright student and that's the way we want things to stay. Actually, if you'd like, I could arrange for another student to tutor you before the next test. Just to get you back on track."

"Honestly, Mr. Haves, it's fine. I've got everything completely under control." Mia managed to shoot him a faint smile before she walked out of the classroom. She was about to become the laughingstock of the entire school, and she was fairly certain talking to a teacher or getting some tutoring wasn't going to change that.

"So how bad?" Candice demanded the minute Mia stepped into the hallway and shut the door behind her.

"Bad," she said with a shudder. "Not only did I fail the last two tests, but even Mr. Haves has noticed that Rob and Samantha are getting close. This is serious, Candice. I think we're going to need more than a push-up bra to fix it."

Another great read from Amanda Ashby,

FAIRY BAD DAY

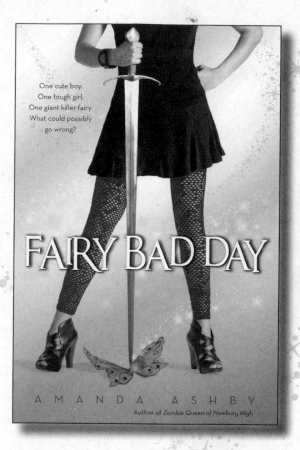

One cute boy.
One tough girl.
One giant killer fairy.
What could possibly
go wrong?

FAIRY BAD DAY

AMANDA ASHBY
Author of *Zombie Queen of Newbury High*

"Laced with humor, danger, and romance, this book will
have readers smiling all the way to the last page."
—*Publishers Weekly*